Mandrakes from the Holy Land

Aharon Megged

Mandrakes from the Holy Land

TRANSLATED FROM THE HEBREW BY

Sondra Silverston

The Toby Press

The Toby Press LLC, 2005

POB 8531, New Milford, CT 06776-8531, USA
& POB 2455, London W1A 5WY, England
www.tobypress.com

Originally published as *Dudai'im min Ha'aretz
Hakdosha*, ("Love-Flowers from the Holy Land").

litscene@ithl.org.il, www.ithl.org.il
POB 10051, Ramat Gan, 52001, Israel
Tel: 972-3-579-6830, Fax: 972-3-579-6832

ISBN 1 59264 057 5 *hardcover* original

A CIP catalogue record for this title
is available from the British Library.

Cover: *Arranging the Flowers* oil painting by Elizabeth Brophy.
Reproduced by kind permission of the artist at www.magilfineart.com

Typeset in Garamond by Jerusalem Typesetting
Printed and bound in the United States by
Thomson-Shore Inc., Michigan

46 Gordon Square
London, 20th July, 1906

Dr. P.D. Morrison
The Fast Hotel,
Jerusalem

Dear Dr. Morrison,

Your letter quite distressed me. I, too, have been feeling some concern for the well being of Beatrice Campbell-Bennett in Palestine, for since her last letter, written on 17th May of this year and sent from the Jewish settlement of Zichron Ya'acov, I've heard nothing from her, not even a reply to my letter of June 1st. But I assumed she was so immersed in her artistic work, and so absorbed in her warm relations with the family of the agronomist, Aaronsohn—the family that had "adopted" her—(in her May 17th letter to me, she wrote that she was happy to be "surrounded by good people," and described the friendship that had developed between her and Mr. Aaronsohn's younger sister, Sarah, whom she praised effusively)—that she was too preoccupied to write letters to far-off London, which, in any case, was far from her thoughts. Now, to learn from your letter that her mental state is so grave that her parents have found it necessary to send you to Palestine especially to inquire into her activities, to persuade her to leave the squalid Arab village she has chosen to live in and return to England, and that it might even be necessary to hospitalise her—why, it's utterly astonishing! Now, upon rereading the six letters she has written to me since her arrival in the Holy Land, I find not even the slightest hint of any emotional upset or attacks of depression. On the contrary, they all indicate that her visits to the biblical sites she had always dreamed of had transported her to a state of near-euphoria.

I

I shall try to answer your questions to the best of my ability:

I first became acquainted with Beatrice four years ago, when she was accepted to the Slade School of Art, which I was also attending. Although her paintings were not particularly original, they possessed a kind of airy transparency and were suffused with an aura of noble-mindedness. All the students—of both genders—liked her once they recognized her sterling qualities, her kindness, her congeniality, her honesty. Was there anything "eccentric" or "odd" about her?—I wouldn't say so, unless her avoidance of the society of young men could be considered an "eccentricity." I attributed it to her lack of self-confidence, to the fact that her figure was fuller than was the fashion, quite the opposite of her attractive, almost doll-like face. I know she had a brief affair with a young solicitor that ended in bitter disappointment.

She regularly attended the weekly meetings, held in our home, of the circle known as "the Bloomsbury Group." Yes, one might say she was an exceptional young lady. Apart from the fact that she was remarkable for her naïveté—a trait not highly respected in this sophisticated group, some of whose members are confirmed cynics—her conservative views were usually not favourably received. As a devout Christian to the depths of her soul—although not the sort that observes ritual commandments—she had reservations about many of the opinions voiced in the group's discussions. I recall that in an exchange we had about William James' book, *The Varieties of Religious Experience*, which was published several years ago, she objected to the idea that spiritual ecstasy is the consequence of a psycho-physical condition. To assume that Paul's revelation on the road to Damascus was caused by an epileptic fit, she claimed, is to say that every sublime spiritual phenomenon—sainthood, prophetic inspiration, spiritual exaltation—is a "disease." Was St. Francis of Assisi (she greatly admired him, and the book, *The Little Flowers of Franciscus*, was very dear to her heart) a psychopath?—she inquired. (And by the way, my sister Virginia is also of the opinion that the line dividing illness from non-illness, normality from abnormality, is very thin and frequently cannot even be discerned.) Beatrice was revolted by droll remarks containing lewd insinuations—quite common in our discussions—and despised gossipy tales of adultery, which were not rare in our circle either. On the other hand, she kept an open mind with regard to novel philosophical ideas and the criticism of social conventions. She occasionally made surprisingly clever remarks. I recall that during one of our discussions on ethics, in response to Lytton Strachey's question, "What common sense is there in 'the good'?" she said that there was no common sense in "the good." It was not a substance found in nature, and must therefore be created each time anew.

She had a naive, almost fundamentalist attitude towards the Scriptures. She once told me about a dream she had, in which her hands and feet were marked with the stigmata, and the sight of the dripping blood filled her with joy. In another dream, she told me with great embarrassment, she was suckling at the breast of St. Margaret of Scotland, and felt such pleasure that she was unable to remove her lips from the nipple, and was afflicted with sorrow upon awakening. (Her mother, who is Scottish, makes pilgrimages to the grave of that saint in Dunfermline.)

As Beatrice's family doctor for several years, you were undoubtedly aware of the tension between the mother, Mrs. Campbell-Bennett—a devout Christian, embittered and alcoholic (and you, as Beatrice told me, succeeded to some extent in breaking her of that addiction)—and her hedonistic husband, one of those gentlemen who hunt foxes when they're in the country, and females when in the city. Beatrice navigated her way with much torment when the storm raged in that strait between Scylla and Charybdis, and I am sure that the antagonism between the worlds of her mother and father left a deep mark on her personality. When she told me, to my surprise, of her intention to travel to Palestine, it occurred to me that she was making the trip to find the Golden Fleece that would extricate her from the tangle of her relationship with her parents and society. When I received the letters she wrote from Palestine, I saw that she was indeed happier in that country than she had ever been here.

It is astonishing, therefore, that you write of "worrying signs of pathological mental disturbance," of "delirium," and it would never have occurred to me that she might condemn herself to isolation in some wretched Arab village, exposed to the heat of the sun and the buzz of mosquitoes, two hundred meters below sea level. (Should I infer from a certain allusion you made—"she has gone astray"—that she has become licentious there?—something I am utterly incapable of grasping!)

Is it the "holiness" of that land that has driven her mad...?

I am enclosing photographic copies of her six letters to me (which I am sending to the Fast Hotel in Jerusalem, where I understand you will be staying for a while until your return to Tiberias), and hope you will succeed in "extricating"—as you put it—her journals from her, and perhaps discover in them the germ that caused disease to spread through her mind.

I would be most grateful if you would inform me of every development regarding her fate.

Yours faithfully,

Vanessa Stephen

P.S. In early September, I shall be travelling with my sister, Virginia, to Greece, where our brothers, Toby and Adrian await us. If you believe there is some point in my meeting and talking with Beatrice, I shall make an effort to leave the group for several days and travel to Palestine on the ship that sails from Piraeus to Jaffa. Please inform me of your opinion by letter to the address shown on the enclosed card.

V.S.

Ramle, 16th April, 1906

Dear Vanessa,*

It is now eight o'clock in the evening, and I am sitting in my small room in the nurses' school near the Franciscan monastery, St. Joseph's, in the town of Ramle, whose name you have certainly never heard before—it is the town of Arimathea mentioned in the New Testament (Matthew, Chapter 27; and this monastery is named after Joseph of Arimathea, who redeemed the body of Jesus from Pilate after the crucifixion and had it buried)—and writing my first letter from the Holy Land to you by the light of a kerosene lamp that sits on a bare, rickety wooden table. I must occasionally stop to crush on my arm or forehead one of the mosquitoes that buzz around me and land on me unmercifully.

This is my second day in this land of wonders (I write "my second day," and cannot believe that only yesterday, I disembarked at the Jaffa port, the vivid, remarkable, constantly changing sights filling my eyes wherever I turned, and my heart overflowing with feelings that caused it to flutter with every step I took on this ancient soil, as if each day were one of the six days of Creation)—and Ramle is the first stop on my way to Jerusalem. Since there are no hotels in this small town—which consists entirely of seven or eight streets of several

* This is the first of six letters written by Miss Campbell-Bennett, kindly sent to me by Miss Vanessa Stephen, which reached me on the 7th of August of this year. I hope that a careful reading of them, examined chronologically in combination with the two notebooks containing her journals, which I was able to take from her more through cunning—God will forgive me for that—than through persuasion, will enable me to comprehend B.'s mental state more profoundly than I did from my conversations with her, during which she revealed a stubborn recalcitrance.—Dr. P.D. Morrison, M.D., D.S.O.

stone and many adobe houses, its population no more than seven thousand—the Mother Superior of the convent was kind enough to put me up in one of the schoolrooms in which Arab girls study during the day. (Can you imagine this: Napoleon himself—the nun informed me—slept in the adjacent room in 1799, when, as is well-known, he failed in his attempt to conquer the country…) At dawn tomorrow, I shall continue my journey eastward, astride a noble steed—his name is Shatr, which, in Arabic, means valiant—accompanied by my drago-man, Aziz, who will be riding a mule bearing my luggage.

But I must tell you of my adventures from the beginning. Yesterday, (was it really only yesterday?) at eight in the morning, our ship, (a steamship from the fleet of Lloyd's of Austria, which had set out from Trieste and made two stops, in Brindisi and at Port Said) docked at the Jaffa shore. I had already gone up to the deck at five to see the sun rise over the Judean hills. During this glorious spectacle, as the light gradually increased, dispersing the darkness, the Jaffa cliff was revealed to me from a distance like a legendary creature rising from the sapphire blue water, and on it, a block of tightly packed houses, rising together like a kind of tower, crowned with a halo of golden rays. This was how I first saw the Holy Land—like a river of light bursting through the mysterious darkness.

The sea was turbulent, bundles of white foam were spread over its entire expanse, like thousands of floating seagulls, and even before the ship had dropped anchor, a dozen or so boats paddled towards us from the shore, moving so rapidly that they seemed to be racing each other. As I was preparing to disembark, scores of Arab sailors climbed onto the deck, agile as monkeys, and grasped the ropes that rolled down to them. Shouting loudly in Arabic, English, German, they swooped down onto the passengers—for a moment, it seemed as if we were being attacked by pirates—and seized our suitcases, boxes and baskets, to lower them into the boats. I had not yet begun to understand what was happening, when two strong men held me by the arms and lifted me over the deck rail into the husky arms of their mates standing in the boat.

I was frightened. I looked around for my two suitcases, but did not see them. The oarsmen reassured me: don't worry, you'll find them on the pier. A dignified looking Viennese Jew with whom I had had an occasional conversation during our five-day voyage—a Zionist activist who was visiting Palestine for the third time—also assuaged my fears: no harm can befall a non-Jewish tourist arriving on the shores of this country who is under the protection of one of the Consulates—British, Austrian, German, Russian. Those who do suffer are the Jewish refugees arriving from Russia or Romania. The Turkish government suspects them of having come to settle here, and makes it difficult for them to enter the country, often returning them to their homelands.

Turkish soldiers in sloven uniforms stood on the pier; most of them with bayonet rifles slung over their shoulders, glittering in the sunlight, and in the doorway to the customs house stood stern-faced government clerks awaiting the arrival of the boats' passengers. I searched amongst those standing on the pier for our consul, Mr. John Dixon, who was supposed to meet me.

I believe I told you that my father knew John Dixon from their school days at Eton and Pembroke College in Cambridge. I myself had met him only once, when he visited our estate in Essex three years ago. Two months before my departure, my father wrote him that I was about to embark upon a voyage to the Holy Land—he also mentioned the purpose of my trip, adding an ironic comment, as is his wont, that, even though I shall be "considering the lilies of the field," I do not know how "to spin my clothing" (yes, he is even more knowledgeable in the Scriptures than I)—and he therefore requested any assistance the consul might be able to provide.*

* During my first meeting with Miss Campbell-Bennett, some five weeks ago, in the village of Magdala—she made no inquiry about her father or mother. When she saw me standing before her in the doorway to her squalid shack, the first words she uttered, emitting a strange, and to my mind, slightly nasty laugh utterly incompatible with her nature, were: "I see you've still got tufts of hair protruding from your ears…" I was stunned. I swallowed the insult and said that her parents, concerned for her welfare, had sent me to her; and when she didn't respond, I saw immediately that her power of judgment was wholly impaired. Looking at her, I asked myself what had befallen her during these last several months since her arrival in the Holy Land. I feel pity for her, but even more for her parents.—P.D.M.

I did not see Mr. Dixon, but several moments after alighting on the pier, still not knowing where to turn, I was greeted by a middle-aged man, dark-complexioned and sporting a thin black moustache, wearing a white European suit and red tarboosh, who inquired: "Miss Campbell-Bennett?" I was surprised. I was unacquainted with this Eastern-looking man. Was my name inscribed on my forehead? Did my fair skin and flaxen hair give away my origins? He extended his hand and introduced himself: Haim Amsaleg, Deputy Consul-General and Dixon's representative in Jaffa; and immediately thereafter, he told me with great sorrow that Mr. Dixon had passed away three weeks earlier, and a new consul, Mr. Edward Charles Blech, had been appointed in his stead. It was Mr. Blech who had asked him to meet me. I expressed my sorrow at the death of Mr. Dixon, of whom my father was quite fond, and asked how he had recognized me. "A sixth sense," he replied, smiling. From his name, I understood that he was Jewish. He was a most courteous individual, who spoke quietly and modestly and had English manners. He took my passport and asked me to wait for him in the shade. He would locate my suitcases immediately, save me from the tortures of quarantine, and make all the arrangements related to my entry into the country. He then went off in the direction of the customs house, and I saw how respectfully he was treated by the Turkish policemen and functionaries, who apparently knew him well.

Not fifteen minutes later, the gentleman returned holding my passport and an entry visa in his hand, followed by an Arab porter carrying my two heavy suitcases on his back. I told Mr. Amsaleg that, before I left England, the travel agency, Cook and Son, had booked a room for me at the Park Hotel, and I asked how to get there. Mr. Amsaleg pointed to a row of carriages on the far side of the port entrance, and suggested that we hire one. He would accompany me to the hotel, which is in the German colony.

After we had seated ourselves in the carriage, he said, "The late Mr. Dixon told me of your purpose in visiting our country. A most noble purpose." I said that I had read the Scriptures, the Old and New Testaments, with my parents from the time I was a child, and the land of the Prophets and of Jesus was in my imagination and my dreams. When I was studying painting at the Slade Academy of Art, I had the idea of painting all the flowers mentioned in the Bible. If I should succeed in that task, I would then collect them into an album that would, so I hoped, be published, with the appropriate verse appearing under each picture. I told him that I had even learned the Hebrew names of many flowers, names that enchanted me, such as *nerd, levona, ohalot*, names that seemed to hold hidden promise. "Are you familiar with the mandrake?" I asked. He smiled. No, he'd never seen the love-flower. He would ask the botany teacher at the agricultural school, *Mikveh Israel*, which is not far from Jaffa, where it could be found, and tell me.

As we rode along the street, lined with colourful shops and crossed from time to time by people astride donkeys and horses, he volunteered some useful information for my journey: the exchange rate for various currencies—piaster, majida, bishlik—(it was different in every city, and the exchange rate of the sterling in Jaffa was 124 piasters, which is about six majidas…for your edification, if you ever come here…); at which of the city's five banks I should exchange my money; how to safeguard against bullies, extortionists and the like. He recommended the Austrian post office for sending letters. It was more trustworthy than the French or German ones; and when he heard that I intended first of all to go to Jerusalem, he said: there are three ways to reach Jerusalem—by train, which leaves twice a day, at seven in the morning and two in the afternoon, and takes three hours and forty minutes; by carriage, known here as a "diligence," which takes twelve hours and which he did not recommend, because of its cramped seating (twelve passengers, and frequently even more, in a carriage), and the jolting ride on the rough road; and the third way—by donkey, camel, or horse…. I immediately said: I choose to go on horseback. He looked at me for a moment in apparent astonishment, and then smiled broadly, convinced I was joking. I told him that I had been a skilled rider from childhood, the horses on our estate were my good friends, and since I wished to make a close study of the flora on the land between Jaffa and Jerusalem, and linger with every flower that caught my eye and my heart, travelling on horseback would be the most suitable way. He continued to look surprised, although after he reconciled himself to the fact that this was what I indeed desired and that I would not reconsider, he said: If so, you must hire a dragoman to accompany you the whole way. You cannot do it alone. Yes, that was clear to me as well, and we agreed to go together to the Cook and Son travel agency and arrange—with a written and signed contract, comprising thirteen clauses, he said—for the hiring of a dragoman.

Even upon our entrance to the Park Hotel—a small clean hotel in the style of the German family lodging houses—he continued to spread a protective wing over me. He saw to it that I was given a room whose window looked out onto the surrounding groves, and did not rest until he saw my suitcases brought to me.

Dear Vanessa, forgive me if I besiege you with so many details, but I am overflowing with impressions, which, against my will, burst onto the page. I shall try to be brief. We went to Cook and Son, signed a contract—yes, thirteen clauses of clearly specified obligations—and it was agreed that, at seven the next morning, waiting for me across from the agency, would be the dragoman—a young Arab who knew English and was an experienced tourist guide—a horse for me, and a mule that would carry my guide and my baggage. It was eleven when we left the office. At six o'clock—said Mr. Amsaleg—he would come to the hotel to take me to his home to dine. He and his wife would be delighted to have me. Would I know how to manage alone in the city until then? I assured him there was no cause for concern: I was accustomed to travelling alone. Just as I had not lost my way walking unaccompanied in Athens, Florence, Rome, and Assisi.

I shall forget neither the marvellous time I spent in Assisi two years ago with you, Virginia and Violet Dickenson, nor your admiration of Giotto when you saw his fresco, St. Francis Preaches to the Birds, in the church there. You said that the greatness of Giotto, in contrast to all his predecessors, lay in his demonstration that the divine is not in the distant heavens, transcending man's grasp, that it is not the province of saints, but can be earthly and dwell within us as a moral essence. Your words moved me, for, until that moment, you had never spoken of paintings of the saints. I thought you disdained them, that they were not to your taste, and now....

When we returned to the church and I remarked on the inclination of Francis's head, bent submissively and humbly, as he spoke to the birds at his feet, and on the movement of his hands, that seemed to be explaining to them the words he was whispering, and on the peasant woman standing at his side, and I said how much human simplicity there was in that painting—you pointed out the deep blue background, saying: yes, although, on the other hand, the lapis lazuli background signifies a noble saintliness that is almost regal…and I thought: how right you are! And how sensitive you are to the sublime, despite your atheistic proclamations…. Later, as we sat in a small cafe near the monastery and, from the summit of that hill, we gazed out upon the valley leading to Perugia, soft fog wandering through its green groves, you said, "Being in a Mediterranean landscape affects me more deeply than being in an English landscape…"

I have just recalled those words of yours.

Jaffa! There is no resemblance, Vanessa, between what I have seen during the many hours I wandered its streets, and the paintings by David Roberts, Bartlett, and Charles Wilson. The tranquil, static paintings of Roberts and Bartlett—in which Jaffa is shown through a thin veil, dreamlike, a kind of desert mirage, a celestial Jaffa—possess none of that city's true, restless, kaleidoscopic spirit. Wilson's lines, however, are darker, stronger, and the scenes he paints are more dramatic. But this is a more exotic, slightly operatic reality that reminds me of St. Saens' *Samson and Delilah*.

The true, earthly Jaffa is a bustling city filled with contrasts: Arabs wearing tarbooshes or kaffiyehs sit on stools near the entrance of small coffee houses, lazily smoking nargilehs, their expressions somnolent—yet there, opposite them, a Bedouin races his horse along the street, a long sword belted at his side, his trailing kaffiyeh and brown caftan, called an *abaya,* flapping in the wind, and he seems to have come rushing headlong from the desert to descend upon his enemies; men wearing European suits and hats—Jews? Armenians? Greeks?—stand in the doorways of their textile shops waiting for customers and, in contrast, like a scene from another world, an Arab peasant woman walks by, wearing a black dress, strands of coins hung round her neck, bearing a pail of thorny, bruised cactus fruit on her head to sell….

I stopped in my tracks, seized with wonder at the sight of that woman: heavyset, the mass of her hips and thighs swaying from side to side like waves, her enormous breasts quivering like fish aspic with every step, her thick arm laden with silver bracelets raised over her head, clutching the rim of the pail—and she strode along the street with such grace, with such ease—with such nobility, I would say!

Those contrasts! On the one hand, in dark alcoves, like gaps in the ruins, sit goldsmiths, cobblers, tailors bent over their labour, as if immersed in arcane occupation, like the scribes in a monastery; and on the other, the fruit and vegetable stalls stand exposed to the powerful light of the sun: piles of merry yellow oranges; bunches of lush lettuce leaves, their greenness glowing; split, sliced watermelons displaying to buyers the redness of their flesh and the gleam of their shiny seeds; and on other stands, fish only just trapped in the nets of the local fishermen flap about, their silver scales playing in the glittering rays of the sun.

Those colourful sights—as remote from the gloomy, depressing drabness of London as day is from night—so inspired me to take up my pencil and brush that I returned to the hotel, removed my drawing pad from my suitcase, went out again into the streets of the city, found a quiet corner near a mosque, sat down on a stone bench and began sketching a camel crouching in the square in front of a shop that sold shiny copper objects. Boxes of gravel rested on his hump, and an Arab boy held its tether, as if he were guarding it.

That camel, whose hide was the colour of golden desert sand, enchanted me. Its long neck was stretched upward, as if yearning for invisible infinity, longing for it, its lower lip drooping, as if reconciled to its fate, and its eyes held a look of primeval woe, like the eyes of the scapegoat in Holman Hunt's painting.

I drew the lines of his form, and then something happened to me that can happen to someone like me only in a foreign country—and perhaps only in this marvellous country: as I sketched, I felt as if someone were standing behind me, looking at my drawing. Upon turning my head, I saw a young man, twenty or twenty-five years old, wearing a wrinkled white shirt open at the neck, and sporting a peaked cap. He smiled at me and spoke, first in Russian, then in German, and when he realised that I knew neither language, he asked, "English?" When I nodded, he said, in school-learned English, that he begged my forgiveness for observing my work without permission, and that he thought the drawing quite beautiful. I thanked him, and, smiling modestly, he said that he too was a painter. This pleasant-looking fellow aroused my curiosity and we began to speak. I learned from our conversation that he had come to this country from Russia over a month ago with a group of "pioneers," that is to say, Jewish Zionists who aspire to do agricultural work in the Jewish settlements—and until he found such employment, he was staying with a family that had immigrated here from his native city a year ago, in a new quarter in northern Jaffa known as Neveh Zedek. Would I care to come with him to see his paintings? "With pleasure!" I replied. And so, only a few hours had passed from the moment I set foot in this country—I rejoiced—and I had already had the opportunity to meet one of its residents and walk about the city with him! And I liked his simple, direct, and unaffected approach to a stranger—so uncommon, so contrary, in fact, to the conventions of our country.

We left the city's central area and crossed the narrow train tracks adjacent to the German colony where my hotel was. An expanse of clean yellow sand spread before my eyes, from where it met the blue sea, sparkling in the sun, northwards, to the horizon. Amongst the mounds of soft sand, in which one sinks to one's ankles, were several dozen unassuming one- or two-story houses with red or grey tiled roofs, arranged in four or five straight rows. This was the neighbourhood in which the "pioneer" at my side resided. Misha, he told me, was his name.

Here was another sight I had seen only in outlying villages: a bare-headed fellow wearing tattered clothing preceded us, his bare feet trudging through the deep sand, and his shoes, their laces tied together, hanging from his shoulder. When we caught up to him, it turned out that he was Misha's friend. They exchanged some words in Russian; Misha introduced me, and appeared to invite him to come along with us. The three of us entered a small room, painted white, that contained an iron bedstead covered with a black duvet, burlap-covered kerosene tins used as chairs, several boxes that served as a kind of pantry or small kitchen, a rickety table and a doorless cupboard in which several items of clothing were hung. We sat on the tins while Misha removed several oil paintings that were hidden behind the clothes in the wardrobe, showed them to me and asked my opinion of them.

The paintings were quite interesting, although amateurish. Colourful fantasies of exotic landscapes, somewhat in the style of Henri Rousseau, possessing a naive humour. Clive Bell would certainly call them "undisciplined." I told him what I thought, and he was so pleased that he put a bottle of vodka and some glasses on the table. The two men drank, chatted in Russian, even argued a bit, and Misha explained the subject of their disagreement: his friend, who had come here several months before him, wanted to return to Russia, for he had not found work here and had no liking whatsoever for the East. Misha was trying to persuade him to stay, not to despair, reproaching him for abandoning his Zionist ideal and for deluding himself that he would find happiness in the Diaspora.

So, as you see, dear Vanessa, on my first day, I purely by chance learned something of the problems besetting the Zionist "pioneers" in Palestine, of whom I had known nothing before my arrival here. Misha accompanied me back to the city, went with me to the bank to exchange some of my sterling for local currency, and it was already two o'clock when we parted. He kissed my hand, bowing, in the manner of the Russian aristocracy, and hoped we would meet again in Jerusalem or one of the settlements.

I will spare you a description of the pleasant and congenial dinner at the Amsalegs, although there too, I learned much about life in this extremely problematic country. Mrs. Amsaleg, a corpulent woman born in Morocco, engulfed me in warmth and affection from the moment I entered their home, as if I were a relative they had not seen in a long time—yet another thing uncommon in our country (a faint smile spread over her dark face—like a crimson sunset in the desert...). At the conclusion of our abundant lamb-and-couscous meal, as we sat in the salon that was lined with Persian carpets and adorned with copper bowls and antique copper lamps, drinking Turkish coffee and eating sweets, Mr. Amsaleg spoke of Sir

Moses Montefiore's seven visits to Palestine during the last century, of his great involvement in building Jewish neighbourhoods outside the Jerusalem walls. He spoke, too, of the obstacles placed by the corrupt Turkish government—all of whose functionaries are tainted with a passion for taking bribes—in the path of the Jews trying to purchase land and build houses, and of their ill treatment of Jewish refugees from the Russian pogroms, who are refused entry into the country. "If the English ruled here, everything would be different," he said, mentioning, of course, George Eliot's *Daniel Deronda*. He then added with a sly smile, "England, you know, is not far from here. They need only cross the Red Sea, as our forefathers crossed it several thousand years ago."

The following day, that is, today, at seven forty-five, I stood across the street from Cook and Son, ready and waiting for my journey, wearing boots and a riding habit I had brought with me.

And then I saw a most astonishing and extraordinary spectacle that was not of this world: a long procession of several hundred shabbily dressed people appeared, moving from the port side towards the city centre, bearded men wearing tattered sheepskin coats and fur hats—as if it were winter—and women clad in long black dresses and white or collared kerchiefs—bent over, carrying sacks on their shoulders. Marching at the head of the procession were priests in black robes and mitres, large crucifixes on their chests, chanting hymns in Russian. They were Russian pilgrims, some of them barefoot, some shod in torn shoes, indigent and pious peasants on their way to the holy city of Jerusalem. When the first members of the procession reached the city square, many of them fell onto the ground and crawled along on their knees, following the priests towards the train station.

As I stood there, astounded by this spectacle, which stirred both awe and compassion, my dragoman arrived—a tall, thin, handsome lad of about eighteen, holding the reins of a horse and a mule. He looked at me curiously for a moment—was I the person who had hired him?—my girth most certainly causing him to doubt that I could ride a horse…. But he smiled at me forthwith and introduced himself: "Aziz, your dragoman, milady." He spoke English with an eastern accent, although fluently, and he wore a bright white kaffiyeh on his head. A smile never left his lips, and there was something gentle about him that I liked from the moment I saw him. I pointed to the dusty procession, and he said: "Yes, we are accustomed to it. Every two or three weeks, a similar procession of poor Russian pilgrims arrives to worship at the graves of the saints in Jerusalem. Especially now, before their Easter holiday." Indicating the bearded men dragging themselves along on their knees, he said: "Some drag themselves like that all the way to Jerusalem, and many die before they get there."

The horse—of the fine Arab breed—was beautiful; grey with a white spot crossing its long face. Its harness was lovely too, inlaid with blue precious stones. The white mule—a kind of tall, large-boned, sturdy donkey, bore on its back sacks that contained—as Aziz explained—provisions for our journey; and his wide saddle also had a place for my two suitcases, as well as for Aziz himself.

Before leaving the city—perhaps the procession of pilgrims had reminded me of this—I asked to see the house of Simon the tanner, which I knew was open to visitors in Jaffa. This is the Simon mentioned in the New Testament, who gave Peter lodging in his house on the seashore, from which he departed to raise Tabitha from the dead with his cry, "Tabitha, rise!" Aziz, of course, knew the place.

Vanessa dear! I know that you'll mock me for the biblical verses I recall and mention from time to time. You were raised in a home where atheism was the keynote, your late father taught his children not to believe in "supernatural" things, but I remember that three or four years ago, when you were still living at 22 Hyde Park Gate, you told me that for three years, from the age of twelve to fifteen, you were very religious, influenced by your friends; you then told me that one day, walking through Kensington Gardens and enjoying the sight of the tall trees, the wide lawns and the lake with its floating swans—suddenly, in a kind of "epiphany" (in its opposite sense), you lost your faith entirely, and told yourself that you would never be religious again. That was something I could not understand. I told you that it is especially in sights of nature—in trees, in flowers, in tiny petals and thin trembling stamens amongst whose calices bees hover to gather pollen, in delicate buds slowly unfolding—that the higher power is, in my opinion, revealed; not "supernatural," but present in nature itself and in all of its marvellous phenomena. You smiled at me and said: "If there is a God, He is indifferent to beauty. It is beneath His dignity to take notice of it. Apart from which, he's busy with other, apparently 'moral' things. It is but we poor mortals who admire beauty…"

Aziz left the animals in the care of a boy, paying him several pennies, and we walked down a lane that led to a kind of tunnel through the back of the port area. We descended some pitted steps and reached a small stone house that looked like a ruin adjoining the tunnel. A small well stood in front of it, sheltered by a water wheel and the branches of a fig tree. This had been the house of Simon the tanner. We went through the narrow door into a dark room, shadows thrown against its walls by the glow of the eternal flame hung from the ceiling. An old Arab, who guarded the site, welcomed us silently. The room was empty but for an icon of Simon, in the Byzantine style, on one of the walls, surrounded by engraved verses in Greek. I stood before the icon, the total silence of the room broken only by the rhythmic murmur of the waves breaking on the shore beyond the wall like a sad melody, and when I closed my eyes they filled with radiant light, and I thought I saw a great sheet descend from heaven like the one Peter saw when he was here.*

(I don't know why, but when I emerged into the light of day, I had a frightening presentiment that evil would befall me in this country. Was this the sort of hidden fear felt by someone in a foreign country whose people and customs are alien to him, and who

---

* It appears that, already on her second day in the Holy Land, Miss Campbell-Bennett was having hallucinations caused by latent hypersensitivity and influenced by stories she had absorbed in her childhood. Her account of her vision of the sheet descending from heaven, enveloped in radiant light, is reminiscent of the story Constantine told his biographer, Eusebius, in which the vision of a crucifix of light crossing the sun appeared to him, and similar cases described in Dr. A.D. Starbuck's compilation. The physical symptoms accompanying such experiences are rapid pulse, shortness of breath, and faintness that may cause a loss of consciousness. I must find out if she experienced photism, or delirium tremens in her childhood.—P.D.M.

occasionally feels he is in a hostile land where danger lurks? Or was I perhaps afraid of myself, lest I bring evil upon myself? Promise me, Vanessa, that no evil will befall me…I do so hope that all will go well…)

We rode to the hotel to pick up my suitcases, and it was nine o'clock when we headed out of the city—Aziz on his mule leading, and I following on my horse. His face held an expression of wonder, and satisfaction, at my practised horsemanship. People on both sides of the street stopped what they were doing and stepped out of the shop doors to watch us, people passing by halted—all were amazed and amused at this apparently rare sight in the East—a woman wearing a riding habit, boots and a wide-brimmed white hat, riding a horse. Many grinned in disdain, mischievous boys in the market shouted after us, and I myself laughed inwardly: here we are, the two of us, a kind of Don Quixote astride his horse and a Sancho Panza on his donkey.

Sun! Strong sun, supreme in its might, pours its light upon this land! There is no hiding from it! East of Jaffa are orange, grape-fruit and lemon groves, orchards planted with fig, pomegranate, date, peach, and apricot trees—their leaves and fruit flashing in the sun. And east of them—fallow land spread with a colourful carpet of wild-flowers, dominated by yellow and red: chrysanthemums, groundsels, marigolds, anemones, poppies, buttercups. Aziz, whom I had already told that flowers were my major interest, said that luck was with me: the rain had come late this year, and it had been plentiful, which is why the earth had brought forth more flowers than in previous years, and they were still far from withering. We stopped occasionally and dismounted to pick flowers—although these were flowers found in our country, and were not "biblical flowers"—which I put into the cardboard flower press I had brought with me. Aziz, seeing me thus, wondered about me. Was I a botany teacher? he inquired. I told him that I was collecting them so I could paint them. "Flowers, flowers," he said, smiling as if reflecting upon something, and a moment later, he quite surprised me by quoting the lines from *Macbeth* spoken by Lady Macbeth to stir her husband on: "Look like the innocent flower/But be the serpent under it." I asked him where he had acquired his knowledge of Shakespeare, and he told me he had attended the English Mission School in Jaffa, and had studied *Macbeth* for an entire year. He knew many passages by heart.

We continued to ride, and on our right, we saw long avenues of palm trees stretching from the main road to a two-storey white house that looked like a manor house, surrounded on all sides by well-tended vegetation. When I read the words printed in Latin letters on the arched gate to this boulevard, "The Mikveh Israel Agricultural School," I remembered what Mr. Amsaleg had said and told Aziz that I wished to tarry there a while.

On one side of the boulevard, a bare-chested youth was harvesting clover with a scythe, and on the other, I saw some Arab women carrying tins containing water on their heads, and Arab children, perhaps ten years old, using them to water the plant nurseries that contained forest saplings, pine, and eucalyptus. Several youngsters were running about, playing ball in front of the house, and speaking French to each other. I asked for the headmaster, and one of them went to call him. A short man with a moustache and small, crafty eyes appeared and, in French, asked what I wanted. I introduced myself: an artist who had come from England to paint the biblical flowers of the Holy Land. Was there a teacher of botany there who could help me locate and identify such flowers? The headmaster, Mr. Lupo was his name, looked at me as if he found this utterly preposterous. "What flowers, for example?" he asked suspiciously. Perhaps he thought me a spy: "For example, *dudai'm*," I said, using the Hebrew name and adding the Latin name, *mandragora*. Mr. Lupo narrowed his gaze. His suspicion apparently increased. No, he had never heard of such a flower. He stopped abruptly and shouted something threatening towards the Arab children, who were frightened by his rebuke and quickened the pace of their work. "As for the botany teacher," he again spoke to me, his expression nasty, "he has gone out into the fields with his students and will not return until noon. Does Mademoiselle wish to wait for him?"

As we continued riding eastward, I saw large fields of yellow and white mustard flowers. It is the same mustard of the Cruciferae family mentioned in Luke, verses 13 and 17 (yes, I am again bothering

19

you with my Scriptures...), in which the Lord says to his disciples: "If you had as much faith as a grain of mustard seed..." and so on. I dismounted and picked a bunch of mustard plants, many of whose fruit had already ripened—they are long, thin pods with prickly edges that contain tiny grains—and as I held them in the palm of my hand, I felt as if I were standing in a field with the people listening to the Lord speak, and I tried to feel—yes, to feel, not only to understand—the meaning of his words.

We stopped to rest in the shade of a fig tree near one of the holy burial sites on the road—a small, domed structure with a trough fastened to its side, cool spring water spouting from it for the refreshment of passers-by. Aziz took some pita bread, olives, and cheese made from sheep's milk from his side pack and placed them on a large piece of cloth he spread on the ground. I ate a bit of this and that, and as he ate, Aziz asked what the *dudaïm* were that I had mentioned. "You studied Shakespeare, but not the Bible?" Yes, they had of course studied the New Testament and chapters from the Old, but he did not recall having read about *dudaïm*. I told him the story from Genesis about Reuben, who found *dudaïm* in the field and brought them to Leah, his mother. Rachel asked Leah to give her a few, for they possess the power to arouse a man's love and passion, but Leah refused at first...and so on. "Do they also arouse a woman's love?" Aziz smiled, blushing. I was momentarily flustered. I said to myself that he was crossing the boundary of what was acceptable in the relationship between a woman tourist and her hired help. But there was something clever and not unpleasant in his face, so I hastened to reply: "But of course! When love is aroused—there is no difference..."*

---

* The matter of the *dudaïm*, the mandrakes, which is apparently an obsession with her, leads us to the assumption that they represent for her—if we remember the biblical tale in its entirety—repressed desire for relations that promise pregnancy and birth, especially in light of the fact that B. has remained unmarried, despite her advanced age. Until now, I have met with Miss B. only three times—once in the village of Magdala and twice in Ein a-Tabiha. Yet I anticipate difficulties in her treatment which, in effect, I should have foreseen from the very beginning: on all my visits to her mother, Mrs. Elizabeth Campbell-Bennett, during

Aziz was silent, and then he looked at me and asked if I were married. I said I was not. He looked at me and asked how old I was. I said to myself that, apparently, it is not impolite in the East to ask a woman her age, and I replied: thirty-one. He smiled shyly and said, "You are pretty. Why are you not married?" I laughed and said that, unmarried, I feel free to behave as I wish. He looked at me as if wondering at my nature, and then I asked, "And you?"—He, it seems, was already engaged to be married, but his fiancée was too young, only twelve, and he was waiting until she grew up to celebrate their nuptials. He also told me that he was born in the village of Ishdod—which is the biblical Ashdod—that his family is well-to-do; they own a fifty-acre citrus grove, as well as a peach and apricot orchard. He was not working as a dragoman in order to earn his livelihood, but because he likes accompanying tourists who come from the four corners of the world, "especially lady tourists," he said, his black eyes twinkling.

Am I naive, Vanessa, to expect that in this country, I will see, in a miraculous moment, the light that unfetters the soul and gives it the wings to fly like a free bird, unencumbered by feelings of guilt or contrition?

Will such a moment ever come?

We stopped three more times on the way, and it was already four o'clock when we reached Ramle. When it became clear to me that there were no hotels in the town, I found shelter for the night in the convent of St. Joseph. Aziz went to tie up the animals in a *khan*, saying he would find lodgings with one of his acquaintances.

As I wrote at the beginning of my letter, the town of Ramle itself is quite wretched, with low houses and streets of sand (Ramle means "sand" in Arabic); but before sunset, one of the sisters at the convent—a pleasant French woman who insisted on speaking Eng-

---

which B. was present, she exhibited an sceptical attitude—if not towards me personally, then towards psychiatry per se—that was expressed more than once in sarcastic remarks. I think that the source of this attitude lay in her opposition to my attempts of several years ago to persuade her to withdraw from London's Bohemian society, and particularly from that circle known as the Bloomsbury Group.—P.D.M.

lish to me—took me to several ancient sites: a thirteenth-century mosque and the Great Mosque, which was originally a Crusader cathedral named after St. John—beneath it is a large subterranean pool, its ceiling supported by columns; and to the White Mosque, from which a high minaret rises some thirty meters. On the way there, the sister told me that Ramle, which was built at the beginning of the eighth century by Caliph Suliman of the Umaya dynasty, had been the largest city in this country before it was destroyed by earthquakes and wars.

These sites were not of great interest to me, but the town is surrounded by marvellous olive groves. Observing those ancient olive trees, their gnarled, twisted, horny and hooked trunks, looking like venerable elders whose bodies preserve traces of their rich life experience and whose faces are wrinkled with the imprint of their wisdom under their silvery crowns, I thought of you: if you were here with me, we would both have placed our easels at the edge of the grove and, as we did then, in Cornwall, facing the waves of the churning sea, so we would have passed our brushes across the canvas and penetrated the heart of this Eastern landscape...

I remember that, as we painted there, facing the sea, you said that it was not the expanse of the sea that interested you, but rather the crests of the foamy waves that seemed to be "crying out" to you. And that is how you painted them, almost "mad." In order to deepen the blue of the sea, you used a red base, in the style of Whistler. Suddenly, a storm blew up, our easels were torn from where they stood, and the canvases took off in the wind. We chased after them, retrieving them only at the door of the house. Virginia was sequestered in her room, locked in her silence, and hardly spoke to me. I thought that she was displeased at my joining you.

I think of you a great deal, Vanessa, and I occasionally recall the "Thursday clubs" at your home in Bloomsbury; the erudite conversations on the art of painting, and the interesting comments made by Clive Bell and our friends from the Royal Academy. I am so far away from all that now.... It seems to me that it is not only the sea that separates me from the group, but whole periods of life as well...those conversations, flowing or hesitating, on Sargent's portraits...on the

Oscar Wilde scandal…on Victorian etiquette that forbids a woman to be alone with a young man in a coffee house…on whether absolute black exists in nature…absolute white…on whether a person can succeed in life without God….

And I recall, too, Virginia's highly meaningful silences. Please give her my regards, and to Katherine Cox, Beatrice Mayor, and Marjorie Strachey as well. Please write soon. I am waiting. My address, until my next letter, at least, is: Poste Restante, the Austrian Post Office, Jerusalem.

Yours with love,
Beatrice.

P.S. An amusing idea for a painting that came to my mind as I was plodding through the sand of the alleyways of Ramle: In one of those alleyways, near the door to a small adobe house (plain wood painted blue), with strings of garlic and red peppers hanging in its windows, there stood a small grey donkey, its head bowed as if in surrender. It was so silent, so uncomplainingly bearing its heavy burden of suffering, that seeing it reminded me of the chapter from Isaiah cited in Matthew (Chapter 8), referring to salvation: "He took our infirmities and bore our diseases." And at that moment, I thought: I will paint that donkey in front of the blue door, the halo of a saint above its head….

Jerusalem, The Olivet Pension
19th April, 1906

It is not yet dawn. Was it the thundering, wailing voice of the muezzin calling the believers to prayer, or heralding the Day of Judgment, that woke me? Or the bells tolling from the many churches in the Old City, echoing each other, their sounds landing like stones beyond the Wall? I leapt from my bed to the window, the massive, sombre Wall facing me still enshrouded in the pre-dawn dusky greyness, majestic and awesome. "Four thousand years look down upon us from on high," Napoleon said to his troops as they stood facing the pyramids in Egypt, and I, facing these walls, can say, "Three thousand years of prophecies of wrath and consolation, of blood, destruction, and apocalyptic visions, of messages of grace and salvation, look down upon me from the top of this Wall."

Crouching on the ground in front of the Jaffa Gate, at the foot of the fortress the Jews call David's Tower, are beggars dressed in rags, peasant women with bowls of some goods or others placed between their legs, and a few camels; donkeys bearing sacks and crates on their backs, their hooves raising dust, arrive from the road that leads to Bethlehem and Hebron, and nimbly enter the gate, peddlers wrapped in kaffiyehs driving them forward.

The dream. Now I remember: I am walking alone down a narrow alley in the Old City, it is the cobblers' or the goldsmiths' street, alcoves on both sides, and I think the alley will close in on me and I won't be able to get out of it. An Arab woman accosts me, half her face covered by a black veil, the exposed half quite beautiful, pallid, her complexion olive, reminiscent of El Greco's paintings, and an aggressive look in her black eyes. Pulling at my sleeve, she asks for alms. She doesn't ask; she demands boldly. I try to evade her grasp, but she will not let me go. I cry for help, but there is no one to turn to. And suddenly, I see that she is pulling the bracelet off my wrist. I cry inwardly: Vanessa gave me that bracelet as a gift! It is more precious to me than anything in the world! But my lips are paralysed. She pulls it from my arm and laughs in my face. I open my mouth to call for a policeman—and then I awaken.

Vanessa. I try to banish her from my being, but she reappears in my waking moments and in my dreams.

"But why Palestine?" she asked me as we stood in the doorway to her house in Gordon Square and I told her of my decision to travel.

"To purify myself," I said.

"Purify yourself?!" she emitted a shriek accompanied by an abbreviated laugh. "Of what?!"

"Of myself," I whispered, feeling tears choking me.

She stared at me for a moment, as if discovering in me a rather irrational oddness she had not previously been aware of, and with a half smile of both concern and compassion, she said:

"Do you want to baptize yourself in the Jordan?"

She spoke with the irony she displayed towards anything that smacked of religious ritual. She had once declared that if ever a child were born to her, she would not baptize it.

"Not in water," I said.

"In what, then?"

"In light," I replied. "There is a purifying light in that land," I said.*

---

* In a theopathic personality such as B., purification through immersion in water is likely to seem most natural, particularly since this method of purification (prevalent not only in Christianity, but in other religions too, such as Judaism, Hinduism, and others) not only symbolizes rebirth, but is also charged with clear erotic-archetypal meaning: the purging of guilt feelings related to sex. Does the announcement of her intention to become purified by "light" attest to her virginity? The question of whether B. had remained a virgin until her arrival in Palestine merits clarification. And how sad it is to read these words in her diary in the light of the knowledge that her end was not purification, but defilement.—P.D.M.

She gazed at me for another moment, gave me an abrupt kiss on the cheek, and entered the house.

The anxiety I felt from the moment we began to ascend the mountain grew stronger with every step that brought us closer to this holy city.

The plain had welcomed me. Extending from Ramle to the foot of the mountains were fields of wild vegetation dotted with yellow and red flowers, barley and oat fields and fields of sunflowers and corn glowing in the sun; poor villages, smoke rising from their bread ovens, scraggly dogs leaping from between the small adobe houses to chase us with angry barks; and the sight—so biblical—of threshing floors and a donkey or camel turning the wheel and dragging the flail over the grains, and the women shaking large sieves, the chaff and straw flying in the hot wind. At noon, we stopped at the Bab-al-Wad *khan* at the opening of the narrow ravine ascending into the Judean mountains to take a light meal and give water to the animals. The *khan* and its surroundings abounded with men and animals—native Arabs, pilgrims from Greece, Serbia, Italy, and Spain, dark-skinned people from some African country or other, Jews clad in work clothes and Jews wearing the traditional black of the devout; and all around, tied to tree trunks or rings on the *khan* wall, were horses, donkeys, here and there a crouched camel. Three wagons stood on the side of the road.

We paid the road tax, called a *darbiya*, for ourselves and our horse and mule, to the Jewish leaseholder of the *khan*, and paid several pennies for a cup of hot, sweetened tea. Shortly after we sat down at the dining table, four or five Turkish soldiers armed with bayonet rifles entered the stone house that was bustling with people coming and going. They moved amongst the crowd asking for papers. Although a kind of fearful silence, a dread of authority, spread through that dark hall, all appeared to go smoothly.

Suddenly, however, two policemen seized a Jewish fellow who apparently had no papers, and began to drag him outside. When he resisted, and another young man, obviously a friend, came to his assistance, the soldiers lashed them with whips, kicked them, struck them on the back with their rifle barrels, and shouting horribly, took them, bleeding, outside and put them on one of the wagons that was headed west, towards Jaffa.

I was seized with trembling. Aziz, observing this, explained that many Jews had come from Russia of late—"Muscovites," he called them—refugees from the recent pogroms, and they intended to remain here, to work or settle the land, even though they did not possess the "red slip" that would grant them the right to stay in Palestine for three months. There was nothing for it, he said, but to expel them forcibly. "The law is the law, lady," he said (he insists on calling me "lady"), although he too cannot bear the Turks, he said.

But my anxiety persisted as we made our way up the mountain, I astride my horse in the lead, and Aziz on the mule walking slowly behind me, "breathing down my neck." I had felt the same sort of anxiety several times in the past. Once at our estate in Torrington, on a cold winter's day when snow covered the garden and all the surrounding fields, my parents went to Colchester for the weekend, leaving me in the big house with only the servants and my cousin, Louise-Anne. I was sixteen then, and she wasn't much older, twenty-two, and we slept together that night in my parents' wide bed that was encircled by a canopy interwoven with silver threads and embroidered with images of does, and when we had extinguished the light and all was silent, I listened to her breathing and could not fall asleep; I did not fall asleep until dawn. My hand was drawn to touch her arm; to stroke her exposed shoulder, so rounded and warm. Her breath intoxicated my senses, the touch of her silky nightgown made my thighs quiver. The ripe fruit was so close to my mouth, and I was forbidden to touch it! The torments of Tantalus! Nonetheless, I was filled with anxiety lest something terrible happen to defile me for all my life. And another time, two years ago, paying a condolence call on Vanessa after her father died, when the family still lived in 22 Hyde Park Gate, and I remained in the room with her stepbrother, George, he held my hand as I sat at his side and stroked it as if to console me, as if I were the one in need of consolation…then too…that anxiety…but different…for I recalled that Vanessa had told me how he used to embrace and caress her, and enter her bed and touch her in private places, occasionally doing so to her sister, Virginia as well…*

Desolate mountains rose on both sides of the road. Low weeds, withered by the heat of the day, thistles with their yellow and purple blooms, Pistacia bushes, occasional carobs and oaks, and limestone rocks glaring in the sun. And I and my anxiety, which did not leave me even when we arrived at the large village of Abu-Gosh and, guided by Aziz, I wandered through the halls of the fortress-like Benedictine monastery built on the foundations of a Crusader fortress in which, according to monastic lore, Richard the Lion-Hearted had prayed when he came to Jerusalem. I went down with him into the secret cave of the monastery cellar, which contained a well of spring water, and then re-ascended and stood facing the Byzantine frescoes and mosaics that depicted the deeds of the apostles. Aziz pointed to the paintings and explained, and I heard nothing he said, feeling pressure in my chest, an oppressive weight. I asked to go outside, outside, I knew not where.

After we had passed through the Arab village of Kolonia and the Jewish village of Motza, Jerusalem appeared in the east like a majestic sight from another world, the sun's rays slanting westward, shattering against its stone walls, shining in myriad slivers from its domes and minarets. Only when I saw this spectacle, appearing before me as if from the remoteness of the past, the depths of memory and the pages of the Holy Scriptures, did the weight lift from my heart, which filled with light. My horse began to gallop as if he smelled his heart's desire approaching and rejoiced at reaching it. Aziz remained far behind, and I did not stop to wait for him until I reached the first houses of the Jewish quarter.

And during all of yesterday, as I plodded at Aziz's side through

---

* These confessions are extraordinarily interesting, and must be clarified regarding B.'s reactions of attraction and rejection vis-à-vis her relations with members of both sexes. Was her friendship with V.S. not merely platonic? I found no allusion to this in the latter's letter to me. And I wonder at myself, how, in all my visits to the Campbell-Bennett house over the years, I never suspected B.'s deviant inclinations.—P.D.M.

the alleys of the Old City, and entered the Church of the Holy Sepulchre with him, mingling with the crowds of worshippers, pilgrims from all over the world, and he wended his way through this labyrinth, with its mixture of styles, to the many chapels—of the Greeks, the Copts, the Abyssinians, the Armenians, and to the Chapel of Mary Magdalene, of Mary the Egyptian, of St. Helena, and of the Forty Martyrs, and returning to the "navel of the world" and the cavern of the Sepulchre itself—I was once again visited by the "evil spirit" and fell into a depression; and when I dragged after him along the Via Dolorosa, past the fourteen Stations of the Cross Jesus passed through bearing his cross on his back, from the Muristan to Hic Flagellabit, and from there to the Ecce Homo Arch, and from there to the Greek Hospice and to the Damascus Gate and the House of Lazarus, and to Golgotha Chapel and the Holy Sepulchre, the same sorrowful route along which the Saviour stumbled three times from the weight of the cross as He walked to His death, I said to myself: it is only fitting that you feel, if only the slightest bit, the suffering endured by the Son of God, whose death on the cross atoned for your sins.

And the constant presence of my dragoman, who explained, walked and explained all that I was seeing, and connected it to what is written in the New Testament—yes, he is knowledgeable, and quite experienced in guiding tourists—was so burdensome that I could barely keep from asking him to leave me alone.

I longed to be alone. Alone with the confusion and storm of emotions that raged within me.

For all along the route, through the labyrinth of the Church of the Holy Sepulchre and the alleys of the Old City, tears permeated my being, drop by drop, as if from a spring whose waters had dried up, and every drop sank within me in a kind of bitter lament: perhaps you were mistaken…perhaps you were mistaken…you will never escape from your loneliness. You fled from your loneliness in the group, from your loneliness with Vanessa—and plunged into the loneliness of being with yourself.

For no loneliness is harsher than that of someone who has not accepted himself.

And how will you become purified?

When I parted from Aziz in the evening, after he had accompanied me to this pension in the new city—a walk of some twenty minutes from the Jaffa Gate—whose owner, Mr. Hansmann, is an Englishman from Liverpool, I told him I would not need him for the next three days, and he was free to do as he wished, I would pay him his wages in any case. An expression of disappointment, insult, perhaps even bitterness, crossed his face as he thanked me with exaggerated, obviously ironic, politeness: "Yes, milady, thank you, milady."

And today, with the help of a detailed map that Mr. Hansmann gave me last night, I will retrace the path I took yesterday, re-enter the Church of the Holy Sepulchre and, if there is time, I will leave the Old City and head eastward to ascend the Mount of Olives. I have been invited to Consul Blech's office at four in the afternoon.

I am thinking of my painting. I must, first of all, accustom my eyes to the strong light of this country before I put any oil or watercolours on canvas. This light has a quality different from any other light I know, not only from that of the north, but also from that of Italy or Greece, which contain a base of the blue of the sea and the green of lush vegetation. Here, the bare light, lacking any shadow, enwraps bodies in a sheer luminescence that seems to derive from an ancient, primal source. In European painting, especially the sort that depicts holy scenes, a mysterious effect is created by the use of dark colours—black, brown, dark green. That is why, when Renaissance artists painted scenes from the life of Jesus and the Apostles, they portrayed Jerusalem as if it were a Medieval city that had temples similar to Romanesque or Gothic churches, exuding darkness and shadows, and on the sides, or background, on the horizon—thick forests or groves, whose concealment infuses the whole painting with an aura of mysteriousness. I am reminded of Piero della Francesca's painting of the crucifixion, in which Jerusalem is a small walled city on the summit of a hill, with tall, narrow two- or three-story houses, cramped so closely together they seemed to be vying for a position closer to the duke's castle. They have red tiled roofs and rectangular windows, and carved, gabled towers protrude from them. The dominant colours in that painting are brown, yellow, and ochre, characteristic of an Italian city. And I remember Giotto's frescoes depicting the charitable deeds of the Apostles, in which thick, towering trees grow out of huge boulders—the sort of trees that grow only in the north.

These paintings—in which shadow predominates over light and which abound with luxuriant vegetation, meadows, and fat sheep feeding peacefully, grazing animals peering out of thick woods—can teach me nothing about painting the flowers of the Holy Land. I shall paint these flowers as holy flowers, flowers of the soul, light emanating from them, and light illuminating them, as is written in Isaiah: "They that dwelt in a land of deep darkness, upon them hath the light shined." The holy rose, the holy lily, the holy thistle and thorn, the holy mandrakes...

I must become accustomed to myself.

Accept myself.

Eight at night.

I spent two full and very interesting hours in Consul Blech's office in an impressive stone house not far from the Abyssinian Church. He is quite an animated young man of about forty, with a straw-collared shock of hair and thin moustache, his azure eyes shining like quicksilver marbles. When I told him of the purpose of my visit to Palestine, he smiled: "Flowers? It is thorns you must paint! This country is entirely prickly thorns! Are you familiar with the cactus plant, the one known here as a *sabra*? You should taste its fruit—a sweet and delicious one, I must admit—and see how it covers your hands with prickles!" He then became carried away with praise—at first, I did not understand why, or why to me, so far removed from politics—of our new prime minister, Sir Henry Campbell-Bannerman, for having so cleverly led the Liberal Party into power after Lord Balfour's resignation, and for having granted benefits to the Boers in South Africa, thereby preventing an intensification of the conflict with them, and so on...but when he realised that I was puzzled by him, he said, "If I am not mistaken, you are related to him..."—"Related? To the prime minister?" I laughed. And suddenly, I understood: His ears, or his eyes, had misled him! Instead of "Campbell-Bennett," he had heard, or seen, "Campbell-Bannerman"…He nonetheless did not give up, and when he remembered that Sir Henry was Scottish, a native of Glasgow, he said, "But you are of Scottish origin, are you not?"—"One of my forebears, I believe," I said, "was born in Inverness, but we have been established in Essex, at Torrington Estate, for three generations." "Torrington…yes, I know the area…" His eyes lit up with longing, "Beautiful pastures, pine forests, fox-hunts…" Then he said, "You have not chosen a very propitious time to paint flowers in the Holy Land." I thought he meant that this was not the most appropriate season, since the summer, which is quite arid here, was approaching, and I said that, fortunately, the rains had come late this year and the land was abundant with flowers. But that was not what he meant. He said with concern that he feared an imminent outbreak of war between the British and the Turks here, on this soil, for both governments were, at this very moment, in the throes of a highly dangerous conflict known as "the Taba Affair."

A large map of the Middle East hung behind his desk, and like a teacher in a classroom, he rose, took a long thin pointer from a corner of the room, and moving it across the map, indicated borders and settlements and explained the nature of the conflict:

Egypt is part of the Ottoman Empire, but for more than seventy years, since the time of Muhammad Ali, the Turks had granted it an autonomous government, headed by the *khediv*, who answered to the Sultan in Constantinople. In effect, we, that is to say, the British—Mr. Blech turned from the map to me—rule Egypt, and the administration of the country (since 1883, if I am not mistaken with regard to the date) is in the hands of Lord Cromer, whose official status—he bestowed a slyly insinuating smile upon me—is that of "the British consul general." The Turks agreed that the entire Sinai peninsula between the Suez Canal and the territory running from El-Arish in the north to Aqaba in the south—he drew his pointer across the map from top to bottom—would be under Egyptian control.

I heard and didn't hear what he said. I could smell my father's tobacco, the brand that had yellowed his moustache. Once, a year ago, he took me to the Atheneum Club, of which he was a member, so that I could see for myself the loftiness of his status. Women were forbidden to enter the club, but a member's daughter was allowed in—particularly during the quiet afternoon hours. And that spacious hall, its entrance lined with Greek columns and its high ceiling carved with ornamental flowers, was indeed majestic. My father introduced me to the elderly doorman of the Club, clad in a black dress coat and a white bow tie, who bowed to him and bestowed a kindly, if somewhat sceptical glance upon me, and then went to the high lectern and wrote our names in the impressively large ledger. We crossed to the far end of the silent hall and sat down on deep leather armchairs. Only a few other people occupied the other armchairs near the walls, each immersed in his newspaper. The walls were covered with oil portraits of prominent people, members of the club from the time of its inception, including a nearly life-size portrait of our King Edward, his face enveloped in a kind of mist of amiability and benevolence, his beard handsomely trimmed, wearing a top hat and shod in boots. My father ordered whiskey with ice for both of us, and only several moments had passed when a distinguished-looking man approached, his grey head bent somewhat, as if pulled down by the weight of his slightly bowed body, and my father proudly introduced him to me—the honourable Duke of Devonshire himself. He joined us, ordered a drink, and the two men became engaged in conversation. I caught snatches of their exchange: the upcoming, worrisome marriage of our King's niece to Alphonso the Eighth, King of Spain…the need to restrict the number of permits to sell alcoholic drinks, since they were being issued to too many pubs…the Boer Rebellion in South Africa…the Empire, the Empire…Out of politeness, the Duke addressed me too, and when I told him that I had studied art at Slade, he again turned to my father and told him that Roger Fry's request to be appointed a professor of art at Cambridge had been rejected because the King had wished Mr. Waldstein to be given the position…Could it be so? my father wondered, what a pity…such a gifted critic…

And I said to myself: I must flee all of this, go far, far away.*

---

* Flee from what? From the dignified atmosphere of high society? Or perhaps from the father? During my visits to their home, when only the two were present, I noticed B.'s ambivalent attitude towards her father, the factitious, strained

Five months ago—Mr. Blech continued his dreary lecture—using his long pointer, which he now and then tapped against the wall map—the Khediv, Abass II, sent two regiments of cavalrymen mounted on camels under the command of General Bromley, against lawbreakers amongst the Bedouin tribes. It then became clear that the Turks had sent a garrison to Taba, which is located west of Aqaba, that is to say, within the territory governed by Egypt…The Foreign Secretary, Edward Grey, exhorted the Sultan Abd al-Hamid II to remove his army from Taba. The Sultan refused…Lord Cromer dispatched the ship, Diana (Diana? I was surprised. Is it fitting to name a warship after the goddess of the forest, the hunt, and wildlife?) to Taba with an Anglo-Egyptian force on board to be put ashore there, but the Turkish garrison prevented this…And so London decided to send the ships of the British fleet to the Mediterranean, off the shore of Constantinople, and threatened to bomb the city…. At this very moment—Blech's quicksilver marbles glittered—these ships were sailing to their destination in the Straits of Bosphorus …

Seeing the concern on my face, he reassured me: "Despite all of this, I believe the Turks will ultimately be deterred. Abd al-Hamid, who is both a paranoid and a coward, will not dare to become entangled in a war with Great Britain."

His face then became suffused with ire and loathing as he spoke with condemnation of the Turks: they are suspicious beyond reason, imagining that all foreign citizens have come here to undermine their rule; they plant spies and detectives throughout their empire. It is rumoured that, in Turkey itself, half of the residents of Constantinople are spying on the other half; those considered suspect are held without trial and are exiled, or executed by hanging. Here, in this country, they harass and persecute natives and immigrants, officials

---

atmosphere between them, the tension visible on both their faces. Arthur did try to be genial and unconstrained, but B. was silent, her expression impervious, as if hostile. May we consider this an Oedipal case?—While I do differ with the new "gospel" of that Jewish-Viennese braggart, Dr. Freud, whose sensational "findings" have caused quite a to-do—parts of his theory even disgust me—I must admit that there is something to his doctrine with regard to the "Oedipal complex," and I may not ignore it.—P.D.M.

extort taxes and bribes from them, and the police flog them cruelly for every minor infringement...

I told him about the scene I witnessed at the *khan* at Bab-al-Wad, when policemen had whipped two young Jewish men until they bled.

He smiled. "Yes...the Zionists...the Turks fear them more than the others...convinced they are coming here to establish a Jewish state. The Zionist leader, Dr. Herzl, who died two years ago—quite a naive man, apparently—thought he could use money to purchase a Jewish state in Palestine from Sultan al-Hamid. He met with him twice at the Upper Gate, and the sultan, who is deeply in debt, but cleverer than Herzl, led him down the garden path...but, in fact..." He was silent for a moment, with some amusing thought reflected in his smile, "In fact, a Jewish state in Palestine is likely to benefit us. It would be like a thorn in the flesh of the Turks, a wedge between Syria and Egypt, and since they are already turning to us for help in realizing their Zionist aim, having despaired of Kaiser Wilhelm II and Austro-Hungary, and Lord Rothschild every now and then knocks on the doors of this minister or that, they can only achieve their goal with our support, which means that..."

(And suddenly, in the middle of his speech, I felt my heart contract: Vanessa. No, she doesn't love me.)

Then he told me that, in recent years, the number of Jews in Palestine had increased greatly. In Jerusalem itself, they now numbered some fifty thousand, constituting the majority of the population; they had built most of the new neighbourhoods located outside the wall. And he spoke of the Jewish agricultural settlements on the plain and in the Galilee, established with the assistance and support of Baron Rothschild. The settlers planted vineyards and citrus groves, almond and apple orchards, and they had wineries and factories...

(A childhood memory: Liza and I, both of us six or seven years old, are running across the cornfield on the far side of the river. Summer. Red poppies dot the field, we fall on top of one another in the soft grass, laughing, hugging, we hear the far-off sound of my mother calling me, but do not emerge from our hiding place, we feel good as we are, sweet. Liza says don't get up, we'll stay here until the evening, and I kiss her fervently, lingeringly…)

"The Turks prohibit the Jews from buying land and building houses"—I hear Mr. Blech say—"but the Jews are cunning, and extraordinarily skilful at circumventing the law," he said, grinning. "They have formed several British-Jewish companies in Egypt, owned by Ottoman citizens, which cannot be prevented from buying land."

He then said that we, the English, help them in various ways, through the missionary societies, which have been active here for nearly a hundred years. The late consul, James Finn, and his wife Elizabeth—he said—did much over the last forty years for the Jews in Jerusalem. The number of Jews they converted can be counted on the fingers of two hands, but they trained many of them in various professions and helped them build one of the first neighbourhoods outside the wall.

"Lady Elizabeth, who is eighty now, still serves as the secretary of the Society for the Assisting of Persecuted Jews in Palestine, which assists the refugees who have fled from persecution in Russia and Romania. Only quite recently, she asked our ambassador in Constantinople, Sir Nicholas O'Connor, to persuade the Sultan to exempt from customs duties the packages of food and clothing meant for these refugees, and to confirm the appointment of Lord Amherst of Hackney as president of the society."

"I know Lord Amherst," I said.

"Do you really?" His eyes opened wide, either in puzzlement or admiration.

I told him that Lord Amherst used to visit our home, and that I attended art school with his daughter.

For some reason, Mr. Blech was wonder-struck. I saw that I had now risen in his esteem after his initial disappointment in discovering that I was not related to the prime minister.

"I myself am not acquainted with him," he said in a low voice. After a brief silence he resumed, "I assume that if Lady Elizabeth Finn recommends him, she knows what attitude he holds towards the Jews." Then he said, "We must remember that we, the English, were the first Zionists. We preached the return of the Jews to their ancient land quite some time before they themselves considered it. A very long time before their Dr. Herzl did. Remember George Eliot's *Daniel Deronda*, Charlotte Elizabeth's *Judah's Lion*, and Palmerston's initiative, when he was Foreign Secretary some sixty years ago, to encourage the return of the Jews to their land. It was he who instructed our first consul in Jerusalem, Mr. Young, to sponsor the Jews of the city. Yes," he reiterated his initial assertion, "we were Zionists before the Zionists!"

When he finally asked about my plans for the coming days, I told him that I would be travelling across the country and collecting flowers. I asked if he knew anyone who could help me in identifying the flowers that grew in this land and did not grow in England. He pondered for several moments, and then, as if he had discovered a great treasure, cried: "Yes! Mr. Shimoni! The botany teacher at the Jewish girl's school, Lemel, ten minutes from here! I met him during a visit to that school! I have no doubt he can help you! No one can match his knowledge of the flora of this country!"

On a piece of consulate stationery he wrote the teacher's name and the name of the school, and drew a street map of the immediate vicinity to make it easier for me to find my way there.

It was dark when I reached the pension.

The high night sky of Jerusalem! The host of glittering stars! Only here can one understand the words in the Psalms—"The heavens declare the glory of God, and the firmament showeth His handiwork." On the land, nearby and on the far horizon, a tiny light here, a tiny light there, flicker as if peeking out from between the cliffs and fallow fields that humble themselves before the beauty of the heavenly stars. You look up at that sky, with its glittering multitude of secrets, and you think—in an instant it will open, as in John's vision—and angels will burst forth, fly downward and spread their wings over the wall of Jerusalem and over the graves of the saints.

Jerusalem, The Olivet Pension
23rd April, 1906

Dear Vanessa,

Three of the most exciting days of my life!

How can I describe to you what I have experienced over these three days?

I went, for the second time—alone this time, unescorted by my dragoman—to the Church of the Holy Sepulchre in the Old City.

My previous visit was a nightmare. Turkish soldiers armed with bayonets had stood at the entrance, their eyes searching the entrants, as if poised to snatch the suspect from amongst them and hurl them into a dungeon. Mobs of people pushed their way in, most of them shabbily dressed Russian pilgrims. The space of the large hall resounded with the clamour, a mixture of prayers, whispers and rebukes; in one corner, a quarrel broke out, perhaps those charged with keeping order had tried to eject someone. I trudged along behind my dragoman from hall to hall, from chapel to chapel, astonished at what I was seeing, at what I was hearing, feeling slightly nauseous, not knowing what I had stumbled upon, feeling as if I were not in a holy place, but in an impure one.

This time, I left home—the pension I am staying in—early in the morning, before sunrise, and entered the Old City through the Jaffa Gate. The narrow streets of the Christian quarter were still silent, my steps echoing on the stone-paved, slippery streets, damp with dew; here and there a shopkeeper raised the metal shutters of his shop. I occasionally stopped one of the few passers-by to ask the way through the tangle of winding alleys. Girls in black dresses with white collars, apparently pupils in a convent school, hurried two-by-two, to their destination.

The great hall of the church was redolent with the scent of incense, and in one corner, some fifty or sixty people sat on chairs before the altar and listened to the verses of the morning mass being celebrated by a Greek priest. I tread carefully, so as not to disturb the silence that enveloped the worshippers. I walked around the thick columns supporting the ceiling that was hung with gold and silver chandeliers, in which red embers glowed. I walked the length of the walls—their ancient stones reminiscent of the unpolished, unhewn stones of a fortress—flanked with galleries that encircled the hall and adorned with paintings of saints and with carpets and curtains.

I walked from hall to hall, from chapel to chapel. I descended the stairs to the long corridor on whose floor beggars sat and lay, that led to the crypt of St. Helena—the fourth-century Byzantine queen who discovered the sepulchre and built the church above it. It is a kind of large cave, shrouded in darkness, a shaft of light invading it from above like the diagonal light that illuminates the mysteriousness in Rembrandt's paintings.

Do you recall, Vanessa, the conversation we had, in your house, about light? Virginia said that in literature, as in art, it is the inner light of the creator that insinuates itself into his creation, even if he is unaware of it, and it insinuates itself, too, into his protagonists and is reflected by them as, for example, in the old woman's wrinkles in Giorgione's painting, in the sparkling ocean waves of Turner's paintings, in Claude Monet's luminescent lake with its floating water lilies. The same holds true for Beatrice's face, in Dante's *Divine Comedy*, whose light guided him from hell to paradise. When this light is absent from the creator's soul—she said—whatever he paints or writes will be lacklustre, like a mirror whose back coating has faded or peeled.

To the question of where the light was in the books of Charlotte Bronte, Virginia replied: "It is hidden in the spaces between the words." She then said that the darkness of mystery is created by the force of shafts of light that slip modestly into it. As in the paintings of El Greco.

After that conversation, which so impressed me, I reread the thirty-first Canto of *Paradiso* and found Dante's poem about the flower that is "so white, no snow unto that limit doth attain," about the angels flying like bees amongst the petals, their wings burning with the flame of love, and about Beatrice herself, whom he sees crowned in glory when he gazes upward, "reflecting from herself the eternal rays."

Upon returning to the main hall of the church, called the Catholikon, I was greeted by an appalling sight: in front of the rock of Golgotha, upon which, according to tradition, Jesus' cross was placed, five women knelt or lay prostrate—Russian, judging by their appearance, for they were clad in grey peasant dresses and wore white kerchiefs on their heads—kissing the stone devotedly, tears flowing from their eyes. And as they knelt, they keened in Russian, a monotonic melody, and beat their breasts with their fists. Their wailing went on and on, a clear, unremitting lament, accompanied by bitter weeping. So heart-rending was this sight that I was seized with a persistent trembling and could barely contain my own tears.

Dear Vanessa. I have read the story of crucifixion countless times, and I have listened in exaltation to the heavenly music of Bach's Passions, but only here, at the foot of the Golgotha stone, at the sight of those peasant women's faces, wrinkled as dried figs, upon which a brightness seemed to pour as they looked upward—ostensibly at the cross—a mournful melody on their lips—only here was I stirred to feel such great pity for His having borne "our diseases," as if I had heard Him whisper with his last breath, "My God, my God, why hast thou forsaken me," as if I had seen the curtain of the temple torn in two and the rocks split apart: and I was filled with pity for us as well, for our lives are vanity, and we return to dust.

It was a long while before I could move from where I stood, and when I left the church, a hand seemed to take hold of me and draw me towards the Via Dolorosa. I decided to walk the entire length of that sorrowful road, from the beginning at the praetorium, within whose walls Jesus was condemned to death, to Golgotha, beside which I was standing at that moment.

Only in Jerusalem can so otherworldly a spectacle as the one I saw on the Via Dolorosa take place. It is a narrow, winding street lined with high, stone walls that provide shade from the sunlight, only a strip of blue shining above.

As I walked from the Church of the Flagellation—this is the place where, as written in John, "he struck him on the cheek"—to the Monastery of the Sisters of Zion, over which the Roman stone arch connects the two sides of the street like a bridge—this is the Ecce Homo station—I heard behind me what sounded like warning cries in Arabic. Turning my head, I became rooted to the spot by my shock: a tall, gaunt person wearing a long, faded and tattered robe, was coming towards me from the end of the street. A black beard and long black hair encircled his face, and he was carrying a heavy wooden cross on his back! He was walking heavily, step after step, and uttering words incomprehensible to me. Passers-by, as stunned as I, pushed up against the walls to make way for him. As he passed me, I shuddered: the man did not have a nose! He had, instead, a kind of crushed button with two holes that protruded from the centre of his face, and his eyes were as beady as those of a mouse. Behind the place I stood was a shop that sold religious items—rosary beads, icons, statues—and I asked the shopkeeper who was standing in the doorway and watching the spectacle, as we all were, who the bearer of the cross was. He told me the man was a leper who had taken leave of his senses and had fled from the leper house outside the wall. Once a week, on Fridays, he walked the length of the Via Dolorosa to the Church of the Holy Sepulchre. At first, he was ridiculed, and efforts were made to remove him from the street. But, since he persisted in returning, ignoring the cries of derision directed at him by youths—who sometimes threw stones at him too—as well as the rebukes and insults of the older people, he was left alone.

"O Jerusalem, Jerusalem, killing the prophets and stoning those who are sent to you!"

It was already noon when I emerged from the wall through the Lions' Gate and went down to the Kidron stream and the Jehoshaphat Valley. This is the brook where—as written in the book of Kings—King Asa burned the abominable idol made by his mother; and this is the valley where, on the day of judgment, all the nations will be gathered and judged—as written in the book of Joel—and where the dead will be resurrected, according to both Christian and Jewish belief.

I stood facing the Mount of Olives, the strong noon light spilling onto its stony desolation, only olive and carob trees randomly scattered amongst the dry thorns, and the sun's rays shattering against the hundreds of gravestones of the Jewish cemetery on the side of the mount.

And suddenly, Vanessa, I felt suffocated in the face of the expanse that surrounded me. I am imprisoned, imprisoned...Can you imagine it? Here, of all places, in this great expanse, to be overwhelmed by the feeling you are caught in a trap? And I was afraid, as if thousands of years of history lay upon my shoulders, and the full power of the holiness of these sites that surrounded me so oppressed me, so burdened me, that I was unable to breathe.

I had to flee that place.

I went down to Gethsemane, where the Church of St. Anne now stands. The stones there are permeated with tears, sighs, and profound sorrow, for that is where Jesus, together with his disciples, spent the last night before Judas Iscariot turned him over to the Roman soldiers. That is the place where Peter sought to pray, lest he be tempted, for "the spirit is willing, but the flesh is weak," and the time was near...

I am once again besieging you with quotations from the Scriptures, Vanessa, and I know that this may cause you to find my letters loathsome—but how can I desist, when, with every step I take, I seem to be to walking in the footsteps of the ancients, who walked here two and three thousand years ago, and whose spirits live with us. How can I desist when every stone I touch holds such stirring memories?

I entered the Crusader Franciscan church named after Anne, Mary's mother, and walked through it to the crypt—the "cavern of sorrow"—where the disciples of Jesus slept when he went out to be alone in the garden, knowing what was to come. I stood alone in that dark grotto—which was like an alcove in the rock and contained a number of small, modest altars upon which statues stood, dimly illuminated by the light of copper lamps—and I thought of those same twelve disciples who, here, on the floor of this cave, slept the sleep of the innocent, unsuspecting of the evil that would occur in only a few hours, just as we, today, and always, numb our senses so as not to confront evil, fooling ourselves into believing that this will prevent its coming.*

The garden of Gethsemane is also there—just a few steps from the church. It is a small garden, enclosed by a white fence on which "The Way of the Cross" is painted. In it are eight olive trees that look quite ancient, perhaps survivors of that time when, at night, Jesus walked and contemplated his death and resurrection—and there are small beds of anemones and myrtles.

You visited our estate in Torrington several times, Vanessa, and were filled with admiration for the large flowers in the garden that extended from the front of the house. "Monstrous blossoming!" you cried when you visited in June and saw the densely flowering profusion of red, yellow, citron and white roses, whose velvety petals seemed to explode with the joy of life; and the marvellous calices of hundreds of tulips stretching their necks towards the sky and drinking in the light; and the beds of narcissi, the pink and purple irises, the unpretentious pansies, and the stellaria peeking from the green lawn…everything so luxuriantly healthy, so lush and glorious, a gorgeous carpet spread before our manor house, extending to the edge of the forest. Here, on this holy ground, such abundance does not exist. This is impoverished, tortured, suffering earth. Trees and flowers grow sparingly in it. They struggle against dryness, heat, the intractability of the land. Growing amongst the thistles and nettles are oaks, carobs, olive trees, a few cypress trees—bayonets that penetrate the horizon of the Mount of Olives—and anemones, groundsels, and chrysanthemums—so difficult is their struggle to survive that they appear to be on the verge of withering.

And that is how I want to paint these flowers: tormented, fighting for their lives, their faces marked with the suffering of the

---

* I am quite fearful that her immersion in such thoughts bearing on the revelation of evil, on unexpected disasters, on illusions that will prevent their occurrence—thoughts that cause her to suffer from guilt feelings to the point of self-flagellation—is itself a symptom of latent manic depressive illness. (I may use B.'s case in a comprehensive essay on ecstatic hallucinations amongst women in isolated estates in eastern England.)—P.D.M.

persecuted—cursed prophets, crucified messiahs, apostles cast into dungeons.

And I hope to find here not only mandrakes—the love-flowers—but also the white lily—the pure, innocent flower.*

(And at this moment, I recall the story your sister, Virginia, read to us from her notebook, "Kew Gardens." With what a fine perception—almost microscopic, I would say—did she describe the flowers in those gardens! The red, blue, yellow petals, the tops of the stems over the heart-shaped or tongue-shaped leaves; and the light flickering on them when the light breeze rocked them, the red, blue, and yellow leaving spots on the brown earth and shining in the eyes of strollers in the gardens in the month of July; and the rings of light falling upon the pebbles in the stream, on a snail, on a drop of water…Yes, red, blue, yellow, and all their hues dominated her picture, just as they dominate an impressionist painting of a glowing summer landscape.)

The second day was a Saturday, and I decided to spend it touring Jewish sites.

I had met few Jews in Essex and London. Our "Thursday evenings" at your house in Bloomsbury, were attended by one of the Cambridge group—Leonard Woolf was his name—who was thought to be Jewish (he fell in love with Virginia, if I am not mistaken, before he left for Ceylon on some government mission), but I did not see in him any particularly "Jewish" characteristics, neither in his physiognomy—he was a bit dark, but this is common amongst our race as well—nor in his behaviour. You once indicated to me, after our group's discussion on "the essence of beauty," that he is endowed with "intellectual acuity"—a quality possessed by many Jews, you said. My mother, who is a devout Christian, has been quite affected by Charlotte Elizabeth's book, *Judah's Lion*, which was published more than fifty years ago. It tells the story of an assimilated English

---

* This sentence is particularly interesting as regards an understanding of the latent aspects of B.'s personality. On one hand—"the white lily," its stem erect, its crown upon its head, is the consummate phallic symbol. On the other hand—B. longs for it to be innocent and pure…—P.D.M.

Jew by the name of Alick Cohen, who takes a business trip to the East. Prolonged theological debates on Christianity and Judaism take place between him and the Irish captain of the ship, Charles Ryan, who tries to prove to him how much more righteous Christianity is than Judaism. At the end of the journey, Cohen is convinced he must convert to Christianity while, at the same time, remaining a Jew. There was nothing contradictory in this, since the source of Christianity was the Jewish Torah ("Becoming a Christian, do I cease to be a Jew?" he asks in his moving speech). He finds a religious and historical connection between the English and Jewish peoples—the symbol of the lion inscribed on the royal British flag is the "lion of Judah"—and calls for English-Christians to return the Jews from the four corners of the earth to the land of their forefathers—to establish there the kingdom of Judah and rebuild the Temple. My mother, too, believes that England's mission is to further the Jews' return to their country, while, at the same time, returning them to the bosom of the "true faith."

My first stop was the orthodox Jewish quarter, Meah She'arim.

The "new" Jerusalem, the one that is west of the walls and has been under construction for some sixty or seventy years, is a series of neighbourhoods known here as colonies. Several of them are composed of only two or three streets, others are but a group of houses separated by plots of rock-filled, fallow land on which brambles and wildflowers grow amidst cisterns, small quarries, piles of stones, and rubbish. During the day, donkeys, mules, and camels bearing stones, sand and building materials, walk about the neighbourhood streets amongst the builders and stonecutters. There is a clean, beautiful German colony established by the Templars, with straight, lined streets and trees surrounding stone houses that have high attics, gables of the kind found in German villages, and biblical passages carved on their lintels. There is a Greek colony called Katamon, whose houses are built of pink or orange Jerusalem stone, their arched doors supported by columns with Greek or Doric capitals. And there is a small American colony of three or four houses near the Damascus Gate. But most of the neighbourhoods are Jewish, spread over a large area, and expanding. They are different from one another, each bearing the character of its residents, who have come from the ends of the earth, from east and west.

And amongst them, rising here and there from amidst the rocks, are opulent castles—churches and monasteries, hospitals and orphan homes, missions and consulates, and pensions for pilgrims. Yesterday, when I went out through the Jaffa Gate to walk to my pension and passed these substantial buildings, all of which are made of chiselled stone that bespeak distinction and look like ancient fortresses—it seemed to me as if I were walking through the historical cities of Europe: here is Rome, here Avignon, here Constantinople, here Moscow. In a few short steps, I moved from city to city…and here was the unassuming, Romanesque, Anglican St. Paul's Church that reminded me of our country, of the small village church I prayed in during my childhood…

The owner of my pension, Mr. Hansmann, cautioned me not to go to Meah She'arim wearing "immodest" clothing, lest I be stoned. I therefore wore my "pearly," polka dot, long-sleeved dress, and covered my hair with the blue silk kerchief patterned with lilies you once gave me as a gift.

This neighbourhood is made up of closely crowded two-storey houses lined with upper balconies. Between them are paved yards with cisterns to catch rainwater in the centre, and their outer walls are joined, creating a fence with gates on four sides, which are locked at nightfall, against Arab burglars and rowdies.

It was Saturday morning, as I mentioned, and the moment I entered the neighbourhood, the soaring sounds of prayer burst upon me from the doors and windows of the synagogues on both sides of the street—an admixture of single voices and a chorus of voices that rose and fell, sometimes shouting, sometimes whispering, sometimes rapid, sometimes joyful, but all reciting verses in a language I did not understand, in Hebrew.

Most of the residents were apparently already inside the synagogues (it is strange that such a small neighbourhood has such a large number—I think it is every third or fourth house—of synagogues), but many still hurried along the street, obviously late, to join their brethren—men wrapped in prayer shawls, wearing wide-brimmed black hats, or round hats adorned with shaggy brown fur, some hold-ing their small children by the hand, who were hurrying to keep up with the long strides of their fathers—children whose mournful eyes and long, curled side-locks hung down on either side of their pale faces; heavy-set, clumsy women wearing large shoes, black kerchiefs covering their hair; girls in long, colourful dresses and white stock-ings, hurrying in very small, rapid steps to reach this synagogue or that—

How different these Jews were from those few who had crossed our path in London! Or from those whose names we know, for they came into prominence in England as men of wealth or as statesmen. How different they were from the distinguished image we had of them—the Rothschilds, the Montagues, the Isaacs, the Montefiores, or the sculptor, Jacob Epstein—and, of course, Disraeli was a Jew!

It seems as if the Jews of this neighbourhood are of another species, a strange tribe that found its way here from some remote land, or from the darkness of the Middle Ages! Are these the descendants of the biblical Israelites? Is this how their forefathers looked—the tillers of the soil, the shepherds, the high priests, the prophets and Talmudic scholars? And perhaps yes, I thought, perhaps this was in fact the way the Pharisees looked in Jesus' time, when they lived here, on this land…

Though I was "modestly" dressed, people on all sides fixed their gaze on me—those who walked past me and those who stood in the synagogue doorways, women from their windows and children playing in the street. It must have been written on my forehead that I was a foreigner, and I did not know if their stares were curious or hostile.

Looking to the right, I saw a startling sight that was not of this world, not of this time: in one of the inner courtyards beyond the synagogue vestibule, stood a crowd of one or two hundred men huddled closely together, with no space between them—had they assembled for prayer? For a memorial service? To hear a sermon?—and they were a single mass, blacker than black, swaying mechanically from side to side, as if an invisible hand were controlling their move-ments, and they looked to me like a flock of ravens that had landed on a corpse…this sight was so frightening, so demonic, that it stirred all the evil legends about Jews as the children of Satan, from the depths of my memory.

Two young men walked slowly in front of me, clad in light-coloured suits and wearing straw hats, and when I caught up to them, I heard them speaking English. I was glad that other foreigners were in the neighbourhood. Begging their pardon, I asked where they were from. They were happy to talk to me, saying that they had come from the state of Virginia in the United States, and they told me they had come to Jerusalem with a group of Baptists to visit the holy sites and take part in a convention being held in the Fast Hotel. I asked if they thought we were permitted to enter one of the synagogues to observe the prayers. "Try it," they laughed.

The three of us stood in the doorway of one of those synagogues, which was but a large room, painted white, at the back of which was an Ark covered with a blue velvet cloth, the form of the Tables of the Covenant embroidered with gold thread on it, depicting a deer mounted on one side and a lion on the other. The room was crowded with worshippers, sitting and standing, reading loudly and singing from the prayer books in their hands as their bodies swayed ardently. One of them came up to us and asked what we wanted in a language that the Americans said was Yiddish. We asked if we were allowed to listen to their prayers. Another person, wrapped in a prayer shawl, who understood English, approached and said that women were forbidden to be there in the company of men, that there was a special section for them in the synagogue. He indicated a side room separated from the hall by a transparent curtain, and told me to go there. We stood there in embarrassment for a moment or two, and then returned to the street.

And now, as I write you these words, I ask myself why that sight of crowded worshippers, and the blend of voices rising from them as if they were competing to see which would overpower the other, and the strange smell—the smell of clothing? Perspiration? Candle wax? The mustiness of worn pages?—why did they arouse such distaste in me that I wanted to flee that place? Was it the absence of beauty? Was it the din, so lacking in grace or majesty, which filled the synagogue? Was it because I am accustomed to English churches, in which the silence of holiness prevails, whose walls depict the honour of apostles and martyrs, and the sight of the cross over the altar inspires awe and causes one to reflect on the insignificance of man and his hope of salvation?

And as I continue to think on this matter, I say to myself: it was not the sights and sounds that repelled so much as the feeling that mercy, softness, gentleness were absent in that male community.

It is no wonder that Jesus was alien to the Jews!

The two Americans asked where I was headed, and when I told them I wished to see the Wailing Wall, they said they would accompany me there. They knew the way, and if I went alone, I would get lost amongst the alleys. Their company was quite amusing. They were twins, identical not only in dress, but also in physiognomy, differing only in that one of them, Angus, was taciturn and the other, Henry, was talkative and laughed a great deal. He asked where I was from, what I did, and the like, and when I began to reply, he said: "No, don't answer. Let me guess." He therefore "guessed" that I was English, that I was born in…one of the Channel Islands ("Why the Channel Islands, of all places?" I laughed.—"Because there is something insular about you…"), that I was married to a well-to-do man—a banker or a barrister—and the mother of one child, and that I liked books and animals. When I told them I had come to this country to paint biblical flowers, they stopped in their tracks, amazed and deferent. "Are there still flowers that have survived from biblical times?" the silent one wondered. "Biblical flowers," I said, "are immortal." The two stared at me wide-eyed, as if they had suddenly discovered that an important personage was standing before them.

We passed through the fetid, rubbish-strewn alleyways of the Jewish quarter of the Old City—leftover vegetables, debris from workshops, papers, feathers everywhere. Since it was the Sabbath, the shops and workshops were closed, and the doorways of the cramped houses looked like cavern openings. After a long walk through the winding alleyways, we reached the opening that led to the small square—it too looked like an alley—in front of the Wailing Wall.

The high wall, clusters of weeds hanging from the cracks in the enormous stones—the only vestige of the Temple destroyed by the Romans—is awesome. A hundred or more worshippers stood before it, wearing all manner of soft-brimmed hats, fur hats, tarbooshes, clad in shiny silk caftans and black, white, striped, or motley gowns with fur edges, belted with coloured sashes. They stood facing the wall, swaying and bowing. Unlike the worshippers I saw in the synagogue, the Jews here prayed silently, only an occasional cry bursting from the group, a shout of supplication, a cry of mourning, or a plea for mercy.

The twins whispered that they had to leave to take part in a meeting of their convention, and asked if I could find my way back by myself. I assured them that I would not get lost, and parted from them.

For a long while, I stood transfixed by the sight of the worshippers standing before the wall, wrapped in prayer shawls. Some had pressed their faces against the wall; others banged their foreheads on it, while still others bowed deeply and fervently before it. Standing in front of their Holy Ark was the rabbi or cantor, wearing a fur hat and an embroidered vest. He had a long white beard that reached his breast and apparently, owing to the weakness of his advanced age, his voice could barely be heard. The anguished ardour with which these worshippers address their God—I thought—held the suffering of that persecuted people exiled from their land after the destruction of the Temple, as well as the hope for redemption and the restoration of ancient times. I looked up at the top of the wall and asked myself whether it is called the Wailing Wall because of the tears that had been shed upon it by this people for hundreds of years, or because the wall itself weeps, the weeds growing down from it its flowing tears.

One of the worshippers—I couldn't see who it was—suddenly emitted a deep, heart-breaking sigh, and I was breathless with wonder. A moment later, a child burst into bitter tears, which did not stop until his father and those standing near him silenced him.

Something so horrible that it shocked me to the depths of my being happened to me as I stood in the square of the holy place known in Arabic as Haram-a-Sharif.

I went through Bab El-Silsila, the Gate of the Chain, up to this holy site, so well known from its appearance in paintings and photographs of Jerusalem, in the centre of which is the golden dome of the Omar Mosque. The moment I stepped onto that square, as I stood under the high arch resting on marble columns, strong light assaulted my eyes, making me so dizzy that I could not see anything around me—not the opulent, octagonal mosque of the Dome of the Rock, not the huge rectangular mosque, called Al-Aqsa, on the southern side of the square, and not the domes of the smaller mosques scattered here and there like palm trees in the desert.

The large square that extended before me, white, gleaming in the sun's rays like the desert of light, an angel—was it Gabriel?—had borne here on its wings from the furthermost part of the Arabian Peninsula and placed on Mount Moriah, where the Holy Temple had stood in ancient times—this square blinded me.

I felt a powerful radiance on my face, and I did not know whether its shafts bore death, or whether it was the glow of a world of perfect goodness.

That was on Saturday. The following day, Sunday, I went to morning prayers at the Church of St. Paul—only some thirty people were there, most of whom, I think, were Arabs—and immediately after prayers, I set out for Mount Zion to visit David's Tomb.

But this is a long story, so I shall end here. I shall write of what happened to me on Sunday in my next letter, after, I hope, receiving your longed-for letter.

Tomorrow, barring any mishaps, I shall leave on horseback, with my dragoman, for Bethlehem and Hebron. But that, too, is for my next letter.

Yours with love,
Beatrice

P.S. I shall also tell you of a sad encounter I had that same Saturday. Walking back from the Wailing Wall to my pension—I must have lost my way somewhat, and instead of reaching the Jaffa Gate, I found myself at the Damascus Gate. A large crowd stood before it—donkeys and camels raised dust with their hooves, beggars lay on the ground at the base of the wall, peddlers hawked their wares, black, bare-chested men bore leather bottles on their backs, offering water for sale in the cups they carried in their hands, or a clay-coloured drink known as Tamar Hindi, poured into the cups from copper jugs with carved spouts. And amidst this mob walked Bedouins with daggers in their belts, Russian priests, nuns, and Arab women with veils over their faces. I did not find my way to the new city, and I was confused about which direction to take. When I had extricated myself from the dust and the mob, I stopped a woman who looked European to me—she was wearing a long grey dress of the kind worn by the peasant women in Germany and Austria, and her hair was gathered in a coil on the back of her neck (she reminded me very much of your wood carving of Emily Bronte's *Wuthering Heights*)—and I asked her if she could show me the way to the street of the consulates or to Jaffa Road. The woman, whose face was gaunt, as if she suffered from hunger, and whose lips were pale, spoke fluent English. I asked her where she was from, and she told me, in an outpouring of the bitterness of her heart, the following story:

She had been living for some fifteen years in a place called the American Colony—not far from where we stood, near Golgotha Hill. In truth, she said, this was the Swedish Colony, for it had been established by some fifty Swedish farmers from the United States who, led by a devout Christian, Mrs. Gordon from Chicago, had decided to immigrate to the Holy Land and do godly deeds of charity. They were joined by another several dozen farmers who moved here from Sweden itself, they and their wives and children and elderly parents—an entire village—led by the village pastor. All were devout Protestants. They lived their lives sparingly. They grew vegetables and fruit around their houses, earned their livelihoods by doing various kinds of handicrafts—carving wood utensils, weaving baskets, embroidering and knitting—and did all the housework themselves. But they devoted most of their time and energy to treating the sick, the crippled, the leprous, and by succouring the poor of all religions.

"And look at what happened to us in this holy city," the modest, Swedish farm woman lamented bitterly, wrinkled with suffering, "Catholics who believe, as we do, in the Father, the Son and the Holy

Ghost, were envious of the great affection the poor and the wretched feel for us and the great esteem in which we are held by all those we help. They spread the most appalling slander about us, that we live in sin, licentiousness, and adultery, that we are incestuous and profligate...and caused us to become ostracized in the city, untouchable. Those who see us must turn away from us. We are unclean..."

She said that the rumour spread through the city like wildfire, and all the other Christian sects banned them. They were expelled from the hospital in which they worked, and could no longer earn their livelihoods. Some of them died of hunger and disease. Many returned to their homelands.

I asked if they were the only ones treated this way, and the woman pursed her lips, a bitter look filling her eyes, and said: In this city, everyone hates everyone else. The Catholics hate the Protestants, the Methodists hate the Lutherans, the Greek Orthodox hate the Catholics, the Russian Orthodox hate the Copts, and so on. The same was true for the Jews and the Muslims, of course, and within their own sects...Everyone is jealous of everyone else, and they all compete with each other, spread lies about each other, proselytise, persecute and are persecuted ceaselessly, "and all to honour God," she said, "a city that devours its residents."

Imagine how I felt upon hearing these words, after the exaltation I had experienced during my visit to the holy sites. Should I return to the vision of William Blake, who, in his mind's eye, saw the fields of Islington and Marylebone and Primrose Hill and St. John's Wood supported by the golden columns of Jerusalem? Or should I vow, as he did, that:

I will not cease from mental fight
Nor shall my sword sleep in my hand.
Till we have built Jerusalem
In England's green and pleasant land.

Could it really have been sunstroke?

When I woke up in this Arab house in Jericho, from whose arched windows a bounty of red bougainvillea blossoms gaze in at me, that nice fellow with the metal-framed round glasses—Kobi? Robbie?—his name escapes me, for some reason—told me it was sunstroke. The sun beat down on my head, and that is why I fainted, lost consciousness. And they carried me, heavy as I am, on an improvised stretcher made from branches, for a mile or two along the blazing, bleached dirt road—to Jericho.

The shame of it! And then to lie for hours in this strange room, on a strange bed, Arab children peeking in at me inquisitively from the window, and a fat Arab woman wearing a blue satin dress ornately embroidered with gold thread—a kind-hearted woman, very kind-hearted, motherly, her large breasts made to nurse Gargantua—wiping my face with a wet cloth, comforting me with words in Arabic that apparently mean, "it will pass…you'll soon be better…" something like that, judging from the tone.

But was it really sunstroke? Throughout that whole tiring, surprise-filled hike—amongst the mountain rocks, along the wadis and the deep ravine whose cool stream water and shady trees revived us, and again, up the arid mountain—I felt so good, and my white, broad-brimmed hat shaded me from the sun…

Only when we sat down to rest in the shade of a spreading acacia—we sat in a semi-circle, and opposite me, sitting cross-legged—was that beautiful young woman, Eva, leaning against the tree trunk, her head inclined upwards, her eyes closed, as if drinking in the sunlight longingly, the rings of light that fell through the net of the branches playing on her delicate cheeks, her slender figure, and on the angles of her pursed lips that seemed to hold an inscrutable

sadness, and her white dress, rolled back, exposing legs flushed from
the heat of the sun, to the whiteness of her thighs, to the hidden
secret of her groin—

And then, that faintness, that sinking into oblivion—

I fell backwards, unconscious.

And it had all begun so well. Promising to be one of the happiest days of my life.*

Two days earlier, I had gone to the botany teacher Shimoni's house in
the new Jewish quarter in the western part of the city. About thirty-five
years old, with cropped red hair and alert, smiling eyes, he opened
the door for me and led me into a room in which books lined one
wall and were piled haphazardly on his desk; there was also a globe,
some fossils, notebooks and all manner of thorns in jars scattered
amongst them. I told him of the purpose of my voyage to Palestine,
and said that our consul, Mr. Blech, had suggested that I speak to
him about perhaps coming to my assistance. "Biblical flowers..." his
eyes smiled at me affectionately, "an excellent idea. Have you read
the books of G.J. Balfour and P. Coates on biblical flora?"—"Cer-

---

* The incident described here confirms the assumption that B.'s condition does
indeed require psychiatric treatment. To her credit, I must point out that, despite
her sceptical attitude towards psychology—which she expressed several times
during my visit to Torrington—here, she herself discerned that her "fainting"
was not caused by sunstroke, but by something else she only hints at, and that
we must consider it an attempt to flee to the limbo of her unconscious, out of
fear of confronting her guilt feelings. Since this "coma" occurred in the Holy
Land, and what's more, in a place close to the mouth of the Jordan, B. could
become a link in the geographic chain of the saints and prophets who "swooned"
as they had their visions, and we must assume that, if she were Catholic, Pope
Pius x would bestow upon her the title "St. Beatrice of Torrington"... In time,
she might even take up her place in heaven alongside such a neurotic saint as
Theresa of Lisieux, known as "the little flower."

The more immersed I become in reading the diary and these letters, the
greater my desire to write a comprehensive essay on this interesting case, leaving
the patient unnamed, of course, (and perhaps, following Josef Breuer, who used
the letter preceding the actual initials of his patient's name, Berta Pappenheim,
calling her "Anna O.," I shall call my patient "Angela B."...)—an essay that I
hope will be published in the *British Psychological Quarterly.*—P.D.M.

tainly!" I said, "I did my homework carefully before coming here!"
He looked at me, his smiling eyes examining me, and then said: "Are
you up to a small adventure?" I said I had been an adventure-lover
from childhood. He then told me that on Thursday, a small group
of some five young men—he amongst them—and three girls, all
"greenhorns" in Palestine, who had arrived from Russia only several
months ago—were going on a hike to Jericho and the Dead Sea, a
long and difficult route that would take some twelve hours, and
would require them to spend the night in Jericho. "It won't be too
difficult for you?" He scrutinized my large body, as if doubting my
stamina. When I assured him that I was much more agile than most
people believe me to be by looking at me, he smiled and said, "In
that area, in the plains of the Jordan and by the shores of the Dead
Sea, you will find many rare biblical plants. Nerd and saffron, myrrh
and aloes, and many others…" I restrained myself from showing the
happiness bubbling up inside me: to inadvertently run across such
an opportunity! A hike from Jerusalem to the Jordan and the Dead
Sea! Could I have expected anything more exciting? "And mandrakes?"
I said, "Will I also find mandrakes there?" Mr. Shimoni burst out
laughing: "If you bring us luck, we'll find mandrakes too!" I asked
what I should bring with me, and he said: sturdy shoes, light clothing, head-covering against the sun, and goodwill. They would bring
provisions—food and water—so I need not concern myself with that.
"And if robbers should fall upon us on the way," he said jokingly, "I
am taking a revolver with me. We shall defeat them!"

When I returned to the guesthouse, I met two silver-haired
English ladies in the lobby, both from the London Society for the
Dissemination of Christianity Amongst the Jews, who had come on
a visit to Jerusalem two weeks earlier. They invited me to take tea and
biscuits with them, and after we had spoken of this and that, they
asked me if I had chanced to meet any Jews since my arrival in the
country. I told them of my few encounters with them, saying that
those I did meet had made a good impression on me. Intelligent and
amiable, I said. "And braggarts," sniggered Lady Ashley. And after
a brief silence, Miss Hollander said: "The Bible says they are a stiff-
necked people, and that is the most fitting designation for them. A

stiff-necked people." She recounted an event that had occurred: A mortally ill Jewish woman collapsed in one of the alleys of the Old City. Some nurses took her to the mission hospital, where both they and the doctors did their best to heal her. Her condition, however, was hopeless, and she died several days later. The hospital administration asked the Jewish burial society to take her body to the Jewish cemetery. They, however, refused to touch her. Because she had been hospitalised in a Christian hospital, they considered her defiled and cast her out of their congregation. She had to be buried in the no man's land east of the wall. "The chosen people..." Miss Hollander shook her head, her wrinkled, blue-veined hands folded on her lap. And Lady Ashley—the colour of her hair somewhere between grey and blue—said that, in contrast, more and more Arabs—numbering in the hundreds—have been adopting our religion, and many young Arab girls—who are modest and obedient—are already serving as nurses in Christian hospitals, while others are assiduously learning other vocations. They were quite astonished to hear that I was planning to go on a hike to Jericho in the company of several Jews. Miss Hollander cautioned me: the Turkish government now follows the movements of all British subjects in Palestine, mainly because of the Taba conflict and the danger that war might break out any day. If they were to discover that I was associating with Jews, all of whom they suspect of secretly supporting their enemies' countries, they would suspect me of being a spy, and those suspected of spying are executed without a trial.... Lady Ashley, a blue jumper spotted with tiny crosses around her shoulders, said they were leaving for England a week earlier than planned because of the danger of war. Lord Cromer had sent a warning to the Grand Vizier, Farid Pasha, telling him to withdraw his soldiers from Taba, but the Turks had not yielded. As far as they were concerned, Taba and Aqaba were meant to be fortresses that would defend the Hejaz railroad tracks, which were being laid... "And we have no desire to place our necks between those murderous pincers."

I, perhaps imprudently, did not heed these warnings at all. The entire matter of this ostensibly expected war seemed utterly fanciful to me.

About an hour later, Aziz came to ask about the tour planned for the next day. When I told him that he would be free of me for the next three days, since I was going on a hike to Jericho with a group of young Jerusalemites, his face took on such an irate expression—his eyes reddened, as if the whites were flooded with blood—that I was frightened. This Arab might harm me, I feared. He stared silently at me for a long minute, and then spat out: "What group?" I told him it was a group of young Jews, new in the country, led by a botany teacher. Following another silence, he said in a hostile voice: "Are you not afraid?"—"Afraid of what?" I asked. He looked at me as if I were a profligate, and then turned and left without saying good-bye.

Aziz's attitude towards me is disturbing. Several times during our tours of Bethlehem and Hebron, I said to myself: he allows himself too many liberties! He steps over the line! Every time I mounted my horse, he would support me by my buttocks, as if to hasten the movement of my body, even after I told him it was unnecessary, that I could manage by myself, that I was well trained in mounting and dismounting. He held my arm as we descended step after step of the Chapel of the Manger in the Church of the Nativity in Bethlehem, and did not loosen his grasp when we stood facing the manger itself, where, tradition says, Jesus was born. I was so unnerved by his touch that I lost any sense of the sanctity of that holy place I had so looked forward to seeing. He reached the height of impudence as we stood near the Magi's altar of sanctification. When I looked down into the deep, narrow well at his feet, into which, according to legend, the star that had guided the Magi to Bethlehem had fallen, Aziz joked: "Do you think you will be able to see the star? The legend says that it is revealed only to virgins…" I was so filled with rage that I almost lashed out: "Leave me immediately! I do not wish to see you again!" But a spark of sense stopped me: how would I continue my journey without him, with no knowledge of the country or the language its people speak? And what would I do with the horse I had rented!

Later, on the way to Hebron, when we stopped to eat near Solomon's Pools, as he bit into an apple, he began talking about my spinsterhood. Why don't I marry? He would find a husband for me. He would arrange a meeting between me and the sheik of the

Azazme Bedouin tribe, whose valiant son, a heroic archer, a gallant swordsman, who rides his horse as if he were astride the wings of an eagle, was not yet betrothed, and would be happy to hear that a lovely young English maiden…And we, the Arabs, love women with full bodies…like wide-hipped clay jugs…" He gave me a look of obscene desire. This was all said in fun, of course, but I did not like that sort of jocularity, and I did not respond to it with even a smile. Silently, I dragged along behind him through the alleys of the Hebron market, amongst the stands displaying jewellery, glass and copper objects, embroidered dresses and shawls and carpets, and I was most displeased when he bought a necklace of coloured beads made of Hebron glass at one of the stands, and fastened it around my neck, as a gift. It was like a harness around my neck that would enable him to pull me after him, leaving me powerless to escape…And as we stood at the foot of the large Herodian fortress, the "Hiram," which contains the Cave of the Machpelah that Abraham bought from Ephron the Hittite, as recorded in Genesis, and where, according to tradition, Abraham, Isaac, Jacob, Sarah, Rebecca and Leah are buried—he said that, although it was forbidden for non-Muslims to enter that holy place—which serves as a mosque—he would arrange permission for me to do so. I laughed. Such permission had been granted, more than twenty years ago, only to Edward, King of England, when he was still the Prince of Wales, so I had read, and even then, only after much intercession…. "With baksheesh," he winked, "you can buy even the Sultan…" I thought he was mocking me. My tourist guide tells how rigidly the mosque guards and their trustees enforce the prohibition against entering it, particularly for women, and all the more so, a Christian woman. But he had boasted several times during our tours of his own connections with Turkish government functionaries, and those bought with the bribes given by his father, that man of property. He asked me to wait for him, and a moment later, I saw him rushing about, importantly, amongst the mosque guards, armed Arabs and Turks, then he disappeared from sight. I stood and waited for him in the shade of the kiosk.

A hot wind from the east blew up clouds of grey dust, and seeing the adobe and white stone houses crowding up against each other on the surrounding hillsides, shrouded in haze and blazing air—it seemed to me as if I were standing in some remote border outpost on the edge of the desert. A caravan of camels passed in front of me, swaying from side to side. A woman clad in black rode on the hump of one of them, only her eyes visible above the black veil that covered her face; strings of coins, crescents, pendants, and amulets adorned her head, her neck, her breast—like Rebecca astride a camel on her way from Haran to Canaan, that is what she looked like to me. My heart was burdened by a kind of inescapable loneliness; abandoned and forlorn, I stood in an arid, ancient land, not knowing how I had come to be here, or even what the day or month were…. Heat of a sort I had never experienced burned my face, and when I remembered Vanessa—how far away she is now, how far from me!—tears veiled my eyes, blurring everything around me. Vanessa, Vanessa, I cried inwardly, if only I could lay my head in the hollow between your throat and shoulder, and feel your warm, perfumed breath redolent of mandrakes, on my face.

No matter how much I pleaded with her to join me on this journey to the Holy Land, she refused, saying that the Arab east did not interest her. Moreover, she had to be with her sister who, since the death of their father, was subject to attacks of "evil spirit" and severe depression. I see her large eyes, gazing upon me as she spoke with utter honesty, but with determination as well.

What was it that drew me towards her so intensely that I was unable to break the tie that bound me to her, even though I was worlds away from her? No, not the light she radiated. It was the dark riddle concealed in the tiny wrinkles gathered at the corners of her mouth when she smiled her thin smile; the riddle hidden in the spark that lit up the pupils of her eyes, like a distant star, when she spoke of her first love—when she was fourteen—young Henry Emery of the golden curls; the riddle in the ringing, bell-like laughter that occasionally burst from her mouth, only to be suddenly broken off for no apparent reason; the riddle concealed from me in the tangle of the hair of her armpits, in the hidden forest of her mount of Venus.

Once, two years ago, I succeeded in persuading her to make an overnight visit to our estate in Torrington. We spent the entire afternoon strolling through the fields and groves north of the estate, picking raspberries from the bushes and colouring our lips with them. Reaching the village, we entered the small church and stood looking at the painting of the holy virgin that hung above the altar, the babe on her lap, her eyes gazing down at him. I told Vanessa that she was looking at him in amazement, as if astonished that this child, destined to redeem the world, had been born of her womb. Vanessa looked at the painting in silence, and she remained silent even after we left the church.

Arriving home, I went into the bathroom with her, filled the tub, gave her a towel and soap, and hoped she would undress and get into the water. The steam rising from the water and the perfume of the soap dizzied me. But she waited for me to leave, and then locked the door after her.

And at night, when she went to bed in the guest bedroom adjoining my own, I could not close an eye. I tossed and turned until dawn.

I must purify myself.*

꙰

* B.'s relationship with Vanessa Stephen is most frankly described in this diary, and it was to have been expected, if we take into account the influence of the milieu and the ideas of the Bloomsbury Group, into which she had, unfortunately, stumbled. It is no wonder that she, too, was caught up in a "love that dare not call its name," since she spent entire nights in the company of such perverts as Lytton Strachey, Maynard Keynes, Duncan Grant and their fellows, and was perhaps present during the orgies that took place at the home of Lady Ottoline Morrell in Garsington...

    The most complex aspect here, and the one that requires rigorous investigation, is the relationship between her and her Arab dragoman. This young man undoubtedly felt a strong erotic attraction to her. (Not to mention the fact that Arabs, as is well known, are excessively attracted to fat women); in contrast, it seems to me that her repeated attempts to rid herself of him, to separate from him for short periods of time—these are symptoms of what has been diagnosed, psychologically, as "unconscious motivation"; and in this case, the motivation is to defend herself against a temptation that, were she to submit to it, would necessarily cause guilt feelings. It is clear that such a situation might result in the inability to morally discriminate between good and bad.—P.D.M.

Arabs wearing their heavy brown *abayas*, wrapped in *kaffiyehs*, Jews in black hats or skull caps, passed before me, many of them casting angry looks at me in my riding trousers and boots—clear disrespect of the customs of their religion—and I fixed my gaze on the walls of the enormous, august Herodian fortress, whose stones were larger than those of the Jerusalem wall, all of it bespeaking antiquity and the fine art of building. Looking behind me, I asked the kiosk owner—a Jewish women, from her look, a black headdress covering her hair—for a cold drink, and when she had poured me a cup of *gazoz*, as it is called here, red and bubbly, she asked in Yiddish—which I was able to understand from my knowledge of German—where I was from. From England, I said. A tourist? she asked. Yes, a tourist. She pointed to a sign at the doorway of a building on the street opposite me, on which the English words, *Anglo-Palestine Bank*, and a line of Hebrew letters followed by another one of Arabic letters appeared. The woman said—so I understood—that I could exchange money at this bank if I needed to. I asked who owned the bank, and she said Jews. "Zionists," she added, smiling. I asked if there were many Jews in Hebron, and she replied: "Oh, many! More than two thousand!" and told me that they had three synagogues and a religious seminary called a *yeshiva*, attended by some two hundred students. When I asked how the Jews in the city earned their livelihood, she raised her hand towards the sky, as if to say, God takes care of us. She then said that the Bedouins and the farmers from the whole area, even from the Negev, come to buy their provisions in the city. Many of the shops are owned by Jews, and "we can live somehow, with God's help." She said that the Jews also had vineyards in the outskirts of the city. I asked about their relations with the Arabs, but before she could reply, Aziz appeared and hurried me along with him.

On the way to the Haram, he said that although they had not granted me permission to enter the mosque and the cave in which the patriarchs and matriarchs were buried, his many efforts had yielded permission for me to ascend with him the first seven steps leading to the gate of the holy place, and from here, I could look down onto the cave from the small window in the wall.

We walked past the guards who, signalled by Aziz, did not stop us, and I walked up the seven high, wide stone steps with him, like a pilgrim ascending to the temple.

It was not possible to see very much through the window, apart from the small hall, shrouded in darkness, containing blocks of rectangular stone that looked like gravestones. But Aziz provided explanations for what my eyes did not see, as he described the rooms of the cave, in which the ancients are buried, each couple in its own room—Abraham and Sarah, Isaac and Rebecca, Jacob and Leah... and according to legend, even Adam and Eve are buried there as well.

To compensate me for my disappointment in not seeing the inside of the mosque in all its glory, he decided we should go to the tree the Jews call Abraham's Tamarisk, *Sindian al-Halil* in Arabic. Tradition has it that it is one of the "oaks of Mamre" under which Abraham set up his tent, when the three angels appeared before him to tell him that Sarah would become pregnant and give birth to his son. We made our way along the narrow paths between the vineyards, surrounded by stone fences, and in the middle of each one, a watchman's hut, a kind of tent made of stones removed from the vineyard soil. As we passed there, my soles crunching on the small stones on the path, and the green of the vine leaves shining in my eyes with every step I took, I recalled a beautiful verse from Isaiah, "My beloved had a vineyard...he dug it and cleared it of stones...he built a watchtower in the midst of it..." How much the sight of these vineyards reminded me of that description!

Abraham's tamarisk, its trunk encircled by a stone fence built by the Russian monks who own the field in which it is planted, is a gigantic oak: the circumference of its trunk is twenty-three feet, so it says in my guidebook, and its branches extend up to ninety feet! We sat down at the foot of the tree to rest, and Aziz told me that it was the only vestige that remained of a primeval forest that had been destroyed. Some fifty years earlier, he said, one of the large branches had broken under the weight of the snow that had fallen that winter. The branch was cut into pieces to be sent to Jerusalem to be used for heating. There was so much wood and it was so heavy that it took nine camels to carry them. He added that one of the logs cut from that branch had been transported to England.

"To your homeland," he said, placing his hand on my knee.

I rose, saying that we had to return to Jerusalem.

We rode all the way back in silence.

That evening, in the guesthouse, I feared that Aziz hated me.

Was it an attack of sunstroke that caused me to lose consciousness? The day had been so beautiful, so rich with impressions, and throughout the entire hike, amongst the mountain rocks and in the wadis, and along the banks of the stream that flows through a deep ravine, I gathered scores of flowers that Shimoni called by their names, quoting the biblical verses in Hebrew and English that mentions many of them—juniper, genista, acacia, nard, and many others—and that group of marvellous people who surrounded me with affection.

And that lovely young woman, Eva, whom I could not stop looking at…the only one who seemed to ignore me, but then darting the occasional thin, somewhat rueful smile at me. And as I walked behind her along the path, my palms were drawn to take hold of her long black braid and wind it around her neck, or mine…

That perfect face I could hardly keep from drawing on a page of the sketch pad I had taken with me: delicate skin drawn tightly over the smooth cheekbones and high, proud forehead infused with pallor, like a small cloud at daybreak; the thin arches of the eyebrows that seemed to have been inscribed by an angel; the almond-shaped ellipses of the eyes, whose black pupils were large and had a look of profound sorrow; the delicate straight line of the nose; and the fingers…. long, sensual fingers for plucking the strings of a harp…

But after several polite remarks of introduction at my first meeting with the members of the group, she did not address me again. I heard her laughter several times from one side of the group or another, in response to some amusing comment, apparently. The clear, spring-like laughter of pure, flowing water…

And all along the way—longing; longing that incessantly gnawed at me, eating away my heart…

1st May 1906, Jerusalem

My dear Vanessa,

Today is May Day, the spring festival in Albion, and it was amongst the delightful abundance of vividly coloured flowers glowing in the sun in the gleaming flower beds of Regent's Park, and along the spacious lawns that have only now awakened, in a celebration of intense greenness, from their long hibernation that we walked and talked about whatever caught our fancy—what did we not talk about?—I, chattering on, you mostly silent—the pre-Raphaelites, Rosetti, Whistler's river landscapes, Ruskin's "Modern Painters," the chances of being accepted to the Academy school, our friends—the Cambridge "apostles," your sister, me, our relationship…

And here, from early morning, a blazing east wind, called *hamsin*, benumbs the earth with its fiery blasts; withering plants droop in submission, houses are choked by the haze, people wilt with perspiration and exhaustion as they go about their business—nor does this heat abate even now, in the evening. There is barely any air to breathe in my small room in the guesthouse. If you open the window, the hot wind rushes in, bent on its evil designs.

Even though I have promised myself not to write until I receive a letter from you, here I am, once again unable to restrain myself from telling you about the exhilarating experience I had several days ago on a long hike to Jericho and the Dead Sea with a party of young Jews.

It is largely about that splendid group I wish to tell you.

I think I have already written you that, at the recommendation of our consul, Mr. Blech, I contacted a botany teacher named Shimoni and asked if he would assist me in identifying biblical flowers. I met with him at his home, where the most wonderful and unexpected opportunity presented itself. He invited me to join him, four other

67

young men, and three young women on a day-long outing during which, he said, I would certainly run across biblical flowers.

Early in the morning, before dawn, I left here to go to the meeting place on the Hill of Golgotha, north of the Damascus Gate. I was the first to arrive, and soon, the other eight had gathered. All of them—apart from the teacher, Shimoni—were new in the country, having arrived some six or eight months earlier, and they spoke Russian and Hebrew amongst themselves. They welcomed me warmly, saying they were happy to have me join their expedition, as if the presence of an English woman in their group were an honour. Hearing that the purpose of my visit to Palestine was to collect and paint biblical flowers, they grew even more friendly. Only two of them, Shimoni and Shneurson, an older, bespectacled man of about forty, whose forehead rose to meet a balding pate, spoke English well. All the others, however, made an effort to speak English to me so I would feel one of them. Traipsing with them for many hours along rough paths and through fallow fields, climbing hills and descending wadis, and sitting together in the shade of a tree or a bush to rest briefly or to eat or drink, I came to know them, and even more, their views, their aspirations and their state of mind.

This was so interesting, so novel and exciting, Vanessa, that I could not wait to share my enthusiasm with you.

We were headed north-eastward, and after almost an hour's walking through hilly, quite desolate country, we reached the Arab village of Anta, which is the ancient Anathoth, birthplace of the prophet Jeremiah. The village itself is quite wretched, some twenty small adobe houses that look like ruins, devoid of greenery, only rocks and stones everywhere, mangy dogs barking, filthy, naked children running about amongst the houses, foul-smelling smoke rising from an indoor oven, and at the edge of the village, the ruins of an ancient fortress and marble columns that lie forgotten amongst the thorns. But these sights filled Shimoni with enthusiasm, and a stream of historical memories flowed from him like the waters of a spring.

Try to imagine this scene: a thin, spry man, wearing the sort of hat shepherds wear, standing on a rock overlooking a large expanse of land, a Bible in one hand, the other extended before him, pointing out a cluster of small, distant houses on the horizon (but barely perceptible in the strong, blinding light of the sun)—the land of the tribe of Benjamin, explaining: That is the Arab village of Jib, the biblical Gibeon, and there is the Arab village of Makhmash, the biblical Michmash, and over there is Maqrun, which is Migron, and that is Ramoun, which is Rimmon, and so on. Further away, in the shimmering waves of blazing air, are several indistinct huts clinging to this and that hillside, the Bethel and Ofrah of antiquity, and now this is the land of Ephraim. Whenever he mentions the name of a place, he opens the Bible and reads from the books of Joshua, Judges, Isaiah, or Jeremiah, and then recounts to his listeners the episode of the concubine in Gibeah, Sennacherib's siege of Jerusalem—his army had passed through this area—and the dispute between Jeremiah and the people of his village, who warned him against prophesying, and sought to slay him, for which he cursed them, saying that one day they would all die by the sword and by famine, and not one of them would be left.... And there, the village in front of us—he points to the desolate, sun-struck village of Anta—it seemed to me that now, too, a curse lay upon it.... Nevertheless, Shimoni marvels at the fact that the Arabs had preserved the biblical names of villages and cities for so many generations and, smirking, speculates that they may be "us, our own flesh and blood," descendants of the ancient Hebrews...and, when he comes down from his stone platform, and we continue on our way, he translates this entire lecture into English for me, including the biblical verses.

We continued north-eastward from there—walking along narrow paths on stony terrain, amongst white limestone rocks glaring in the sun, with only an occasional fig or olive tree rising out of this desolate land of thorns, a sparse herd of goats visible in the distance, grazing on the withered grass that grew on the mountainside, watched over by their goatherd—to Wadi Farah, the ancient stream of Prath, where Jeremiah hid his linen girdle in the crevice of a rock, as God had commanded him. Upon reaching the high ridge over the ravine, we suddenly saw before us, in the distant southeast—like a desert mirage—the gleaming surface of the Dead Sea, an azure mirror glittering with a myriad sparks, white mounds, like pillars of salt, on the near shore, and on the far shore, the bluish Moab Mountains.

We walked down a steep incline—ever so cautiously, along a serpentine path—to the bottom of the wadi, a narrow ravine encircled by tall mountains, and when we reached the bottom—another surprise, an exhilarating one, in complete contrast to everything we had seen on our way: greenery, trees, and dense shrubbery lining the banks of a conduit, and fresh water leaping gaily over rocks, splashing against them, splattering into small burbling cascades, rushing headlong from the spring that was its source, eastward along the ravine. So surprising and invigorating was this sight, that those young people cheered with happiness, like children, *hey and ho and high-dee-lo-lo*, the sound echoing and re-echoing from mountain to mountain in that deep ravine.

And on the summit of the tall mountain, as if hewn into the stone, was a monastery whose windows looked like the openings of the caves that surrounded it, like eagles' aeries. Its inhabitants—so Shimoni explained—were Greek Orthodox monks who, he joked "are apparently descendants of the Essenes, or ancient Christians, who also hid in these caves."

We fell upon the cool water to quench our thirst, drinking until we were full, and then sat down to rest and eat on the bank of the stream, to the sound of its merry burble. Several members of the group removed their shoes and dipped their feet in the refreshing water, splashing and laughing like children.

You might find this description odd, Vanessa, even absurd: what impressed me so? What was there in these things—so commonplace to any English school trip—that I found so engaging and worthy of recording?

But you must remember how very different this country is from ours. Since it is mostly barren, every spring, every stream, every grove, is an event in its life, images inscribed upon its features! This is a land thirsty for water and shade, and that is why anyone chancing upon them as he walks about, revels in them! How precious are these things here, which we, in England, take for granted and squander so thoughtlessly! Many times during this outing, the sun beating down on my head, my throat and lips parched, my legs weak, I gazed upon the desolate expanse, thinking that the abstract God, the One who has neither a body nor the image of a body—is present here, between the cloudless skies and the blazing soil. This is the only place in which He exists, for in our country, with its scores of streams and forests, its grassy meadows and carpets of flowers, it is the Celtic gods, or the Greek gods of Byron, Keats, and Shelley, that frolic in the hills...

As we were sitting near the stream, drinking and eating fruit, the members of the group talked and laughed amongst themselves and, since they were speaking Hebrew sprinkled with an occasional Russian sentence, Shneurson volunteered to explain what they were talking and laughing about. One of them, he said, had had the amusing notion of establishing a settlement there, on both sides of the stream, planting a vineyard and producing wine they would sell in Jerusalem and offer to the cloistered monks in the monastery above us. This was the idea they were tossing about so hilariously.

We walked for some four hours along the ravine, called Wadi Qelt, which is watered by the Farah spring and two others. Its varied, albeit sparse, vegetation grew in its bed, and Shimoni made sure to point out to me every shrub and tree and grass and herb characteristic of this part of the country, naming them in Hebrew and Latin, sometimes in Arabic as well. Here was the Desert Juniper, a shrub taller than a man, its finger-like branches glowing with thousands of sweet-smelling white flowers; and this was the thorny Negev Acacia, with its unruly foliage and comb-like leaves; and here was the Desert Scorpion Sting, that had yellow and white flowers and wide leaves; and here and there, rising high above the rocks, is the *Pistacia Atlantica*, that the Arabs call *dom*, with its thick trunk and foliage, and its curved thorns and hard, round fruit that resembles olives.

It is interesting how legends about ancient heroes have become associated with certain plants: legend has it that the crown of thorns placed on Jesus' head was made from the buckthorn; it was the *Cercis silliquastrum*, an exquisitely beautiful bush covered with pink, butterfly-shaped flowers, from which the Jew, Judas Iscariot, hanged himself in remorse for having betrayed the saviour; Abraham's bush, with its blue flowers and finger-like leaves, was the thicket in which the ram was caught by its horns as Abraham was about to sacrifice his son...

However, it was not the plants I wanted to tell you about, but the people.

Shneurson, who walked beside me for long stretches, made a concentrated effort to enlighten me about the group I had joined: he told me of their aspirations and opinions, and about Zionism in general—as if it were important to him that I, whom he apparently considered a representative of the British Empire, should understand it and perhaps become their advocate at Westminster...

And so, as I picked herbs and thorns and wildflowers and placed them in my rucksack, occasionally stumbling over patches of pebbles and sharp flint stones, he told me the following:

He and the rest of the group live together in a two-room flat in Jerusalem; they share everything equally, both income and expenses, do the housework together, and are responsible for one another. Two of them work in a quarry and are learning to be stonemasons; one works in a bakery; and he himself—in a printing house. One of the young women is a kindergarten teacher, another works in a tree nursery, and the third is responsible for managing their household. Imagine: all are educated people, high-school graduates and former students in the universities of White Russia and the Ukraine, who left their homes and their families, where they had never wanted for anything, and came here! It was not material deprivation that brought them here, but the conviction that this was what Jewish young people must do now: leave the countries of their exile, where they are a persecuted minority, victims of anti-Semitism and pogroms, and live "a life of freedom, a life of liberty" in their ancestral homeland—the cradle of their culture and language, from whence they were exiled nineteen centuries ago—which is the Land of Israel.

He also delivered an edifying lecture on Zionism, or to be more precise, on socialistic Zionism, for the members of that group were not merely Zionists, but socialists as well...Should I repeat that educated Jew's long lecture? (He would have been eagerly accepted into our Fabian Society, I thought, listening to him and stealing an occasional glance at his balding pate, his bespectacled eyes shining with ideological ardour as he spoke, beads of perspiration glistening on his brow, thick spittle gathering at the corners of his mouth...) His words would bore you, and, in any case, my memory of them has become quite muddled, since I was distracted by the countryside, and what he called its "Syrian-African" vegetation. All I recall is that he did talk about the Jews wandering from country to country, an abnormal people in their exile, most of them earning their livelihoods from such insubstantial occupations as commerce, brokering, money-lending (meaning, more or less, that they were "Shylocks")...He said something I did not quite understand about "the inverse pyramid" that had to be set right...and about the aspiration to once again become a "normal" people, living by the sweat of their brow...he even slipped in the Marxist slogan that society must be based on the principle of "From each according to his ability, to each according to his needs."

This group—he told me—aspires to establish an agricultural settlement, known in Hebrew as a *kibbutz*, based on these socialistic principles, and it is their dream to settle in the Galilee or on the banks of the Sea of Galilee, to work the earth there and live a communal life.

These ideas, which reminded me of Thomas More's *Utopia*, are as far removed from me, Vanessa, as my parents' Torrington estate is from Robert Owen's "New Lanark," the failed cooperative village he established in the last century. But my encounter with the idealistic members of this group, their marvellous spirit of brotherhood and solidarity, and their naive, youthful enthusiasm for their dream have given me ample cause to admire them. Young people hungry for knowledge, helping each other as would the members of a family, ready to sacrifice their own personal welfare for the sake of the ideal they seek to realise.... And with what unaffected simplicity they relate to one another, and to me, too!* (These Jews—are they, in fact,

---

*   The excessive affection B. demonstrates for the Jews here—can it be a reaction to her father's anti-Semitic views? However, in contrast to this idyllic and

Jews? I asked myself as I observed them, listening to the melody of their speech, their songs, in Hebrew and Russian, as we walked in the heat of the sun…)

And the next day, when we returned to the city from Jericho and the Dead Sea—I will tell you about that later—I reflected on the enormous difference between that group and our Bloomsbury group. You know, Vanessa, how much I respect and value all the people in our circle, and with what interest and curiosity I listened to what they said, even though I rarely participated in the discussions. And yet, when I think back, it seems to me that our endless thrashing of abstract experiences was basically sterile. Time and time again, we discussed the essence of beauty, happiness, honesty, friendship; we would condemn Victorian hypocrisy, imperialism, organized religion (I recall that Maynard Keynes once said that our view of morality and human relations is "the new religion" we should adopt…); and how many words we expended on examining the essence of "the good," following George Moore's *Principia Ethica*. Was "the good" an entity in itself, like the forms and colours we perceive with our senses, or was it perhaps an entity conditioned by our moral concepts, and so on, the speakers expressing themselves with great self-confidence, quite arrogantly, I would say, out of a feeling that they were superior to everything beyond the walls of 46 Gordon Square. But did we become "better" people in our daily lives after these profound discussions on the essence of "the good"? Were we in any way "more honest" after our discussions that praised honesty and censured Victorian hypocrisy? Here, on the other hand, in this group of "pioneers," as they call themselves—"the good" and "honesty," which are not spoken of at all, are actually realised in their relationships to one another and in their aspirations to create a communal society. That was my impression from having been in their company for two days and a night.

idealistic description of this group of Jewish "pioneers," I have heard Consul Blech's secretary, as well as the priest of the Franciscan church in Tiberias, say that these groups, imbued with revolutionary ideas of equality and socialism, influenced by anarchistic groups in Russia, are atheists. It is therefore curious that a young woman with the religious sensitivities of B. should feel such sympathy for them.—P.D.M.

Let me tell you about it: In Jericho, we found a small hotel called Gilgal, barely large enough to hold all of us—the four young women in one room, and the men in another, and the lavatory—quite filthy—was in the courtyard. Having walked for twelve hours, we all had swollen feet. One of the girls in the group had blisters that were so painful when they burst that she feared she would not be able to continue walking the next day. One of the young men, who carried a rucksack containing first aid supplies, knelt beside her bed and bandaged her sores. The owner of the hotel, who saw this, apparently thought he was a doctor, and asked if he would be so kind as to examine his daughter, who had malaria and was burning up with high fever, since there was no doctors in the town. (Malaria is quite prevalent in Palestine, because of the millions of mosquitoes flying about wherever there is stagnant water, and most of the people I met told me they had fallen ill once or twice with this disease, which has killed a great many.)

I went with the young man to the room in which the sick girl lay, her eyes misted with fever, her body shaking with cold. I saw him sit down beside her, check her temperature and pulse, and ask them to bring him a damp cloth, which he put round her head. He took a quinine tablet from his rucksack—a must on every outing in this country—giving it to her with a swallow of water. He left a packet of these tablets with her father, and continued to sit besides her, stroking her arm, waiting to see if she were better. During those moments—perhaps because we were in Jericho, close to Jordan—this sight reminded me of the New Testament story about Jesus, who, when in Capernaum, was approached by one of the synagogue elders and asked to heal his feverish, twelve-year-old daughter, who was already at death's door. When he reached the house where she lay, everyone thought she was already dead, but he said she was only sleeping, and cried, "Talitha, arise!"—and she rose and was healed.

The next day we reached the banks of the Jordan—the river that disappoints all the tourists, who imagine it to be wide and large, with a powerful current, like the Thames or the Seine, only to find that it is a slow-moving, modest stream hidden amongst a tangle of reeds and tamarisks. When I saw the Russian pilgrims, those poor, wretched and oppressed *muzjiks*, hoping to inherit the kingdom of heaven, immerse themselves in it, splashing the holy water on their bodies and taking some away to bring with them to their homeland, I saw in my mind's eye a picture of Jesus, being baptized by John, and as he rose from the water, the heavens opened and the Holy Spirit descended upon him in the form of a dove and landed on his shoulder.

Riding back to Jerusalem in a diligence we hired—and the young men and women so high spirited that they sang the whole way—I thought that they themselves, more than any of us, who were christened in childhood, live and conduct themselves like the early Christians of this land in the time of Jesus, actually practising what he preached in his Sermon on the Mount, for they do not "lay up treasures upon earth," nor do they "serve mammon," but they share amongst themselves the scanty loaf they earn with the sweat of their brow, and are as content with their lot as the "fowls of the air."

(There are, nonetheless, spots on this sun: at one of our stops on the way to Jericho, as we sat resting in the shade of some juniper bushes, a blue-eyed young man with an unruly shock of flaxen hair sat down beside me, and whispered: "I saw that our philosopher, Shneurson, was tormenting you with his fiery speeches all the way. I wanted to rescue you from him, but did not dare. We are used to him. He talks and talks, as he aspires to become a leader of the workers, and practises his rhetoric on whoever he encounters. Yes, his preaching is quite fine…" So they too are not perfect…Even though, the Epistle to the Hebrews, says, "Let brotherly love continue…" However, woe the weakness of man…)

Nevertheless, believe me, Vanessa: never, neither at home, nor in any other place I reached in my travels, have I ever felt so good, so comfortable in the company of others, never has my contact with people been so simple, so natural and direct—as it was with that group!

(And in a whisper, I add Vanessa, that no, I did not immerse myself in the Jordan…I say this, because I remember that before I left, you asked me—ironically, of course—whether I intended to do so to purify myself. Well, I did not become purified…)

I must end this letter now. As for biblical flowers—I did not find mandrakes, or white lilies; on the other hand, I have enriched my treasury with a "Rose of Jericho," a rare, extraordinary plant with parasol-shaped flowers; a "Sodom Apple"—a shrub with broad, stiff leaves and mauve flowers, from whose apple-like fruit, according to an Arab legend, the daughters of Lot made the wine with which they intoxicated their father and committed their sin; the "Balm of Gilead" mentioned in the Song of Songs—which is balsam—from which the Arabs extract a healing oil they sell to pilgrims; and I collected many stalks of "nard," also mentioned in the Song of Songs, and of the "briar" that is mentioned in Isaiah, and many, many more, so that this hike has benefited me greatly.

I am enclosing a drawing of the biblical nettle, which is a very picturesque and expressive thorn, seemingly innocent, but quite vile, that I sketched quickly on the bleached path from Jericho to the Jordan River. (I just remembered that your sister once told me about an idea she had of writing a play in which all the characters would be talking flowers...)

I am awaiting your letter "as the hart longs for flowing streams" (a verse from Psalm 42, which was frequently repeated on our hike through this harsh, parched land).

Yours,
Beatrice

P.S. And yet another piece of information that perhaps bodes well for me: Advised by the teacher, Shimoni, I wrote to Mr. Aharon Aaronsohn, a world-famous agronomist who lives in a Jewish settlement called Zichron Ya'acov, not far from Haifa, and has the largest collection of Palestinian, Trans-Jordanian and Syrian flora. I asked his leave to visit and see the collection, and I am impatiently awaiting his reply.

Jerusalem, 2nd May, 1906

In the morning—with Aziz, on horseback—to the Mar Saba monasteries in the Judean desert. Like a dream—or a nightmare—of the time before creation or the End of Days. A blinding glare spilled over the desolate white mountains. The sun dominates everything. After two and a half hours of riding through dust and blazing heat, we reached those monasteries: white buildings, piled one on the other, enclosed by a fortress wall. Facing the deep ravine of the Kidron stream were the dark, gaping mouths of caves in which monks were sequestered, each alone in his separate cave. Ancient chapels. In one of them, paintings and a Byzantine mosaic. In another—the skulls of monks slaughtered hundreds of years ago by the Persians or Arab conquerors. Absolute silence. Monks in black—Greek Orthodox, long-bearded Russians—walk about like shadows in this fortified reserve, completely removed from the world. In one of the hovels are the "naturalists," whose only activity is feeding birds, amongst them, a rare black bird with yellow wings. Legend has it that in the fifth century, St. Saba, after whom this place is named, lived in one of the caves, together with lion cubs. One of the palm trees in the garden cultivated by the monks, where fig and olive trees also grow, was planted by Saba, and its fruit has no stones. This bewitched place is shrouded in death.

Aziz is hostile to me—that is obvious. Especially after my outing with the group of young Jews. Throughout the day, he was coldly polite, excessively polite: he arrived with a letter of recommendation already in his hand—signed by the *Kaimakam* of Jerusalem—without which it is forbidden to enter the monastery area; upon our arrival there, he paid the entrance fee for both of us, three francs for each, and another twelve piasters to the administrator and six for the gatekeeper for each of us, and refused to take a penny from me. When we were inside the fortified area, he took pains to translate every one of the monk's explanations, which were in Arabic.

While I waited outside for him to arrange matters in the monastery office, I saw something that upset me greatly, even frightened me, I would say, although I don't know why. In the shade of the wall stood a scrawny little donkey licking at the dust, as if inhaling it. Looking at it, I saw that its organ was growing longer and thicker, hanging down like a hose, or a viper. It was so long and so thick—almost touching the ground—that I said to myself, in astonishment that bordered on alarm: this is unnatural! It is bigger than nature! How can so large an organ extend from so scrawny a donkey? And while my gaze was still riveted on it—despite my desire to avert my eyes—the donkey erected its large organ, and bounced it against its stomach, striking his belly with it.

And yet, there was no expression of sexual desire or passion on its face! Its eyes were turbid, indifferent. I told myself that this was the embodiment of bestiality, vulgarity in all of its hideousness.

I was nauseated.

When Aziz came out of the office, I was relieved that he had not observed this spectacle.*

On our way back, near Bethlehem, Aziz saved me from imprisonment. We passed a company of Turkish policemen marching on the dirt road, unkempt, in tattered uniforms, and the rare sight of a foreign woman riding a horse aroused their suspicion. The officer stopped us and asked for our papers. I had neither taken them with me, nor my passport or entry visa into the country, and the officer

---

* This sickening description of bestial lewdness raises the fear that B. was suffering from neurotic anxiety about penetration by the male organ, stemming from some childhood memory or other. It may be that the appropriate therapy in such a case is mesmerism, which, in all likelihood, would restore the suppressed trauma to her consciousness, thereby releasing her from it. It is interesting to compare this description to the description of the donkey in her first letter to V.S. from the town of Ramle, in which she saw it as "holy" (perhaps influenced by the well-known saying of Francis of Assisi—"I have sinned against my brother the donkey"). Apparently, the complex, ambivalent relationship, filled with repressed libidinousness, that developed between her and her dragoman, is what caused this change in her attitude towards that animal.—P.D.M.

ordered us to follow him to the police station in Bethlehem. Upon our arrival there, I was taken to the station commander's office, who began to question me with the help of an interpreter, who knew a bit of English. It was a coarse, aggressive interrogation, attended by threats and warnings: why had I come from England? What was I doing in this area? What other places had I visited? Had I been to Aqaba or Taba? And when I told him (because of my naiveté, because of the strict education I had received at home, because of my devout mother who trained me to "always speak the truth") that I had gone to Jericho and the Dead Sea with a group of young Jews, their suspicion grew even greater, and they told me to remove all the contents of my rucksack. My sketchpads and drawings of plants also aroused their suspicion, and when I said I was painting biblical flowers, this was almost conclusive proof that I was a spy.... I asked them to contact our consulate in Jerusalem, but they ridiculed the idea: was it not clear that the consulate would protect a spy operating in its name?

They were about to put me in a cell, when Aziz entered the room, held a short, whispered conversation with the station commander—perhaps buying him off with a baksheesh—and I was released.

Yes, Aziz did more than was required of him in his job of seeing that all went well on our journey, and I am grateful to him for that. But he did it with no warmth, as he had at the beginning. He smiled constantly as he spoke to me, but his smiles were cold, as if concealing hostility towards me. And I did not understand why he occasionally recited—as if to himself, as if in jest—the witches' curse from *Macbeth*—"Fair is foul and foul is fair"—as if my beauty had become loathsome to him, as if to provoke me.

Here, in the evening, the English ladies sat conversing in the lobby, ensconced into two facing armchairs, their faces bitter. I did not accept their invitation to join them, but went up to my room.

How far away I have come from the world I left only twenty days ago!

Image after image cross my mind's eye:

Dinner at the Carlton Hotel, attended by many distinguished members of the Conservative Party. The glow of the lamps pours over the white cloths and the sparkling silverware on the round tables in the large hall. I was my father's escort, for my mother refused to accompany him to public events from the time, some years ago, when it became known he had a mistress in London. At the request of the master of ceremonies, everyone rose and lifted his glass of wine in a toast, "Long live the King." Speeches. Joseph Chamberlain speaks against free trade and for giving customs allowances to the colonials; the Duke of Devonshire speaks in favour of free trade; the Secretary of the Treasury, Asquith, speaks for limiting permits to sell alcoholic beverages...Lord Balfour has not yet resigned as Prime Minister, and all await his speech. He is sitting at the table to our left—quite an impressive man, intellectual looking, so different from the others—and to his right was a young woman of about thirty—was she the daughter of his brother, a scientist?—long golden hair, a claret-coloured velvet gown gliding over her body. The speeches bore me, I do not listen. My glance is fastened on Lord Balfour's escort. (No, she is not his mistress. That eternal bachelor was known to be a puritan in his relations with women.) I try to catch her eye, but she does not turn towards me. She is looking at the speakers, either interested or lost in a daydream. With my eyes, I stroke the soft, elegant velvet gown that envelops her full, ripe breast, greatly attracted by the sight of her.

It is too late for a train to Colchester when the conference ends, so my father books a room for me in the hotel where the dinner was held. He gives me a parting kiss, saying he would fetch me in the morning.

And I know where he is spending the night. I even know the address from a letter I found hidden amongst the pages of a book in his library, signed by "Your Lillian": 12 Cheyney Walk, Chelsea. I lie awake all night, picturing him having sex with a young wanton—perhaps an actress or dancer from Covent Garden—whose face I am unable to conjure up. And for the thousandth time, I could see that terrifying image from so many years ago, when I was twelve: he, bent over Henrietta, our fat cook, on the bench in the garden pavilion, jasmine winding along its planks, his hands on every part of her, his pants pulled down, and his face so red it seemed about to burst. I bolted that place and vomited up my guts.*

And between images, I see the sparkle of the soft, elegant, claret-coloured velvet dress that reveals arms, hips. And I see the longing—for whom? for what?—luminous face of that dreamer sitting so near and yet so far, unattainable.

It was no wonder my mother became an incurable alcoholic. It was no wonder she devoted most of her time to organizing charity bazaars in the church, to decorating the altar with fresh flowers—which she replaced every other day—from our garden, her beautiful face gradually becoming drier, more severe.

Was it her decision alone to send me to the Bury Saint Edmonds convent school, or did my father also desire that, to have me far away from the tense atmosphere of the house? During holidays, I would run across the meadows, the spacious lawns, to the flower beds that surrounded the pond, where broad-leafed water-lilies floated and ducks sailed serenely; or I would ride a horse to the woods, and from there—even farther away, far from the house, far from the atmosphere thick with resentment and hate and jealousy and silences.

For my seventeenth birthday, my father gave me Peter Farlow's *History of Nature*, filled with marvellous paintings of flowers and animals, and my mother gave me the six-volume, complete works of John Milton, elegantly bound in leather, never imagining how great an influence *Paradise Lost* would have on me, for that exalted poem became engraved on my heart as a continuation of the passages of the Old and New Testament we used to read together evenings and Sundays. When I was a child of eight, nine, ten, I would turn the pages illustrated by Martin Westall, the stories of Adam and Eve in the Garden of Eden, the flood, the sacrifice of Isaac, Samson and Delilah, the good Samaritan, Mary Magdalene washing the feet of

---

*   Although it is a well-known fact that Mr. Campbell-Bennett is an inveterate womanizer, this information, that he had a "kept woman" in Chelsea, was not known to me. Nor did I imagine that he could sink so low as to have sex with his cook.—P.D.M.

Jesus, the crucifixion—all these pictures had been engraved on my mind, and I tried to draw them on paper.

My seventeenth birthday party took place on a beautiful, sunny day, and the guests, friends from neighbouring estates and Colchester, sat round the tables outside on the grass, in the shade of the pine trees, my mother and father making a great effort to hide their mutual enmity behind a facade of cordial smiles, pleasant words, and compliments. Nicest of all, my teacher, the nun—whom I had asked my parents to invite to this event, for she was the only one of all the teachers I liked—announced to all those present, after having drunk quite a bit—wine makes everyone kind—that God had graced me with a great talent for painting, and to develop it was a sacred obligation. This talent was still but a grain—like the grain of mustard, smaller than any other seed—but once planted, it would grow into a spectacular tree in the eyes of all those who beheld it. My mother, so knowledgeable in the Scriptures, added laughingly, "'And then, the birds of the air nest on their branches....' But who knows what sort of bird it will be?"

It was perhaps because of that teacher that my parents agreed to send me to London and enrol me in the Slade Academy of Art, where I met Vanessa.

Vanessa, for whom my heart yearns—

Very polite to me. Yes, polite. And attentive. And tolerant.

And I am immeasurably grateful to her.

For *"Love caused my body to tremble/ Like mountain wind/ Besieging the oak trees."*

We had a nude model in our painting classes—Felicia, an Italian girl—and I was so captivated by the swarthy roundness of her arms and thighs, which exuded a bold and proud sensuality, that the pencil in my hand trembled with excitement, deviating from the lines I intended it to draw, and the sketch looked more like an open-throated orchid than a likeness of the subject. When Professor Tonk, who was a strict conservative-academic, looked at what I had done, he said reprovingly, "Are you trying to be surrealistic?"

I later thought that there was indeed something surrealistic about me, not in my paintings however, but in my proclivities.

I remember that wretched, depressing affair with Herbert Lewis Hill, the thought of which, even now, embarrasses me. My father, concerned about my indifference to boys and my unresponsiveness to the attentions of two or three sons of our acquaintances, attributed it to my shyness, and tried to make a match for me with a young man he liked, who was destined for a distinguished future. One day, when he was in London, he invited me to the Café Royal, and when I arrived there in the evening, I found him in the company of a young man wearing an elegant suit and a dark tie dotted with stars, his black hair neatly combed with a side-part, his complexion fair and his expression somewhat melancholy. My father introduced him: Herbert Lewis Hill, a barrister with the well-known firm of Johnson and Woodhead in Lincolns Inn in the City, a young man for whom a "parliamentary future" was predicted. After some thirty minutes of aimless talk, during which my intended beau directed scrutinizing glances and seemingly interested questions at me concerning my art studies—my father rose, excused himself on the pretext of having to hurry off to a meeting, and left us alone.

Thus began our fictitious "courtship," which continued for five months. Five months of suffering and torment.

I recall our meetings with self-loathing and shame. Herbert was a gentleman, courteous and considerate. He never pressed me to do anything he felt I did not wish to do. "Come with me to the opera tomorrow evening?" he said hesitatingly, and a moment later: "No, I see you don't have a great desire to do so. Then...when could I hope you would be available to meet again?" I, of course, decide the time of our next meeting, for I do not find the courage to break off our relationship, he is so courteous and considerate... A week later, therefore, we meet again. He comes to fetch me from my house in Dover Street, the carriage waiting, and he takes me to an exclusive, sumptuous Italian restaurant in Grovesnor Square. We spend three hours over five or six courses of the best Italian cuisine, then over a bottle of port, and the entire time, I am forced—as I chew and sip—to strain the muscles of my cheeks in order to smile at him when he tells me a joke about the intrigues amongst the various factions of the Conservative party, and reveals secrets about the relationship between Lord Rosbury and Campbell-Bannerman; and I have to respond with my own remarks, trying to make them witty, sprinkling my speech—so as not to suffer by comparison, not to sound uneducated or Philistine—with a rhyme from some poem or other, or a famous aphorism, and demonstrating knowledge about the world as well…And so, at our next meeting, during a pleasant walk on the promenade along the Thames, or drinking afternoon tea in a café near the Serpentine in Hyde Park, or watching a horse race at Ascot, for which he had acquired two tickets through his good, secret connections…Those forced smiles! Those forced words; the forced attentiveness to his smooth, pleasantly flowing speech in which I had no interest, and throughout it, I find myself in a thoroughly wretched mood.

To his credit—and the truth is that he must be favourably judged!—one must add that he was so cautious about touching me that he never went further than a light kiss on my cheek when we parted.

Who was that Herbert Lewis, really? Was he truly what he seemed? Was he honest? Was he in love with me, or interested only in my father's connections, which would have granted him a serious political advantage, or in the property he would gain from marriage to me?

No, I don't know who Herbert Lewis Hill was, never having concentrated my thoughts on him, for I never really took an interest in him.

When I became close to Vanessa, I broke off with him abruptly. Without any complications or pangs of conscience. I refused his invitations to meet once, and then again, until he stopped asking. He understood on his own, and disappeared from the horizon of my life like a drifting cloud, as if he had never been. I forgot him completely.

And now, too, in the night silence of the holy city, Jerusalem—from outside, with only the persistent chirping of a cricket in the grass, and in my room, the faint buzzing of a fly or mosquito—there, beyond the wall, the churches, mosques, synagogues, and tombs of the saints are alone now with their hidden secrets, not a living soul in their vicinity—even now, I see her noble, enigmatic face. Her sorrowful gaze, scrutinizing everything she sees, pondering, as if to say: is this truly what I sought? And yet—somewhat bewildered, unsure of herself; and her large eyes, clear as lake water, looking off into the distance, as if at something that was disappearing from sight. "A saint," her sister Virginia called her, because of her passion for the truth. Perhaps she called her this with a tinge of mockery, and said, perhaps with a tinge of envy, that only one fervent desire burned within Vanessa, for "paint and turpentine, paint and turpentine..."

I see her riding her bicycle to school in South Kensington, her long skirt flapping in the wind, which suddenly whipped her large hat over her head, leaving her black hair blowing wildly, and she stops, gets off her bicycle, and chases after it, as it rolls away from her.

I see her furnishing and decorating their new flat in Bloomsbury, at 46 Gordon Square, diligent, utterly sure of what she wants: the walls must be painted white, so that the flat will be filled with light, in contrast to the former dark family home in Hyde Park Gate, and the furniture must be light too, and sparse, only what is absolutely necessary, and Indian throws would cover the armchairs, a red carpet would lie on the dining room floor...She organized all this by herself, having sent her sister to Cambridge to recover from the crisis she had suffered, staying in bed for days and refusing to speak to anyone...When the work was done, she put her arm around my shoulder and led me to the window that looked out into the yard: "Look at how much light there is on the trees, the grass..."

And when I invite her to come with me to our house in Torrington for a Sunday tea party with my mother and her friends from the district, she says she "loathes society matrons." Only once did she come to our estate for a day and night, and I was ill at ease most of the time, because I did not know what we would talk about, and she made no effort to initiate a conversation between us, as if to show that she had come against her will, simply not to offend me. And at night...that was a terrible night for me.

And she hates gifts. When I brought her a silver, butterfly-shaped locket, she held it in her hand, looked at it smilingly, as if expecting it to fly from the palm of her hand to some flower, and then, saying how beautiful it was, she returned it to me: "You wear it, it suits you better…"

A long-time family friend, the aristocratic Violet Dixon—a large, generous woman brimming with strength and courage—admires her. "She is a genius!" she once told me.

And during the Bloomsbury group's Thursday night gatherings (which have become mostly Friday night gatherings), she speaks little, keeping her thoughts for herself alone. But when she does speak a few words, the sound of her voice in the room is like the clear ringing of a bell in the meadow, eliciting attentive silence.

Do I long for those gatherings?

But for her voice, her eyes—

Oscar Wilde wrote, "Where there is sorrow, there is holy ground."*

---

* B.'s frank stories of her romantic adventures in art school, of her perverted "falling in love" with V.S., of her failure to form a relationship with the young male barrister, all arouse my compassion and empathy. They are, however, the strongest possible proof of what a fatal error it was to lead this good, innocent soul into London bohemia, so utterly defiled by moral corruption and sexual perversion. How ironic it is that a teacher-nun from Bury Saint Edmonds opened before her the gates of Sodom, where homosexuality is common and respected, while the anti-patriotic "apostles" of Cambridge were her prophets.—P.D.M.

My dear Vanessa,

What a happy surprise! This morning, in the Austrian post office—two letters! And your handwriting on one of them! "Belated happiness is the greatest happiness."

The other letter was from the agronomist, Aaronsohn, who lives in the Jewish settlement of Zichron Ya'acov, and I almost jumped with joy when I read the three lines he wrote: "I will try to help you as much as I can. Please come to the settlement on the fifth or sixth of the month, because on the seventh, I am leaving on a tour for several days to the east of the Sea of Galilee. If you would like to join this tour, I would be happy to take you with us." Was the hand of Providence in this, providing me with such unexpected, longed-for opportunities in the Holy Land?

And to the Sea of Galilee, on whose waters our Lord walked! Who would have thought that such a chance would come my way!

Returning to my room, I became immersed in reading your letter, which saddened me. First, I was sorry to hear about Virginia's nervous breakdown—the third one, I think, since your father's death two years ago. I remember how close they were, even when he was old and infirm, already deaf and surly, his mental faculties so impaired that he would scold her for every little thing. She spoke a great deal about how much she missed him after you moved to your new house in Bloomsbury. Am I wrong in saying that it was this longing, and her separation from the man who symbolised her connection to earthly reality, that led to her hallucinatory mental state? I once heard her say that she listened to the birds in the garden, and they spoke Greek...and another time, she said she had seen King Edward VII leap out from amongst the bushes, uttering obscene words to her...

I often think of Virginia, and because of her extraordinary

sensitivity, she seems to me like a rose whose silky petals tremble with every light breeze, and if the breeze should become a bit stronger, they would break away from their stem, fall to the ground and wither. When the three of us were together in your house, with such witty, amusing words flowing from her—I used to look at her pale, transparent face and say to myself: that face is purification of matter, spirituality itself, as in Raphael's paintings of the virgin.

But I am astonished that you say she refuses to eat, believing that her eating, which she thinks is excessive, is driving her mad!

And I am sorry that the entire burden of caring for her has now fallen on you, in addition to the burden of managing the household, which you have always taken upon yourself. And it is you, too, who organizes the meetings of the group in your house, welcoming the members and providing the refreshments, serving the biscuits and cocoa, taking the guests' coats when they arrive and returning them when they go, and taking responsibility for the course of the conversation. In fact, I remember that you, much more than your sister, ministered to your sick father, (he once told me that women interested in the arts, in painting or writing, who become intellectuals, lose something of their femininity…), bathed him, dressed him.

I know it is difficult with your sister now, and I am consoled by the fact that Violet Dixon—that angel, a true friend of your family, who, from the time your mother was alive, has been prepared to do anything to support and help you at any moment—is helping you now too. I am happy to hear that she will accompany you on your journey to Greece in September, and I very much hope that Virginia will have regained her strength by then.

I was also saddened by the doubts you express in your letter regarding Clive Bell's marriage proposal. Why "doubts"? This is not the first time he has asked for your hand. He has been pursuing you for four years, from the time he sent you those partridges as a gift, of which you told me so gleefully, and later, when you were with your brother Toby in Paris and met him there. You rejected him all those previous times. And wisely so. Why now, tell me, does doubt "gnaw at your heart," as you put it?

I think I have come to know Clive well in our many meetings

at your house. His charm is, in my opinion, deceptive. There is no denying that he is handsome, and has a pleasing, agile body, and when he voices his opinions during our group discussions—on painting, sculpture, music, art in general, on what not?—his comments are impressive, not so much for their content, which is rather superficial, as for his impassioned tone, which sounds as if he has invested his entire soul in what he is saying, for the great self-confidence with which he speaks and, of course, for the captivating, scintillating humour of his remarks. But a careful, critical listener discerns their hypocrisy, the slight odour of falseness they exude, which is like perfume in the nostrils of the gullible.

True, Clive is quite an educated man—and perhaps he has a future as an art critic—but he is frivolous, Vanessa. He flatters his audience, and panders to women. Were I in your place, I would not trust him. In truth, when he came from Cambridge to the first meetings of the group, I thought he was in love with Virginia. He would sit beside her, exchange whispers with her, shower her with compliments—as far as I was able to hear—on her charm and beauty, as well as on her articles published in the *Atheneum*, and after several weeks, when he realised he would not win her heart, it was rumoured that he was courting Miss Raven-Hill…. Even Lady Ottoline, who tended to like him, said—so I heard—that he was "unfaithful, possessed of the fickle charm of flattery."

I am telling you all of this because I think you would be making a grave mistake—that might beget much trouble—if you accept his marriage proposal.

I was happy to hear that Roger Fry plans to organize a post-Impressionist exhibit in the Grafton Gallery. I admire Cezanne and Manet.

My painting occupies my mind a great deal. I think about it even during my outings, when riding. I think about the effect of the light on objects in this country. The changes from hour to hour, as the sun moves in its path, are much more intense than in England. When, for example, the pink and orange and grey Jerusalem stone absorbs and reflects the light, its whole nature changes. Before day-break, the wall of the Old City, which I see from my window, is as sombre and severe as wrathful prophesy; two or three hours later, when the sun is already in its zenith, the wall, bathed in the strong light, becomes agitated, as if suffering with fateful submissiveness, to the blows being rained down upon it; and at twilight, when the sun slants westward—it emanates such softness! Consoling prophecy. Serenity. A time of grace.

The same is true of the stones in the field, and of the flowers. There is something cruel about the sight of thorns at noon, amongst the arid rocks. On the way from Bethlehem to the Mar Saba monastery, I rode past juniper trees and thorn-bushes, the hot wind that passed through their branches sounding a lament—for their loneliness, their thirst, the pitiless heaven and earth. I sometimes think that the plants, like the sequestered monks, mortify themselves in this holy land.

And what do I want to express in my paintings of these flowers? Love. For love of the beauty of creation is love of God. For in love there is hope, glad tidings. Will my paintings succeed in generating this consoling harmony that is everlasting, eternal?

For the entire purpose of my visit to this country is to find the source of purity, which I have not found in my native country.

I must end now, for at dawn tomorrow, I will be setting out on horseback, accompanied by my dragoman, for the settlement of Zichron Ya'acov, through Nablus, which is the biblical Shechem, and Tul-Karem. A long way on horseback.

Yours,

Beatrice

p.s. For your amusement: Yesterday, returning to the city from a tour of the Judean Desert, I met the teacher, Shimoni, of whom I have written to you, and he told me that a Jewish professor from Bulgaria, whose name is Schatz, is about to open a school for painting and fine arts in Jerusalem, and is looking for teachers. "What do you think about joining his school as a teacher?" I laughed, saying that I myself still have much to learn.

Mr. William Holman Hunt
In Care of The National Gallery
Trafalgar Square, London

Dear Mr. Hunt,*

In London, I would not dare approach an admired artist such as yourself, either in person or in a letter. Here, however, in Jerusalem, seeing the house in which you lived for two or three years, and inspired by my impressions of the landscape of the Holy Land, my heart was filled with "the spirit of counsel and strength," as written in Isaiah, and, you can see, I have plucked up my courage and am writing to you…

I came to Palestine three weeks ago to paint biblical flowers—and I must say, that to some extent, although not from the beginning, I set out upon this journey in your footsteps. I became acquainted with your paintings while studying at Slade, and was impressed with your theory that a painter must know the subjects of his paintings intimately, in their most trivial details, as they are in reality—even if he desires to portray them symbolically, or religiously. And when I saw "The Finding of Christ in the Temple", "Light of the World", "Victory of the Innocents", and several other paintings of yours, I understood

---

* I found this letter amongst the pages of Miss B.'s diary. It is not clear to me whether it is the original, which, for some reason or other, was not sent to its destination, or whether it is a copy she kept for herself. Whichever the case may be—it is of great interest in constructing the writer's highly contradictory personality. (Did she, as a student at the Slade, consider him—who, based on his age, could have been her father—the knight of her dreams, as did many young women, since, as rumour has it, he did not deny himself their Favours…?)—P.D.M.

why you made four journeys to the Holy Land, and even stayed here for a prolonged period, despite the harsh conditions.

Before sunrise this morning, accompanied by two English ladies also staying in the Olivet Pension (emissaries of the London Society for the Dissemination of Christianity amongst the Jews), I saw the house in which you lived with your family some thirty years ago. Yes, it is still standing in the same place, that lovely, two-story stone house, in a small lane emerging from the Street of the Consulates, fronted by a lavish garden with pear, fig, and pomegranate trees, ferns intertwined on its walls. I stood before the silent house now inhabited, I have been told, by a Russian nun who tended to you when you were ill, and I thought about the painter I so admired, and his work.

I regularly attend meetings of the Bloomsbury group, some of whose members are painters, and, as you are most certainly aware, they are highly critical of the pre-Raphaelite style. During one of our discussions on John Ruskin's book, *Modern Painters*, and his theories regarding "truthfulness to nature" someone mentioned his assertion that you are the great religious painter of our time. Responses to this were mocking and sarcastic. They said that your paintings are "sermons in line and colour," that you are more preacher than artist, that you are mainly interested in the moral message of your paintings, and so on. I protested, citing as an example your painting, "The Awakening Conscience", which, although it does have a "moral message"—it depicts an innocent maid quite astonished or embarrassed by the brazenness of her piano teacher, who has placed her on his lap and has begun to vulgarly make love to her (her expression indicates that she will succeed in resisting his seduction)—I saw how much artistic thought and meticulous attention to detail was given to painting the background—both the girl's and the man's clothing, the embroidered shawl, the curtains, the carpets and the shapes woven into them, and especially the erotic atmosphere, accentuated by the glowing red that dominates the picture. Moreover—I asked—what is wrong with a "moral message"? This question received no response.

I, in any case, do not think that the description, "religious painter" is an odious one. And, in my opinion, you should not be denounced for your support of the Jews' return to their ancestral land.

Several days ago, while touring the Old City and seeing the Jewish worshippers at the Wailing Wall, as well as in the two or three small synagogues in the Jewish quarter I saw, I was reminded of your painting, "The Finding of Christ in the Temple". The supplicants in your painting—standing or seated on the ground, some wearing skullcaps, others with a kind of turban, wrapped in prayer shawls, bearded, their eyes burning, and amongst them, the young Jesus in a striped robe, an expression of astonishment and innocence in his eyes—these are all startlingly similar to the Oriental worshippers I saw that day in their synagogue. And as I stood looking down on the Kidron stream, I recalled your painting, "The Scapegoat", in which the goat dispatched to the ravine in the wilderness is so pathetic, so wretched, the hair of his coat so sparse and scraggly, his eyes filled with tears, his acceptance of the judgment so pitiful—that I felt compassion for him and the goats I see wandering amongst the arid rocks on the slopes of the Mount of Olives.

These paintings of yours, like your other biblical paintings, are an actualisation of your theoretical principles: they are naturalistic in their realistic details, while nevertheless suffused with profound religiosity. To my understanding, this is an enormous change, one might even call it a revolution—compared to the romantic, biblical and historical paintings so cut off from the everyday life of the periods they were depicting. Even in your painting, "The Light of the World"—which Carlyle said was far from realistic, for Jesus is shown wearing a priest's robe, a crown of thorns on his head—I found "religious realism" in the small details, such as the wild vegetation, which I know so well now (thistles, if I am not mistaken, from the tall, thin stems and the parasol-like blossoms), growing at the base of the door to the house, or the lines of the face of Jesus, which are those of a tormented Jew of that time and this.

I have not yet wandered much in this surprise-filled Holy Land. I have been as far as Jericho in the east and Hebron in the south. In the next several days, I shall set out northward, and hope to tread in your footsteps through the alleyways of Nazareth and along the paths of Mount Tabor and Capernaum. My eyes are filled with the light of this country, and my heart is filled with its wonders.

If my paintings of biblical flowers are successful—I shall, with your permission, show them to you when I return to London.

Forgive my impudence in troubling you to read this letter of mine,

Yours faithfully,

Beatrice Campbell-Bennett

A night, a day, and another night have already passed—the horror has not yet been erased from my mind, and I am overwhelmed by what happened to me that dreadful night on my way here. Tomorrow morning, I leave with Mr. Aaronsohn on the trip I so hoped to take, not knowing how I will recover by then, and how I will survive that five-day outing without collapsing.

There are moments—walking through the streets of this lovely colony, which looks like a French village, with its small, red-roofed houses, its yards surrounded by stone fences, enclosing a stable or cow shed, ploughs, wagons, chickens wandering freely; or gazing upon the magnificent landscape of the forest-covered Carmel Mountains, and the bluish Samarian Mountains on the horizon, eternal peacefulness everywhere—when I forget the horror. But only for a few moments, for, like the heavy blow of a hammer on my head, the memory of that appalling humiliation returns and strikes me, and I am enshrouded by darkness.

I cannot separate myself from my body!

Aaron's beautiful sister, Sarah—sixteen years old, she looks and behaves like a twenty-year-old—discerns, perhaps because of my pallor, that something happened to me, and she has already asked me several times if I feel well, if she can help me with anything, or if we should go to the local clinic. I shrug off her concern, saying that it is mere fatigue from the long ride from Jerusalem.

I sit in Aaron Aaronsohn's round library, all the walls covered with science books in French, German, and English, silence prevailing this evening in this house, as well as in the family's house, which is in the same yard, and an air of importance emanates from the thick books, and the bunches of dried grains—oats or barley—placed on the shelf to be examined by the researcher. I sit at the oak desk imported from another country, writing these words in my notebook—and how far is this world—thousands of light years!—from the nightmarish world I fled some forty hours ago!

How can I rid myself of the shame that engulfs me here, of all places, in the Holy Land?

There were no warning signs of the evil about to befall me.

The day before yesterday, at daybreak, we rode north from the square in front of the Damascus Gate. It was a lovely day, and the scenery—how different in its greenness from the Judean Mountains! Olive groves, oaks, and carobs dotted the hills, and amongst them, vineyards, cultivated fields and vegetable gardens. A populated land. We rode through small and large villages—Shuafat, Nebi Samuel, Beit Hanina, Dir Naballah, Hirbet el-Atra, El-Birah, and others; I recorded all their names in my notebook—and when we reached Ramallah, which is quite a large town, impressively prosperous—we saw two- and three-storey stone houses with arched windows and metal shutters painted green or blue, fronted by gardens with trees and cultivated flowers; a picturesque market, a variety of fruit and vegetables on its stands, and the abundance of copper objects and embroidered dresses in the shop doorways were breathtaking. Church towers rose on the outskirts of the town…. When was all of this? In the age of innocence before the flood?

We entered a restaurant on the main street to rest and quench our thirst. I took my Baedeker and my Bible out of my bag and opened them to identify, by their names, the places we had passed. Shuafat is Nov, mentioned in Samuel 1, Jib is the Givat Benjamin mentioned in Judges, Hirbat el-Atara is the Atarot mentioned in Joshua; Hebrew tradition has it that Nebi Samuel is where Samuel the Prophet is buried, and so on.

Unlike the previous days, Aziz, my dragoman, was amiable and forthcoming with me. He helped me find the appropriate biblical verses, and read several of them aloud, giving his opinion of them; and when we rose to continue on our way, he suggested—since the town is mostly Christian—that we visit some churches. I did not see any point in this: the churches, Greek Orthodox and Catholic, were not ancient, and, besides, I feared we would be late, and night would fall before we reached Nablus. But he entreated me, so I gave in, and we went to the monastery and church of the Sisters of St. Joseph, and then to the small Anglican Quaker church and its adjoining school and hospital. I conversed with the school headmaster, a Scot from Glasgow, who was delighted to hear of my purpose in coming to Palestine, for he himself was a nature-lover, a plant collector, and when I asked him jokingly if he had, by chance, come upon mandrakes in the area—he rejoiced: certainly! He, too, had looked for and found them!—in the Dotan Valley, north of Nablus! He enthusiastically described the plant, its broad, bumpy leaves, its fruit, which look like small tomatoes, its intoxicating scent, its twin roots that resemble human feet and toes, and he told me of the legends and widely held beliefs concerning the mandrake, and what Josephus Flavius and Dioscorides wrote about it, and he cautioned me not to pull it out by the roots, for legend has it that anyone doing so will be punished by having his life shortened…To his sorrow, he did not have one to show me, although he could show me another plant mentioned in the Bible, in the Book of Isaiah *katzah* or, in Latin, *nigella sativa*, called *kazha* by the Arabs, which grows in the surrounding fields and is used as a spice…He took me to his room and showed it to me protruding from a glass vase on his table—a tall, straight stem hugged by narrow leaves, topped with white flowers.

"I shall find you mandrakes," my dragoman promised—I am no longer able to utter his name—when we were riding again. "He said the Dotan Valley? I know where that is, on the way from Nablus to Jenin." I told him my fear that, if we veered north, we would not reach Nablus before evening. "No," he said, "we will spend the night in Nablus, but before that, we will have dinner at my uncle's house. I have already sent him a message with an acquaintance that I would be arriving with a distinguished lady visitor from England. Tomorrow morning, we will ride to the Dotan Valley, which is not far, and on the way, we will tour Sebastia, the ancient Samariya, where there are many ruins from the time of Herod, the Greeks, and the Romans, and from there, westward. We will have enough time to go to Zammarin—the Arab name for Zichron Ya'acov—a long time before evening. 'And I shall bring love flowers, mandrakes, to my betrothed,'" he laughed, and told me he had seen her only once, and he did not find her pleasing. "Too thin. Like a goat in a drought year…not like you," he said, sizing up my body with a smile. But his father and hers—a wool merchant—had made a betrothal agreement that had something to do with the payment of an old debt, and he could not violate it. Once again, he intoned a verse from *Macbeth*—"The Thane of Fife had a wife/Where is she now?"

We reached a pretty Arab-Christian village, an island of green on a mountainside, a kind of oasis, called Jipna, which had a Latin church we went in to see for a few moments. After riding through another village, Ein Sinia, we reached the edge of a narrow, deep ravine named El-Haramiya and, since it was already noon, and we thought the place so lovely—a spring flowed amongst the rocks, falling in small cascades into the ravine and gathering in a pool, and there were groves all around…. When was all this? In the age of innocence before the banishment from the Garden of Eden?

We tied our animals to the trees, opened our bundles, and sat down to eat. Again, as on the first day of my journey, he asked why I was unmarried, mocking European women—most of whom he had met, he said, when he was their guide—who sought to be independent and forgot the function nature meant them to perform, to be wives, housekeepers, and mothers. "And to be good to their husbands," he added, winking. If they want to be like men—let them grow a beard!—he said. "A Muslim woman could never conduct herself like a man. Do you know why? Have you ever seen how a Muslim man kneels when is praying?" he laughed.

Three young Arabs holding long shepherd's staffs, descended the hill, stopped near us and, casting glances at me, exchanged words with my escort. From their facial expressions and the tone of their voices, I understood that they were admonishing him for something, and then seemed to threaten him, as they looked at me. He spoke quietly, then rose, answered them quite angrily and, finally losing patience, drove them off with vehement gesticulations. As they left, still hurling insults, I asked what the row had been about. In these rural areas, he explained, far from Jerusalem and Jaffa, where the inhabitants rarely came across tourists, they were not used to seeing a young Arab man in the company of a foreign woman, especially in the fields outside the villages. The man would be considered an adulterer and the woman a prostitute. "I told them"—he laughed—"that I was carrying out an order given by the imam and the *Kaimakam*."

When we were riding again, I asked the location of the village of Bitin, which, according to my guidebook, is Bethel. "We passed the turn-off to Bitin a long time ago!"—he said—"We had to turn east!" But why was I asking? There was, in any case, nothing to see there! I said I wanted to be in the place where Jacob dreamed he saw the angels ascending and descending the ladder set upon the earth. "The ladder is no longer there," he joked, "the Crusaders took it…" He said the ride back and forth would take at least another hour of our time. I insisted, saying that I was particularly interested in going there, for the stone Jacob placed under his head had been taken to England and was in London's Westminster Church. "Ah! Richard the Lion-Hearted brought it to you!" he cried, "All right, we will turn back." He pulled the mule's halter, "And if we find one of the rungs of the ladder there, take it back as a gift for King Edward VII."

There were only a few scattered ruins amongst the small, shoddy houses of Bitin. The ruins of a fortress, the foundations of a Byzantine church, yellow-budded thistles and stinging nettles grew amongst the sun-washed rocks, and a cactus hedge marked the border of the village, where scrawny, filthy dogs wandered. But on the top of a hill, we looked out upon a large expanse of land to a mountain ridge in the north, to a bleached valley in the blazing east, to green olive groves in the west, to hills in the south, and as I stood there, under the high, cloudless sky, Jacob's words of wonder echoed in my mind—"Surely the Lord is in this place; and I knew it not…and this is the gate of heaven."

"Was it worth it?" he asked, mockingly, when we returned to the main road leading to Nablus. I did not reply. As we approached the village of Silon, which is Shiloh, mentioned by John Milton in *Paradise Lost* as a holy village, I asked that we visit it as well. "Both Bethel and Shiloh?" he laughed, "do you want us to reach Nablus after midnight?" I relented, saying, "Do you know that it was in Bethel that the Lord promised Jacob this land would belong to him and his seed forever?"—"His seed?" he smiled, "Who are his seed? The Jews?—God kept his promise, but they did not! They left this land!" I said that now, they are returning to it. "Yes, the Zionists, I know, want to establish the Jewish state here." After a long silence, he said, "If you welcome a guest into your house, give him a room to sleep in, share your bread with him, make him feel at home—what do you expect him to do? To thank you, is that not so? But if, instead, he conspires to take over your whole house, perhaps even drive you out of it—what is such a person called?—But the Jews are now returning to their own homes, from which they were expelled almost two thousand years ago!—Where have they been all this time? Why did they not return? Were they not allowed to do so?" He was again silent for a long while, and then turned to me: "If a person leaves his wife and his house to wander in all sorts of countries, and does not write or ask how she is, or send money for her and the children, and after thirty or forty years, he returns to her and wants her to accept him—will she? No! Perhaps, in the meantime, she has found someone else who she loves…the country does not want them! It has someone else!" He laughed, then he added, "In any event, they will not succeed."—"In what?"—"In building their state here." When he saw I did not understand, he explained his words: the Jews do not like to work. Not far from his village, Ishdod, there are three Jewish settlements. Who works in their vineyards and orchards? Arabs from the neighbouring villages! Who does the work in their houses and yards, who washes their clothes, cleans, tends to their chickens, picks their fruit? Arab women and children! The Zionists come from Russia and Poland to work on the land. Seeing that the work is hard, the summer is hot, there are mosquitoes and malaria, and wages are insufficient—they run back to the countries they came from! How will they build a state?"—"There are other Jews," I said, remembering the group I had hiked with.

Did I make a fateful error by asking to ride up Mount Gerizim when the sun was already beginning to set?

We arrived at the outskirts of Nablus a short while before sunset. The city was spread across a narrow valley between Mount

Gerizim and Mount Ebal. Before entering it, he pointed to a group of trees—several palms amongst them—on the right side of the road, the dome of a mosque rising above them. He said it was a spot called Jacob's Well. And he pointed out another mosque, further away, which he said stood on the site where Joseph, Jacob's son, was buried. His bones had been brought there from Egypt. I looked up at the peak of Mount Gerizim on our left and—recalling the story from Judges I loved so much as a child, about Jotham, who stood on the top of this mountain and told his parable about the trees that want to anoint a king to rule them—I asked to ride up the mountain. "Now?" he gave me a lopsided, sceptical smile. "Yes, why not?"—"Don't you think it is getting late?" I don't know what I was thinking at that moment, some demon tempted me to insist that we ascend the mountain straight away, and not the next morning, as he tried to suggest. "All right," he said, grinning.

The mountain, Jabal a-Tur in Arabic—was taller than it seemed when one stood at its foot, and the tired horse climbed slowly up the path that wound amongst the rocks. My escort, whom I was following, knew the mountain well, having been there several times when he was guiding tourists, and relatives from Nablus. We stopped now and then to look at the view, which broadened as we rose higher on the mountain, and from the top, we could see as far as the snowy peaks of Mount Hermon in the north, and the blue strip of the Mediterranean Sea in the west. We stopped near the ruins of a square fortress that had thick stone walls, the foundations of an octagonal Byzantine church in its centre, and a Muslim mosque called *Sheikh Ghanim* beside it. On the mountain top, we came to the Samarian "temple"—which is nothing but a stone altar, and beside it, several rectangular pits carved into the stone, in which, my dragoman explained, the Samarians sacrifice seven white sheep on their Passover festival. Twilight had already fallen on the valley below, on the city and the olive groves in its outskirts, on the scattered villages wrapped in fog, on Mount Ebal opposite us, a cloud resting on its peak. He stood at my side and explained some things, the customs of the Samarians, their white-robed priests, their ancient Torah, their separateness from the Jews…But I barely heard what he was saying. I was lost in a vision. I saw Jotham, a poor lad, whose brothers were slain on a single stone, leaving only him. He had stood in the place I was now standing, and below, at the foot of the mountain, were the people of Shechem, who hated him and wanted to take his life, and he, a young boy of courageous spirit spoke his parable to them…and I thought about the picture I would paint when I arrived in Zichron Ya'acov: an olive tree, a fig tree, and a grapevine, three trees laden with their ripe, juicy fruit, their branches and foliage intertwined, like children holding hands in a dance—and in front of them, the bramble, a prickly shrub that had never sinned, that had never been guilty, going up in flames.

It was almost nightfall. Below, from the city, small lights flickered in windows. I held my horse's reins, and my dragoman held his mule's halter. Before we mounted, he put his arm on my shoulder, and with his other hand pointed to some far-off point: "Do you see that dark peak?" I removed his arm from my shoulder and turned towards my horse, and then he said: "You know the Bible very well, is that not true? So tell me, why did the sons of Jacob kill all the men of Shechem after they had circumcised themselves, and were bleeding? Why did they slaughter them, and rob them of their goats, their cows, their donkeys, and why did they take their women and children?" He looked at me, sneering.

When we had descended to the streets of the city, I said that, as it was late, it would be best for me to arrange lodgings for myself in a hotel before we went to his uncle's house. There is no need, he said, there were two hotels in the city, the Nablus and the Samariya, as well as the Latin Mission's hostel, and there were undoubtedly few tourists now, so lodgings could be found at any time.

It is evening now, and tomorrow I must get up and go with Mr. Aaronsohn on a long journey beyond the Sea of Galilee, and I wonder where I find the strength to write, detail after detail, the things that happened to me that day, when I had no presentiment of evil, and on that terrible night…If my mother knew, if Vanessa knew…But I shall never tell a soul how, in one moment of darkness, my life collapsed around me….

We left the animals in the *khan* near the police station, took our two suitcases with us, and I followed him to his uncle's house through the alleys of the Casbah, whose stones were lit only by the dim light of lamps hanging in the shop doorways. We entered a stone house, wedged between other houses, and a short old man with a thick grey moustache and a deeply lined face welcomed us. He and his nephew kissed, greeted each other, and then I was introduced to the host, who greeted me in Arabic and shook my hand, and after several moments, his wife entered—a stout woman, short, as he was, her broad, bright face encircled by a purple kerchief—and she too greeted me.

This was my first visit to an Arab family. A lamp hanging from the high ceiling lit up a large room whose walls were painted—the bottom half green and the top half white—and hung with two family photographs. Over the sideboard hung a watercolour of Abraham sacrificing his son—Ishmael, in the Arab version—a ram peering out from amongst branches. The floor was a checkerboard of orange tiles with pictures of leaves, circles, and triangles, and a long wooden table stood in the middle of the room, with a large bowl filled with oranges, figs, and dates. The woman, whose words were translated by my dragoman, said I must certainly be hungry, and she was just about to bring food to the table. She led me to the small washroom in the back, painted green and containing a basin, a tap, a toilet, and a towel for my use.

The air was thick with the smell of urine and laundry soap, the paint on the walls was peeling, and as I stood before the mirror, I asked myself how I happened to be here against my will, and why I had not insisted on going directly to the hotel. The kerosene lamp on the shelf spread gloom in the narrow room. I thought: If only I could get away from this house with some excuse or other…

The woman served a chopped vegetable salad, lamb, rice and millet, called *burghul*, and our hosts did their best to make our visit pleasant. They asked many questions about my family in England, our estate, its crops and horses, expressed amazement at my riding skills, attested to by my escort, and asked about life in London, and what I thought of the country I was now visiting…I said that, because I had spent much time in my childhood reading the Scriptures, and I knew their stories almost by heart, I was travelling in a familiar landscape.... Their nephew confirmed this, saying that I also remembered God's promise to Jacob to leave this land to him and his seed. The master of the house glanced at me smilingly—the wrinkles on his face deepened when he smiled or laughed—and after a short silence, asked if there was any truth to the rumour that England was about to take the country away from the Turks. I laughed and said I hadn't heard about it. The woman, who was bringing sweets to the table, said that even if they tried, they would not succeed, just as the Crusaders had not succeeded, but were defeated by Saladin, for the east belongs to the Muslims and will always belong to them. Entreating me to taste the Turkish Delight, she asked whether, as a woman, I did not fear travelling alone, unescorted, to a far-off, foreign country. My dragoman translated her words, and replied in my stead, saying that I was a brave woman, and moreover, he was protecting me.

I thanked my hosts for the delicious and satisfying meal, and asked my dragoman to take me to one of the hotels. When the master of the house heard this, he protested, saying in Arabic, translated simultaneously for me, that I was their guest and they would not allow me to leave their house at such an hour, and why should I pay twenty or thirty bishliks for a hotel, when they had already prepared a place for me to sleep in their house: their oldest son, who is a tax collector, had been called to Damascus by the government and would not be back for several days, and his wife had gone with their daughter to her parents in Jenin. His apartment, which adjoined their house, was empty, and the bed there had already been made up for me.

I tried to refuse, but my hosts protested once again, saying that it would be an affront to them if I did not accept.

Their nephew stood on the side and watched me silently, a faint smile on his lips.

And against my will, I agreed.

Their nephew carried my two suitcases, and the three of them went out of the house with me. Some ten steps from there, they unlocked the door of their son's house, and the father lit the kerosene lamp.

My room, which was at the end of a narrow corridor, although not large, was pleasant enough. A colourful patchwork carpet was spread on the floor, a round table stood in the middle of the room, and on it, a copper pitcher and small coffee cups on a large copper plate engraved with Arabic letters; a double-door clothes cupboard painted white was placed near the back door; a cabinet with an elliptical mirror stood against one wall, and a wide bed, already made up, was placed against the opposite wall.

My hosts showed me where the lavatory was, and left, saying that, the following day, they would be getting up before dawn, for they had to pick peas in their field, which was outside the city. Their nephew stayed several more minutes, inspected the room, inspected me, asked if I needed anything, said I was probably very tired, so he would not wake me early, but would come at seven or seven-thirty to continue our journey. He wished me a good night and went out.

I was indeed very tired. I undressed, lay down on the bed and extinguished the oil-lamp. Dim light coming from the street fell across the floor. I was filled with a warm, pleasant feeling. The place and the people may have been foreign to me, but their gracious hospitality warmed my heart. My Baedeker says that the people of Shechem are known for their fanaticism and contentiousness, but my hosts had been perfectly cordial to me. I sank into sleep.

I woke with a start, frightened by the touch of a body lying next to mine, and I shouted, "Who is it?!" But a strong hand forcefully covered my mouth, and then, my eyes opened wide with the shock of seeing his face—him? It could not be!—bending over mine, his eyes glittering with a fire I had never seen in them before. "Are you mad! What are you doing?" My voice was choked off as he threw his arm across my breast. "Sh-h-h…I will make you happy, don't shout," he silenced me. "Get away from me! Get away!" my cry was stifled by his hand as he stretched over me. "Quiet, quiet…" he uttered through clenched lips, pulling at my nightgown, trying to roll it up to my hips, struggling to subdue me as I tried to ward him off with my arms, and kicked at him with my legs, at the same time, silencing me: "Quiet, quiet, nothing will happen…" And when I shouted, "You will not…you will not do this!" he crushed my face with his hand, "Do you want people to come in from the street? They would stone you!"—And, pinning my arms to the bed, his mouth on mine, he forcibly spread my legs, panting and moaning like a bellows, and I suddenly felt a burning skewer penetrating me—

I was paralysed. I did not know what was happening inside me. When he fell on me, breathing his final gasps, I rolled him off the bed to the floor and said, "Take the horse back to Jaffa. You will never see me again."

He rose, put on his trousers, and sniggered, "I did not think you were a virgin," and left.

I lay on the bed, vanquished, humiliated, defiled, loathing my violated body, my entire being.

I had turned to stone. One hour, two hours. I lay as if I were a prisoner in chains. No one to save me. No place to hide. No escape. When the faint light of day from the street slipped through the window, I raised myself slightly to look at the sheet. I was astonished almost beyond reason: not even a drop of blood stained it.

Stunned, I sat on the bed, understanding nothing.*

---

* The description of the rape raises several fundamental questions as to its truth:

1. Why did B. persuade the dragoman to ascend Mount Gerizim even though darkness had already fallen? Did she not fear being alone with him in the dark, in an isolated spot, with not another living soul present? (And, according to her description, it was he, not she, who did not wish to ride up the mountain!)

2. Why was she not forewarned when he placed his arm on her shoulder as they stood on the mountain?

3. Why did she not insist upon going to a hotel, agreeing instead to spend the night in a strange house whose owners she did not know?

4. Why did the dragoman, hired through a world-famous travel agency, risk raping an English tourist from a distinguished family known to the consul—a crime punishable by death by hanging, especially in a Muslim country ruled by a government known for its tyranny?

5. Why did B. not contact the local police the first thing in the morning, to inform them of the crime and demand the criminal's capture?

6. And most curious—shocking! sensational!—of all is her account of the absence of blood after intercourse! Is it possible that the entire rape took place in her imagination? That it was simply a fantasy stemming from both her erotic attraction to the good-looking Arab youth and her fear of having

I got up and dressed, repulsed by my body, took my two suitcases, went outside and stood at the door. Several passers-by cast glances at me, at my suitcases, and continued on their way. I recalled that, when we came down from the mountain last night—in another era, in another life—we had passed a coach station in the city. I stopped a boy who looked to be about ten years old, gave him ten piasters and asked him, using my hands and the few Arab words I had learned, to carry my suitcases to where the coaches were.

A morning mist enshrouded the city. A carriage stood at the edge of the square, harnessed to a grey horse, its muzzle thrust into a sack that hung around its neck. I stood beside the coach with my suitcases, and after several moments, the driver appeared, a jovial-looking Arab of about forty, wearing a fringed turban, and asked where I wanted to go. I remembered the Arab name for Zichron Ya'acov, and said, "to Zammarin." Zammarin? He searched his memory for a moment, then pointed west, and said jokingly, "Far! Far! On the Carmel! *Yahud*! He stated his price: fifty majidas—and I did not argue. He put my suitcases into the coach, told me to sit in the back seat, and whipped his horse.

It took four long hours to reach the next city, Tul-Karem. We ascended mountains, descended ravines, passed through picturesque villages filled with trees and greenery, flocks of goats grazing on the hills, women bearing jugs of spring water on their head, camels dragging water wheels, little streams flowing along the edges of orchards and groves—but all these sights passed before my eyes as if through the veil of a far-off dream. The driver hummed to himself, occasionally turning to ask if I was well, if my seat was comfortable, if everything was all right. My heart bled. I could not forgive myself for trusting

sexual relations with him? Was it theopathic hysteria resulting from her subliminal desire to identify with the Holy Virgin, whose bed never showed signs of lost virginity?

One way or the other, this story of "rape" is the key to understanding Miss Campbell-Bennett's psychic state. I must delve deeply into this matter in our next meeting. I will, however, be satisfied if she agrees to speak to me of it. Sometimes, when I ask her something, she looks at me as if she does not understand what I am saying, a frozen smile on her face.—P.D.M.

that scoundrel. How could I not have perceived the scheming that lay behind his smiles, behind his polite, refined English. How could I have been so obtuse to the signs that augured evil: his hostility towards me every time I toured without him; his vulgar insinuations; the strange fire in his eyes every time we were alone in a dark place during our travels; his ostensibly good-humoured teasing that masked the profound antagonism he felt towards my opinions. How could I not have suspected anything when he placed his hand on my shoulder as we stood in the twilight on Mount Gerizim, his other hand pointing to the distant view, showing me, like a faithful guide, the peak of Mount Hermon, the Carmel Mountains....

Again and again, all along the way, I relived that horrifying moment of panic, as my flesh chilled at the touch of a strange body pressed up against mine—that deadly fear!

Only once before, when I was about seven, had I felt such heart-stopping panic. It happened one evening when I went down to the wood shack at our Torrington estate to see whether my cat, which had run away, was hiding there. When I opened the door, I emitted a great shout, and my body shuddered with the fear of death, for a monster had appeared before me from out of the darkness, a demon with the face of a wild forest creature, dishevelled black hair covering it head, surrounding its face—I bolted for home, breathless, into my father's arms, sobbing.

He went down to see what had frightened me, and when he returned some fifteen minutes later, he said he had found nothing there. I had seen the monster only in my imagination, he said, because of the many legends I was always reading about demons and monsters.

Only years later, when I was grown-up, did I learn from my mother that it was the livery boy who worked on the neighbouring estate, Atwood Hall, who used the place for clandestine sexual relations with one of our servant girls, and they were both let go the next day.

To this very day, however, my entire body shudders whenever I recall that moment of panic.

The past cannot be erased. What happened to me in Shechem is branded on my flesh forever.

Looking at the painting, "Virgin with Child", in St. Catherine's Church in Bethlehem, I understood how exalted is the idea of "immaculate conception."

Mary is seen kneeling, the child in her extended arms, as if she is offering Him to God. Her back is erect, and a prayer of thanksgiving is on her lips. Joseph kneels on one side of her, Elisheva on the other, and angels hover above her, children with wings, blessing her and singing her glory. The entire scene is suffused with a misty luminescence that breaks through the surrounding darkness.

Seeing that woman, looking ahead courageously, proud of herself, unashamed of her innocence, I thought how true it was that she became with child "sinlessly," and gave birth a virgin—the physical possibility of this is completely irrelevant (can God take on a physical shape?), for it is impossible that the Saviour of the world be conceived through an act that is the contamination of innocence, the defilement, pollution, and corruption of purity, through violent penetration and bleeding.

Mary, the pure, immaculate, eternal virgin! Consolation for the sufferers! Seeing her, my heart weeps as I remember the scene in the Apocalypse when the temple of God opens in the heavens, and she appears to John, wrapped in sun, the moon her footrest, a crown of twelve stars on her head.

When we arrived at Tul-Karem, the driver proposed that we have something to eat in a restaurant.

Having no common language, we could not converse. But he, in high spirits, ordered for both of us—pita bread and humous and all sorts of spicy salads—paid for both of us and refused to take any money from me. Though I did not understand his words, I did understand that his good-humoured banter was intended to raise my spirits and I tried to laugh with him now and then.

The way from there to Zichron Ya'acov was much longer than I thought it would be. We went down to the plain and, after an hour or so, we entered a swampy area we had to circle around. Straw huts were scattered along the edges of the tangled reeds, and bare-buttocked, bleary-eyed children ran about amongst them. Now and then, the coach stopped to ask directions of a resident of the huts—poor peasants dressed in rags. We crossed a small wooden bridge over a stagnant stream and continued travelling north—on both sides of the road were carpets of yellow and white wild flowers, spotted with red anemones and poppies, flocks of birds flying above them—and we reached a sandy strip. The coach sank in the deep, yellow sand, and the driver got out and walked towards the fairly close, black Bedouin tents, to ask for help. He returned with two strong men, and I too stepped out of the coach. The three of them pushed the back wheels, I held the reins, and in several minutes, we were back on the paved road, the Bedouins waving farewell.

The driver's good-humour never left him, and when he was again seated on his platform, he continued to hum to himself and make jokes, ignoring the fact that I did not understand what he was saying. After another two hours of travelling, however, troubled by doubt, he stopped at the entrance to a large village. And indeed, after he spoke with one of the inhabitants who was passing by, he realised that we had gone too far north and he should have turned east much earlier. We drove back in the direction we had come, and after three or four miles, the horse climbed eastward up a mountain covered with a grove of oaks and terebinths, and when the carriage stopped in front of the Aaronsohn house, it was already five o'clock.

Six family members stood at the door to the yard to welcome me, as if they had been waiting for me: an elderly man and woman of about sixty, two young men and two young girls. The youths took down my suitcases and carried them inside, saying—in French, the language they and the girls spoke—that their brother, Aaron, had gone to Haifa to return the following day, and had asked the young man to apologize in his name for not being there to greet me. They took me into his house, one of the two family buildings, and said that, in his absence, I could stay in his room. The two girls—Sarah and Rivkah—followed us in, and with great amiability, took pains to show me every little thing in the four rooms of the house, so I would "feel at home." Sarah, the elder of the two, hurried to turn on the water heater in the bathroom—sure I was very tired from the long, exhausting trip, and would want to take a bath before we all sat down to dinner.

I walked through the rooms after they had gone, and although they contained no visible signs of opulence or wealth, I felt—after everything I had gone through that dreadful night and along the rough path—like Cinderella entering the king's castle. I walked from room to room, from the library—which was in a kind of conical tower—whose many books bespoke importance and scholarly seriousness; to the drawing room, whose damask furniture, inlaid with mother-of-pearl, was carved with verses in Arabic, and decorated with copper objects; to the bedroom, which contained a monastic single bed and a small wardrobe and cabinet carved with wheat sheaves, and two porcelain lamps, birds and flowers drawn on their shades; and from there to the large washroom, which had a bathtub, a water heater, a clothes cupboard, a mirror the entire height of the wall, and a toilet. No, not opulence and splendour, but modesty and nobility, and an atmosphere that invited one to sequester oneself in this house to read, or paint...a serene atmosphere that could make me forget the horror, at least for a while.

I filled the bath with hot water, immersed myself in it, and closed my eyes so as not to see my body spread out full length. I rose and quickly wrapped myself in a towel, so as not see my image in the large mirror. Then I made up the bed—Aaron's bed—with the fresh sheets that lay folded on it, and lay down to rest.

A knock on the door woke me from my slumber, filled with fragments of disordered dreams, and the voice of a girl asked if she could take me to dinner. I asked her to wait a few moments, dressed and went out to her.

Sarah—wearing a festive white dress and a large bow tie on her breast, her light hair gathered on her nape by a black ribbon—asked if I had had sufficient rest, and as we walked through the yard to the family house, she said that her brother had told her of my purpose in coming, and she would be happy to show me, the following day, his "herbery"—of which she was in charge and where she was sure I would find what I wanted. Another of her brothers, Alexander, had gone to Algeria to bring a special genus of grapevine plants, and she was sorry I would not have the opportunity of meeting him.

In the drawing room, the table was already set as if for a holiday meal: a white lace cloth was spread on the table, and in its centre were silver candlesticks engraved with buds and flowers. Dinner plates, their edges decorated with pictures of angels, had been placed on the table, shiny silver cutlery and goblets on either side of the plates. I was seated between the two young men, Zvi and Shmuel—both in their twenties—and after the father of the family had made the blessing, in Hebrew, over the bread, goblets were filled with wine made from the grapes of their vineyard and the colony's excellent winery—so they told me—and everyone drank to me.

The wine infused me with a mellowness I had not felt for a long time, and in a moment of dizziness, I longed for the time I used to console myself with drink, drowning my sorrow in a glass, and more than once, Vanessa had snatched the glass from my hand and forbade me to take another sip.

The meal lasted for two and a half hours, during which conversation never flagged. I was asked about my family, my life in England, my impressions of the country, where had I already visited and where did I still intend to visit, and they recommended places I had to see. They told me about the colony and its history, especially the activities and achievements of the eldest brother, Aaron, of whom they all spoke with great admiration. The parents, who had come from Romania twenty-three years earlier to settle and establish a farm on this mountain, spoke only Hebrew and Yiddish, and the young people translated their questions and stories into very good French, which is the language of instruction in the local school. The conversation flowed easily and comfortably—I, to my great surprise, was swept into it as if nothing had happened to me only a day earlier—and Sarah, this young girl of sixteen, seemed to be the woman of the house: she served the food, asked each of us what we wanted, and when the meal was over, she removed the dishes, with her sister's help, and stood at the kitchen sink to wash them.

At about ten o'clock, after we had had tea and coffee in the drawing room, whose furniture—a sofa, armchairs, an oval table and a long, glazed cabinet containing porcelain and silver objects—the parents had brought with them from Romania, Sarah escorted me to my room. Before leaving, she told me that she too was a painter, albeit an amateur, and said she would be glad if I stayed in the colony even after I returned from my expedition with her brother, for as long as my schedule permitted. I could stay in the small inn run by the Graff family for tourists, and she would tour the beautiful surrounding countryside with me, all the way to the peak of the Carmel. What was more, I had told them that I ride, and they had two horses, so we could both ride far on them.

I was so grateful to her that I kissed her on the cheek when she left.

Entering the bedroom again, I sat down on the bed, and when my glance fell upon the bottle of wine in the small cabinet, I could not control myself. I did something I should not have done—I took out the bottle and a glass, poured some wine, and drank it down.

I fell into a deep sleep, oblivious to everything.

Waking before daybreak, I dressed and went outside.

How pure everything was. The morning dew on the grass was pure. The towering palm fronds at the gate to the yard were pure. The small white flowers peering out from the branches of the myrtle shrubs were pure. The proud forest on the hill was pure. The fruitful vineyards in the valley were pure. The serene, turquoise sea spread out far below in the west, all the way to the horizon, was pure.

I must write to Vanessa this very night, if only so that she hears my voice, sees my face before her.

Dear, Dear Vanessa,

This letter will be short. It is now eleven-thirty at night, and I must get up early in the morning to leave with Mr. Aaronsohn on a long, five-day journey.

Well, as you can see, I am in the colony of Zichron Ya'acov. I arrived last evening, and the Aaronsohn family—elderly parents, two of the sons and two of the daughters—welcomed me warmly, as if I were a relative. Mr. Aaron Aaronsohn himself was not home when I arrived, and he returned from Haifa only this morning, so I have only just had the pleasure of first acquaintance, but my first impression has been that of a physically and mentally robust man, a courageous man of action, who knows very well what he wants and will not be deterred from realizing his aspirations. He has generously left his house and bedroom for me, and is staying in his parents' home on the other side of the yard.

In order to give you some idea of what this absolutely beautiful colony is like, I would have to paint it for you. It is located on the top of a mountain that overlooks the Mediterranean to the west, and is surrounded on its three other sides by mountains covered with forests of oaks and terebinths, maples and arbutuses. A magnificent, breathtaking sight—regal, I would say. Looking out upon a green expanse from the mountain peak, your heart overflows, giving thanks to the One who created it. There are four paved streets in the colony, lined with red-roofed stone houses with fenced-in back yards. The residents of the colony, established some twenty-five years ago, are Jews of the sort I have never met and never knew existed: Jewish farmers. Owners of vineyards, grain fields, olive groves, cattle sheds, stables and chicken coops. Though many hired employees work their land, mostly Arabs from neighbouring villages, they too—unlike the estate owners in our country—labour alongside the others: they plough and sow and harrow and fertilize and pick their grapes, and bring them to the large winery they built on the mountainside. Many of these farmers are educated, well-read people, and this colony, which has a population of about one thousand, boasts two schools, a hospital, and an imposing synagogue.

"An utterly beautiful colony," I have just written, "a breathtaking view," which makes the heart overflow...

But why should I conceal it from you?—Here too, there are moments...

Today, in the noonday sun, as I stood in the Aaronsohn yard that faces east towards the wooded mountains thinking of the happy circumstance that had brought me to these good people who surround me with affection—a damnable doubt suddenly began to gnaw at my heart, like a worm in an apple, polluting the soul: perhaps I am mistaken. Perhaps I am attributing purity, kindness, honesty to people who happen into my life, when they are only pretending and, in fact, have evil designs...Perhaps this is a weakness of mine, to trust anyone who smiles at me, or speaks pleasantly to me...My mother warned me more than once that I, like Little Red Riding Hood, am liable to be devoured by a wolf, for I will believe his honeyed words...

Perhaps it was the smell of the hay and manure coming from the stable and the sight of the rose bed in this garden that reminded me of our estate, and I remembered our butler, Smith. You met him on your visit to our home, and when he caught your eye as he served breakfast, you exclaimed, "What a good-looking man!" (And the foolish thought crossed my mind that you desired him...) Yes, I too thought he was good-looking and amiable, that tall, sprightly man who had been with us from the time I was a child, and who today is forty-five years old. He was the quintessence of a faithful and obedient servant. He followed my mother's orders scrupulously, and ruled over the two cooks, the two maidservants—who had to polish the banisters "until one could eat off them"—the gardener, the stable boy...In that cold house, where my father was always preoccupied with his own business and utterly inattentive to anything related to me, and my mother so strait-laced, he was my only "friend." He was as kind and gentle with me as he was grave with my mother. He joked with me, flattered me, sometimes smoothed my hair…I even found his vulgarity endearing. I was not offended when he called me his "partridge," because, he said, "a partridge has fat thighs, and, because Christmas is coming, we'll fatten you up and serve you for dinner"; and I was not offended when, patting my rear when I was fifteen, he said to me, "With a bottom like yours, you'll be a great horsewoman! It'll sit right solid on the saddle, that bottom!" And he was, of course, a "good-looking fellow." He had an agile body and a mincing walk, his hands were quick, his eyes often changed expression, from seriousness to laughter, from laughter to dreaminess, and his lips were well shaped, "meant for kissing," and so on. He was, as I have said, my "friend"…I liked and trusted him until…until I discovered that this "friendship" existed only to exploit me as a go-between in his clandestine relationship with a male "friend" who lived in the adjacent village—a strong blacksmith who shoed our horses. He tried to make me his confidante—to use me to covertly pass messages to his friend, to lie to my mother about his whereabouts at various times, in order to camouflage his meeting with that same friend, to be an accomplice in the alibis he invented about his meetings with the blacksmith…When he realised that I refused to be a partner to this surreptitious, deceitful game he was playing, he changed straight away: he was angry and stopped talking to me altogether. Suddenly—here was a different person, utterly unlike the one I had known for so many years! A bad person! Evil!*

Can it be that I understand nothing about people?

What else can I tell you about this colony? The residents, and the people who come to visit, jokingly call it "Little Paris," because

---

* Of course, I know the butler, Smith, and his perversion as well, which is incurable. More than once, I warned Mrs. Elizabeth Campbell-Bennett about him, for I know that such people are capable of all manner of deceit and villainy for, owing to their nature—and the circumstances of their lives—they are tainted by treachery and hypocrisy. I advised her to let him go, and she was inclined to agree, but her husband objected vehemently, claiming that Smith was a devoted and faithful servant, and his sexual proclivities were of no interest to him.—P.D.M.

of the French spoken in its streets, especially by the youth—it is the language used in the schools, along with Hebrew—and because many of them take their holidays in Paris, or continue their studies there, and, upon their return, imitate French customs and manners. This afternoon, when I went out for a walk in the street, I saw a group of young girls walking arm in arm, chattering away in French, wearing dresses and hats in the latest French *mode*...French is also the language of negotiation, both oral and written, used by Baron Rothschild's officials, who are in charge of managing the vineyards and the winery here, since the Baron has taken them under his aegis, and is backing them financially.

As for Aaron Aaronsohn himself, I can say only good things about him. Shall I enumerate for you all the praises lavished upon him by his family?

Imagine this: When Aaronsohn was only seventeen, Baron Rothschild appointed him deputy manager of his properties, in Zichron Ya'acov and in a number of other Jewish colonies, and he supervised two thousand Arab workers who planted vineyards, olive groves and eucalyptus and pine forests.

Owing to his great success, he was sent to France a year later, to study agronomy, and upon his return, having graduated with honours, he was appointed to supervise agricultural work in a colony in the Galilee.

He became renowned in Palestine and throughout the Ottoman Empire as an enterprising and inventive man in improving crops and increasing productivity, and an estate owner in Turkey invited him there to manage a five thousand acre farm...

Shall I continue sketching you his curriculum vitae, the details of which are gathered in my memory like rain water in a Jerusalem cistern? No, I shall not, except to tell you the most important thing of all: he is inspired with a grand idea—to discover the wild wheat that is the source of all species of cultivated wheat, in order to develop a new, more fertile species. That is why he explores the Golan and Horan—areas east of the Jordan. The expedition I will be joining tomorrow is mainly for this purpose too.

Aaron's sixteen-year-old sister Sarah, who admires him even

more than the rest of the family, told me that he sleeps only four or five hours a night, and in his trips to the four corners of the country—some two years ago, he circled the entire Dead Sea—he sleeps on the ground, wrapped in an *abaya*—which is a kind of Arab overcoat—and eats very little. He speaks Arabic and Turkish quite well, moves about amongst the Arabs in their villages, associates with the Druse that live on the Carmel and in Horan, who consider him a brother always ready to come to their assistance. Apart from the plants he collects—she told me—in order to classify, label, and keep comprehensive records of them, he also collects, as a self-taught geologist, quarry stones and samples of rock layers, and is so knowledgeable about them that the government, as well as various entrepreneurs, consult him about the possibilities of exploiting them for industrial purposes.

A man like him—the acme of perfection, according to everything said about him—is certainly worthy of admiration. But I...

You tell me, Vanessa, is it not a shameful trait of mine that I am incapable of admiring people like him—people of action, "positive" in every sense, so beneficial to society, to their people, perhaps to all of humanity—that they are "the acme of perfection"?

During our brief meeting—and he was quite gracious, ready to help me in any way I asked—I realised, to my sorrow—to my shame!—how far apart the world of this "positive" man is from my own. There was something closed and unbending about him, quite "earthy," undoubtedly quite efficient too, and yet...his glance, fixed upon my face, seemed to be focused far beyond me, and his words were occasionally punctuated by short bursts of laughter lacking warmth, which I found incomprehensible...and his chin is too heavy for my taste...

And I—you know this, we spoke about it more than once—look for something else in people. Not for "the acme of perfection." Perhaps the opposite. The nature that has a certain infirmity, a certain incapacity. An incomplete, imperfect circle. Something of a riddle.

You will send me, as you did once, smiling that ironic smile of yours, to the saints. And I will tell you again, as I did then, that I admire only those amongst them who are a riddle to me.

Sarah is a charming girl. I liked her from the moment I saw her. She possesses a rare blend of gentleness and determination, modesty and self-confidence. Her blue eyes are not soft; they express courage and decisiveness, while her voice is warm and bell-like. Standing beside her, you feel that this is a mature personality, intended for great things. She has strong opinions with regard to both the management of the colony and political matters. Yesterday, 5 May, was the last day of the ultimatum our government gave to Sultan Abdul Hamid II to withdraw his troops from Taba on the Sinai border, and Sarah waited excitedly to see whether he would submit or choose to fight the Egyptian army under our command. "I hope he doesn't give in to the ultimatum," a flash of the joy of battle lit up her smiling eyes. She hoped that, as a result, war would break out between Turkey—"the corrupt, cruel, and decadent kingdom"—and Britain, and she did not have the slightest doubt that our army would devastate the Turkish army, which is rotten with decay, conquer Palestine, Trans-Jordan, Syria, and Lebanon, and then, under the enlightened rule of "the English, who were raised on the Bible," (she believes we are the descendants of the tribe of Dan, which, after the exile of the ten tribes, sailed far away to the British Isles, where it settled...), a Jewish state would be established in this land, the cradle of Jewish culture.

A beautiful girl. Three months ago, on the holiday known as Purim, which commemorates the victory of the Jews over the evil Haman, as recorded in the Book of Esther, the local youth performed a play based on this Book, and Sarah played the role of Queen Esther. A photograph of her in this role hangs on the wall of her parents' bedroom: a long silk bridal dress on her tall figure, a gauze bridal veil gliding down both sides of her face, a gold crown on her head, her blonde hair spread across her shoulders, her eyes shining like stars in the heaven of her broad face...The photograph reminded me of the one of Sara Bernhardt in the role of Phaedra.

(By the way, I have asked myself many times why it is so universally accepted that a bridal gown should be white? White is one of the three colours of Mary, Mother of Jesus: turquoise, which is the colour of the sky, purple, which is the colour of royalty, and white, the symbol of virginal purity. And on the wedding night, that purity is already desecrated…)

This morning, I walked beside Sarah along the paths of the wonderful garden behind their house, as she trimmed the rose bushes and helped the Arab worker move plants from one place to another. The Aaronsohns call this garden "the garden of the seven species" after the seven species that the land was blessed with, mentioned in Deuteronomy. However, not seven but seventy-seven kinds of trees, bushes and flowers grow there. As we spoke about my plans to continue my travels in Palestine, she invited me to stay in the colony as long as I wished after returning from my expedition with her brother. I am inclined to accept her invitation, and I may stay here several more days and meticulously examine their rare collection of plants. And I shall paint. Yes, I shall paint a great deal here, Vanessa!

And I shall bring you mandrakes when I return…

There is much to tell about this extraordinary family, but I must end here. It is already half past midnight. When I return from my trip, I shall write to you again, at length.

This country is full of contradictions, Vanessa. As in ancient times, today, too, there are those who profane its holiness. For the spirit of impurity, as written in Matthew, that issues from man wanders in the land of suffering and finds no rest. Who will save us from it? Sometimes I pray: Please come, Lord, and reward every man according to his deeds…

You will mock me: from the moment I entered this colony, surrounded with vineyards, fine wine pouring from its winery, I find I am seduced by the temptation to drink…as "in the good old days…" but throughout these last weeks, since I first stepped onto this land, liquor has not passed my lips. Muslims, in any case, are forbidden to drink alcohol, and there is none to be found where they live…

Good night to you, my dear.

Longing to see your face, to hear your voice—

Beatrice

Tiberias, 7th May, 1906

The trip from Zichron Ya'acov to here took some twelve hours in the covered wagon belonging to a farmer from the colony. We arrived at seven-thirty; Mr. Aaronsohn met with several acquaintances here. Together with an official, Mr. Turov, who will be going on the trip with us, we ate a delicious fish dinner on the shore of the Sea of Galilee, which is also called the *Kinneret* in Hebrew, and I am staying in a hotel owned by a religious Jew, named Grossman. I was given a small room, whitewashed, with a domed ceiling like those in old Arab houses. It is furnished with a metal bed canopied with mosquito netting—against the malaria-carrying anopheles mosquito, which is abundant in this area and, I am told, can be fatal. There is also a small table and rickety chair. A niche in the wall serves as a wardrobe.

We left Zichron Ya'acov after eating breakfast with the rest of the family, who were on their way to work in the vineyard, the wheat field, or in the yard. The wagon was already waiting for us at the gate. We descended into the valley called Wadi Milek, bordered by hills covered with woods, vineyards, and fields abounding with wildflowers. We passed two small, isolated Jewish colonies that appeared to be empty, each consisting of a number of houses surrounded by only a few greening trees—cypress, pine, and eucalyptus. Shffeyah and Bat Shlomo were their names. Mr. Aaronsohn told me that in Shffeyah, a school had been established for orphans from the pogroms that had occurred three years ago in the Russian city of Kishinev.

We rode through this valley for two hours until we reached the eastern slopes of Mount Carmel, where a wide valley spread before us, the Jezreel Valley. Swamps and lakes abundant with reeds glowed in the sun, and a creek wound through them like a snake—the Kishon

Creek, whose name I remembered from the Song of Deborah; it is the creek that swept away Sisera's army in its war against the army of Israel.

The wagon driver, who was quite familiar with the way, having already driven through it several times, knew where to cross the marshy swamp and directed our wagon to a narrow strip of heavy, packed earth amidst the swampy waters. When we had reached the other side, Mr. Aaronsohn stopped our journey for me, saying that here, too, I could find several plants mentioned in the Bible. We stepped out of the wagon, and from the tangle of reeds on the bank of the swamp, he pulled up three long, thin stalks and brought them to me: here was a rush, here a papyrus, and this was cane. The rush—he showed me—the one whose top resembled a horse's tail, is the most fibrous. It is mentioned in Isaiah and Job. The Bedouin, who live in straw huts around the swamps, use it for stringing the fish they catch in the creek. Papyrus, with its fan-shaped head, was used by Jochebed to make Moses' wicker basket, as described in Exodus, and the Egyptians made the parchment from it on which they wrote their hieroglyphics. Today, it is used to make mats, and also plays a role in building huts and light boats, in braiding shoes and producing all manner of tools. The cane, called *kayneh* by the Arabs, the thickest of the three, is mentioned in Isaiah. It is made of a series of joints, and is used mainly in the sugar industry. After he showed it to me, he broke off two joints and gave them to me to chew. I chewed the cane, and my mouth filled with a sweetish juice.

We continued riding, and the road rose into hills forested with oaks. Aaron Aaronsohn—strong, broad-shouldered, with straight black hair and a bold and direct gaze—spoke English well and tried to make our journey interesting and instructive. He spoke thoughtfully and to the point, as if he were taking care not to waste his words on nonsense, and his sentences were precisely formulated. His explanations of what I saw on both sides of the road were quite good, and when he asked about my life in England and my family, and I told him about our estate in Torrington, he asked what we grew in our fields, whether we fertilized them, if we had a thresher, a flour mill, and so on. He listened attentively to my answers, as if they could teach him about his own occupations. He then spoke about the great tasks confronting the Zionists: to cultivate desolate land or reclaimed swamps—like the Jezreel Valley we had crossed—for Jewish colonisation; to mechanize agriculture so that a large population could earn a livelihood from it; to develop industry based on the minerals found in the land and lakes of this country, such as the Dead Sea, which he had recently studied; to build railroad tracks…The Zionist leadership, with whom he was in constant touch, had instructed him to survey the possibilities of building railroad tracks between Jaffa and Haifa, as well as between Haifa and Zemach…Under the rule of the Turks, however, who were not interested in any development—on the contrary, they wished to maintain the backwardness—it was quite difficult to implement these plans, he said. The new governor of Jerusalem, Achram Bey—whom he had met regarding a franchise for developing uncultivated land in the area of Jericho and the Jordan Valley—was an honest, blameless man, a playwright and poet when the occasion arose, yet he nevertheless feared the Jews, lest they establish here "Yehudistan," as he put it, and rebel against the government, as the Kurds, the Armenians and the Bulgarians had. He therefore rejected any agricultural or industrial development enterprise, and made it difficult for Jews to immigrate to Palestine. But if the English governed the country…. Had I read Dr. Herzl's *The Jewish State*, he asked? That pamphlet, which is well worth reading—he would make me a gift of it when we returned to Zichron Ya'acov—describes how the state would actually be established and what it would be like. Herzl also mentions England and its government as a model, naming London the centre for "The Jewish Society," whose role it will be to take the first steps in establishing the state. I looked at him as he spoke, wondering if that countenance, so utterly focused—directed solely to some important purpose—was, in fact, a reflection of his inner self. Occasionally, however, as he described the future he envisioned for this country, his fervour burst forth from his words—like small tongues of fire erupting from a pile of ashes—and attested to the great vision that illuminated his heart.

When we arrived at Nazareth, he announced—for me, the Christian—that we would stop there for an hour so I could see the city in which Joseph and Mary, Jesus' mother and father, had lived and where, according to him, Jesus himself had been born. We would therefore dine there as well.

We left the wagon and driver in a field in the centre of the city, and the two of us went to the main street, a stone-paved street that ascended the mountainside. Crowds of people walked to and fro, as if it were a holiday, and the Arab women, their light-skinned faces exposed, wore embroidered vests, and necklaces of amulets hung around their necks; and the camels and donkeys that now and then moved past, the passers-by making way for them, were adorned with shell necklaces and embroidered pack-saddles. Church towers rose everywhere, along the mountainside and on its peak, amid gardens of olive, fig, and pomegranate trees, enclosed by cactus hedges. Mr. Aaronsohn pointed out the churches… "that one is Greek Orthodox, that is Marronite, the other is Latin, and over there is the Franciscan monastery, and there—the Russian, and there—the Sisters of Saint Joseph…"

And I, with my wounds and my shame burning ceaselessly inside me, I felt the mark of disgrace branded on my forehead. (Dear God make all the evil that befalls me disappear as if it were a nightmare that terrified my errant soul).

Though I am a year or two older than Aaron Aaronsohn, I felt as if he were my older brother. His seriousness dissipated somewhat as we walked along the street, and he now and then made a joking remark. When we passed a carpentry shop, its wide open door revealing the carpenter covered in the sawdust flying from his saw, he said: "You see, that's how Jesus' father looked. Nothing much has changed since then." And as we continued walking up the street, he said: "Well, what do you think, was Jesus born in Nazareth or Bethlehem?" I said that if one were to believe what is written in the Gospels, then it was Bethlehem. That is the common belief of Christian tradition, and that is why the Church of the Nativity was built there…—"Then why was he nonetheless called Jesus of Nazareth, and why were the early Christians called Nazarenes, and not Bethlehemites?"—"Because that was the city of his origins, where his family was!" I said.

We entered the Church of the Annunciation, built on the ruins of a Crusader church and which, according to tradition, stands on the place where the angel announced to the Virgin Mary she had become pregnant by the Holy Spirit. We went through the three chapels, lingering beside the ancient well, and once outside again, Mr. Aaronsohn said, continuing his earlier train of thought, "How do you explain the contradiction that several places in the Gospels mention that Nazareth is 'His birthplace,' and it is recounted that, when He arrived in that city to preach in the synagogue and was expelled, He said, 'Is no man a prophet in his city?'" His knowledge of the New Testament surprised me. When I asked whether he had studied it in school, he said he had read it on his own.

When we left the second church, the Church of the Angel Gabriel, where the stream of the Virgin Mary flows—pilgrims sprinkled their heads and eyes with the spring water flowing in a conduit along the length of the hall—he again surprised me when he mentioned the explanation of this contradiction posited by Ernest Renan in his book, *The Life of Jesus*: While Jesus was undoubtedly born in Nazareth, the fact that he was elevated to the status of "Messiah" by his disciples and followers—and the Messiah, according to the prophets, would be a scion of the tribe of Jesse and a descendant of King David—Jesus therefore had to have been born in the city where David was born, which is Bethlehem.

We dined in a restaurant that looked out onto the busy street, and sitting at the other tables—apart from the local, Arab-speaking people—were many tourists speaking English or German. One woman, wearing a wide-brimmed white hat and a full-length white dress, approached our table and asked me: "Pardon me, didn't we once meet in London?" Her face—beautiful, with shining azure eyes—was unfamiliar to me. "Weren't you at the opening of the Dante Gabriel Rossetti exhibits in the National Gallery?" She smiled at me. I was momentarily frightened by the thought that she might be my father's lover, who had apparently seen me standing by his side at that same opening, and feared to approach us—that same mysterious lover I had never seen, who had appeared with a thousand different faces in my imagination. "No, I'm sorry," I said. "Excuse me, I must be mistaken," she said with a disbelieving, perhaps faintly mocking smile.

During those moments in the "birthplace" of Jesus, not far from the Virgin's spring, I became imbued with an evil spirit of the sort that used to terrify me in my childhood and girlhood, when my father was gone from the house for many days and nights, and my mother would shroud herself in taciturn silence, or try to drown her depression in glass after glass of whiskey after sending me to bed, and I was drawn to the stream that bordered our estate, to drown myself, but it was only a rivulet, whose burbling water was not deep. I used to flee to the small village church—there, under one of the large stones of the floor, a sword in the shape of a cross engraved along its length, lay the sarcophagus of Lord Torrington, who died in 1689—and kneel before the picture of Mary Magdalene, who was also genuflecting at the foot of the crucifix, her supplicating eyes raised towards the merciful heavens, and vow never to be defiled, never...

We returned to the wagon and continued our journey eastward.

This is the Galilee, the land of Jesus, where He went from village to village, from synagogue to synagogue, preaching that we must love our brothers and our enemies, and the growing number of His disciples gathered round Him and followed Him wherever He went. There, to our left, was the village of Cana, where he performed the miracle of turning water to wine at a wedding. Then, during a hurried visit to the Franciscan Church in the village, while Mr. Aaronsohn was reading me the third-century Hebrew inscription in the mosaic floor, a thorn pierced my heart: what will happen if Vanessa accepts Clive Bell's proposal and marries him...She will be lost to me forever. And I—?

A warm wind, carrying the chaff and straw from the abandoned threshing floors on the side of the road that was lined with dry, yellowing fields blew against our faces as we continued our journey. Those are the Horns of Hittin, Mr. Aaronsohn pointed to a double-peaked mountain where, he said, the final battle between the Crusaders and Saladin's army was waged, and the eighty-eight-year Crusader kingdom had ended, never to return.

Suddenly, about an hour later, from the top of the cliff we had reached—like a revelation, as if the heavens had opened—below, spread before us—the immense lake was like a sheet of shimmering turquoise; it rested with divine serenity in the cradle of the mountains encircling it, daydreaming the ancient dream of the time when the Saviour had walked upon it, seeming to hover above the surface of the water—the Sea of Galilee.

Mr. Aaronsohn asked the driver to stop for a short while on the cliff so I could drink in the magnificent sight.

This is the pure land, I said to myself, looking at the expanse of the lake eastward, towards the mountains drenched by the light of the setting sun, and northwards and southwards, to its placid shores, strips of green descending towards it from the mountain slopes, as it licked them with the tongues of its waves. A pure land, undefiled.

The land I had hoped for.

I am writing these lines by candlelight, in a small room of an ancient building in the tiny Jewish colony, Bnei Yehuda.

I slept fitfully last night. Netting protected me from mosquitoes, but not from bad thoughts and tumultuous dreams. I dreamed I leapt from the top of the cliff into an abyss, with snakes swimming in the foul, murky water at its bottom, and the great shout I gave woke—so I fear—not only myself, but also the kind man sleeping on the other side of the wall.

It was eleven o'clock in the morning by the time we went down to the boat to cross the Kinneret to its eastern side. Mr. Aaronsohn had been obliged to first meet with several of his people, and visit the Scottish Hospital to learn the meteorological forecast, activities that took up the entire morning.

I walked alone along the streets of Tiberias, with its houses of black basalt, a small city oppressed by the stifling heat. On a hill to the north rise the ruins of an ancient wall, perhaps from the Crusader era, and close by is the impressive building that houses the Scottish Hospital. Not far from the lake shore is the bustle of the *souk*, crowded with donkeys and camels bearing sacks of wheat and barley and vegetables of all kinds, for the consumption of both men and animals, which are unloaded—with boisterous negotiations in Arabic and Yiddish between buyer and seller—in the doorways of the small shops and at the stands laden with dates, figs, oranges, lemons, and sacks brimming over with corn, rice, and grain. Most of the city's residents—so I was told—are Jews, some from Europe, called *Ashkenazim*, who wear hats and clothes similar to those of their pious brethren in Jerusalem, and others, called *Sephardim,* who are from oriental countries, and dress like the Arabs. In the southern part of the city are Jewish holy burial sites, the tomb of the medieval Jewish philosopher, Maimonides, amongst them, and there are curative hot springs; but I feared going that far, lest I be late for my meeting with Aaronsohn.

At eleven o'clock, Aaronsohn, his friend Turov, and I went down to one of the rowboats on the shore. Several fishing boats sailed serenely on the water, which was calm, smooth and bright as a mirror. Though the sun was already shining high in the sky, its rays glistening on the clear water, the weather was pleasant. At twelve o'clock, we landed on the eastern shore.

While we were in the middle of the lake, and I was looking far off to the north to locate Capernaum—suddenly, like a sword in my heart, I was pierced by the thought that perhaps I had become pregnant by the seed of that villain, and if it turned out to be true—twenty days remained until my next period—what would I do? For a few minutes, the glowing scene that surrounded me became turbid, and I was enveloped by darkness. (Dear God, make all the evil that befalls me disappear as if it were a nightmare that terrifies my errant soul…)

We disembarked on the eastern shore of the lake; it was strewn with pebbles, gravel and shells, and walked eastwards for half an hour, until we reached an Arab village that was baking in the sun, no shade anywhere—Anayib—on the mountainside. An Arab named Toufiq, Aaronsohn's agent in this district, was supposed to be waiting for us there with three horses, on which we would make our way. Since we did not find him, Aaronsohn proposed that we go down to Abas Effendi's orchard to eat our lunch there, in the shade of the trees.

We sat at a table in the shade of a thickly branched lemon tree, surrounded by hibiscus, rose, bougainvillea, and oleander bushes, blossoming in a blaze of red, purple, and pink. There were pomegranate and palm trees, and vine pergolas that lined the gravel paths—an oasis in the heart of this sere landscape, swooning in the sun, of mountains to our left and to our right. The effendi, owner of the white villa in the front of the garden, was not at home, but his black Sudanese servant, who knew Aaronsohn from his earlier visits there, brought us rose-water and fruit, and Mr. Turov removed from his rucksack the provisions he had brought with him. While eating and drinking, Mr. Aaronsohn talked to me about the natural aspects of the area, about the volcanoes to the north and east that had erupted thousands of years ago, covering the entire Golan and eastern Galilee with burning lava that froze and turned into the basalt that is now scattered across that whole expanse. He explained that the Golan had once been quite fruitful, settled by Jews, and this area in particular was considered the granary of the country—on both sides of the Jordan—as well as in the Ginossar Valley that surrounds the Kinneret, which is now almost devoid of fruit-bearing trees. Once, in the time of the Second Temple, the time of Jesus, it was said that the Golan was the Garden of Eden, all green and abounding with sweet fruit, but the many ravaging conquerors, and the Bedouin, who invaded from the east, came to plunder, with no intention of settling on the land permanently and making it bloom.

Mr. Turov, a short, agile man of about fifty, with a round face and round, metal-framed glasses, pestered me with all sorts of questions and insipid jokes, but I shook him off again and again to speak to my mentor.

It was already three o'clock when Toufiq arrived with the three horses. We mounted and rode north along the shore. Toufiq and a Bedouin loaded our baggage onto a donkey, and accompanied us on foot.

(Dear God do not punish your servant for her sin of weakness, for she did not have the strength to repel those who set upon her to violate her innocence…)

When we reached the mouth of the stream, known as the Samach stream, we turned east and climbed a steep mountain strewn with huge basalt boulders. The stream flows along a deep ravine, and Aaronsohn stopped us every now and then, dismounted, and went to examine the nature of the rocks and soil, climbing the ravine walls, leaping from rock to rock, ascending and descending the narrow paths. He collected some stones too, showed them to us, pointed out their geological age and put them in his rucksack. Since I understood very little about this, I found it difficult to follow his explanations.

As we continued on our way, he began to turn his attention to the vegetation, and to me. The three of us dismounted, tied our horses to the tall oaks that grew in that area, and went out onto the fallow fields to collect some of the many flowers that dotted them with splashes of red, purple, white, and yellow. I found no "biblical flowers" amongst them, and Aaronsohn did not discover the "wild wheat" he was looking for, but he called each and every flower by its name and the name of its genus and described its characteristics. When I showed him the ones I had gathered, he told me their names too, many of which amused me, for they were so "zoological": "dog's tail," "eagle's plume," "rooster's comb," "scorpion's sting"… and so on.

At six, we arrived at Bnei Yehuda—a squalid colony of a dozen or so families, where poverty and want had left their mark on its gaunt men and women, with their dull eyes and ragged clothes. The colony had one large, two-story house, which contained many rooms, for public use and to lodge guests; the rest of the houses, small, built of unchisled stone, were scattered amongst the rocks on the craggy, barren ground. Here and there, several olive and pear trees grew amidst the thorns. When we arrived, the settlers gathered in the large room of the public building, and one of them, a black-bearded man with fiery eyes, spoke with great fervour, his words directed at Aaronsohn, Turov and an agronomist named Berman. Aaronsohn responded with a long tirade, his remarks interrupted several times by the shouts from the audience. I understood nothing of what was happening, for they all spoke Hebrew and Yiddish, and only later, after the meeting, did Mr. Turov explain that the settlers were quite bitter that no one had provided them with the funds needed for sowing and planting, as they had been promised, and they were therefore sinking into debt and suffering from hunger, and Mr. Aaronsohn had upbraided them for not cultivating the fields as they were taught when they arrived there, for not drawing water from the many springs in the area for irrigating the orchards, and for wasting the money they had already received on the purchase of things not essential to the development the place.

After a modest meal in the company of my fellow-travellers and two other distinguished men, I went to the room assigned to me on the second floor of the public house.

It is now only ten o'clock. The candle is burning down, and

will soon be extinguished. Another iron bedstead and mosquito net for my use. I will have to get used to these ascetic conditions.

My thoughts give me no rest. I will be thirty-two in August, and I have not established even one permanent relationship. I tread on shaky ground, constantly afraid that, at any moment, a chasm will open up beneath me. "Get thee to a nunnery"—Hamlet exhorted Ophelia in his madness. How many times during my years at the Slade, when I ignored the men who pursued me, and the women students gossiped about me behind my back, did I say to myself: Get thee to a nunnery! But I knew I would wither there, like a sunflower in the desert, without love, without art, without any hope for the future.

But this holy land is a harsh land of stones.

I shall light another candle at the head of my bed and lie down to read the Bible I carry with me wherever I go.

This is a God-forsaken place called Jilin, and I was accommodated for the night in a house whose residents had abandoned it several months earlier, even leaving their dirty dishes in the kitchen sink, where the roaches scurry around...The room contains two beds with thin straw mattresses, but Mr. Farhi and Mr. Ginzburg, the quite cordial managers of this estate, offered me a bed with clean sheets and blankets. What with the fear that scorpions and mice might get into the house through the many cracks and crevices, I am afraid I shall not sleep a wink.

Like Bnei Yehuda, this colony too—called Tiferet Benyamin after Baron Rothschild, who purchased this land, the district known as Horan—has been abandoned by most of its inhabitants, and only five families remain. Thousands of mulberry trees and vineyards are planted on purchased land, but because the Turkish government in Damascus dealt deceitfully with the settlers and placed obstacles in their path, most of them gave up in despair and left. The large, walled yard remains, and most of the stables, cowsheds, and houses in it are now empty.

In the late afternoon, when I arrived at this colony—which adjoins the Arab village of Jilin, surrounded by a thick hedge of cactus—and learned of the fate of its settlers, I thought about the future of the "Zionist vision" that Mr. Aaronsohn spoke so much about during our trip. The Zionists aspire to settle Jews on all of "the Promised Land," including the eastern bank of the Jordan, which was the land of the tribes of Reuben, Gad, and half of the tribe of Manasseh. It is an exalted vision, a vision of "the End of Days" augured by the prophets, when the Israelites would gather from the four corners of the earth into their own land, but the people who were supposed to realise this vision, the Jews, who had been dispersed throughout the world, were of the middle-class and had never engaged in physical labour! Would they succeed in becoming farmers, dedicated to their land despite all the hardships of nature and government oppression? Wasn't this idea incompatible with human nature? Was it likely to so excite people that they would be willing to make such a great revolution in their lives—to leave their native countries, their businesses and posts, to abandon their customs and native languages, to go off to a new land, where a life of poverty, suffering, and hard work awaited them?

(Jesus Christ—save me from the seed of sin. I came to the Holy Land to purify myself and now I have become defiled here; scrub my body clean of the defilement that clings to it.)

We left Bnei Yehuda at seven in the morning and rode northeast. Mr. Turov stayed in the colony, so that only two of us remained, Mr. Aaronsohn and myself, with Toufiq the Bedouin and the donkey bringing up the rear. From the top of the ridge facing west, the thrilling sight of the Kinneret spread before us, nestling serenely amid the mountains; the Jordan winding through the green strips along its banks to the wide delta where it spilled into the lake; and west of them were the soaring Galilee mountains, the valleys that dissected them, the small villages set securely in their bosom, and like a bird's nest atop one of them—the houses huddled together like birds in a frost—was the city of Safed. We rode across a high plateau covered with spacious meadows where goats and camels grazed, and about two hours later, we reached a large village named Skufia, that was surrounded by the lush vegetation of wild grain, as well as clover and chicory. We dismounted and walked in the field. Aaronsohn picked several spikes of wheat, examined their grains, then crushed them and removed their seeds, placing them on the palm of his hand, inspecting them carefully, hoping to find "wild wheat." Giving up in discouragement, he turned to me, looking defeated: "And now, to your 'biblical flowers.' I promised we'd find them here." And he brought me three: flax, whose flowers are blue, which he said is mentioned many times in the Bible: in the Book of Exodus, as one of the crops that was destroyed in the plague of hail; in Joshua, which mentions that Rahab the prostitute dried flax stalks on her roof; in Judges, which says that the ropes used to tie up Samson were made of flax; celery—mentioned in the Book of Esther—which has large, white flowers, and he believed this was the cotton from which cotton wool is made; and galbanum—a tall plant with small, parasol-shaped yellow flowers, mentioned in Exodus as one of the aromatic incenses burned in the Tabernacle.

"You call me Aaron, and I'll call you Beatrice, all right?" he said, as he handed me the flowers.

Since the two of us were alone, I was able to learn more about his character. His speech became a bit gentler, though he seemed to be guarding against excessive closeness and frank conversation. Once, as we were walking in the fields, he asked, as if offhandedly, "Are you married?" And when I asked if he were married, he laughed, "I have no time for it," he said, and immediately went on to talk about the local flora. Sometimes, when I remarked on the view, he looked indifferent, distant, as if he were contemplating something else, and a moment later, he would awaken and agree overmuch. I wrote to Vanessa that I am unable to admire people like him, but I respect him—a man devoted entirely to a single goal that is truly important to him, disregarding as irrelevant anything beyond it.

We reached the village called El-Al at ten, and stayed only long enough for him to show me the remains of columns and capitals engraved with pomegranates and grape clusters that he said testified to the existence of a Jewish colony there during the Talmudic era. After another hour of riding, we came to a round, wide pool of water, a kind of lake, surrounded by swamps—Birkat-Nam in Arabic. A herd of goats, tended by young girls and boys clad in colourful robes and carrying long sticks, encircled the lake like a loincloth, drinking from its waters. Seeing us on our horses, they were seized with paroxysms of delight: they called out to Aaron, laughing, and the girls shrieked, as if pleased by the sight of us. Aaron threw them a few piasters, once again prompting their laughter. I asked him what they were so excited about, and he said they were delighted by the sight of a white woman riding a horse, wearing a riding habit, boots and a wide-brimmed hat, something they had never seen before.

At noon, we arrived at the village of Haspin, and there too were many ruins from the Hasmonean and Talmudic eras: the arch of a doorway, lintels, capitals of columns, stone panels with Greek inscriptions, and a section of the mosaic floor of a synagogue or Byzantine church. In the area around the village, A. found rock fragments that contained, he said, iron oxide, possibly indicating the presence of iron ore—which is suitable for use in industry—as well as flint stone and feldspar. He put all of these in his rucksack.

(Dear God make all the evil that befalls me disappear—make it only a nightmare that terrifies my errant soul.)

We rode for another hour in the highland, until we reached a stream flowing in a deep gully, with dense oleander, laurel and burnet bushes, and acacia and poplar trees growing along its banks—the a-Rokhad stream. We passed the bridge and went down a steep path to the bed. We tied our horses, sat down in the shade of the bushes, and Toufiq unloaded our bag of provisions. I washed my face in the cool stream water and drank of it from my cupped hands, the way the people of Gideon drank from the waters of Ein-Harod. As we ate, A. told me—to my surprise—something about his childhood in Romania and his arrival in Palestine with his Zionist family: he was six years old then, and they, along with several dozen other families, had ridden in ox-drawn wagons up to the village of Zammarin, whose land they had purchased. It was winter, and when the wagons sank in the mud, they pulled them out by hand, and began to build their houses on the barren rocks. At the age of eleven—he said—he stopped attending school and began to work in the vineyard and in the fields. What he learned after that, he learned from private tutors and through his reading, until Baron Rothschild—whom A. had met several times when he visited their colony, and whom he liked and respected—sent him to study agronomy in France. Everything he said about himself—humbly, concisely—astonished me, for the scope of his knowledge was so enormous: botany and geology and meteorology and history and geography and Bible studies and Hebrew linguistics…And I also learned about the activities of an admirable man, an Englishman like myself, Sir Laurence Oliphant—who was enthusiastic about the Zionist idea and, in his desire to promote it, travelled to the Jewish communities in Romania and urged their families to immigrate to Palestine, and later, assisted the first settlers of

Zichron Ya'acov in overcoming the difficulties that confronted them, and contributed his own money to the settlers of Bnei Yehuda.

I must find a copy of the book, *The Land of Gilead*, written by this visionary, who died some twenty years ago. When I return to London, I shall buy it and give it to Vanessa and my mother to read too. (I find it amazing that my mother never mentioned his name, and perhaps knows nothing at all about him.) He is, after all, one of those "proto-Zionists," as consul Blech put it—an Englishman, or a Scot, who came to Zionism out of his Christian faith, and expressed the idea that the Jews should settle the Holy Land, on both sides of the Jordan, perhaps even before Dr. Herzl.

Listening to Mr. Aaronsohn's thrilling conversation, I recalled Vanessa's jesting words to me before my trip here: "To whom can you talk there? You'll meet only Philistines in Palestine…"

The truth is, however, that Vanessa—in contrast to her sister Virginia—did not ridicule "Philistines." She is tolerant and forgiving towards them. When Edna Clark-Hull came to Bloomsbury and heard the witty remarks uttered by Keynes, Strachey, and others, and her eyes—the eyes of a frightened rabbit—bulged with the effort of trying to understand what was being said and why several *bon mots* or vulgar insinuations had provoked such laughter, she asked all sorts of Philistine questions—such as, what is the difference between Impressionism and Post-Impressionism—and Vanessa did not make a show of ignoring her, as her sister did, but quietly and patiently explained to her everything she had difficulty understanding.

Vanessa, despite being a confirmed atheist, is a woman guided by moral principles. She mocks Victorian and Christian-clerical morality, which she believes is corrupt and hypocritical, but, in her relations with others, demands from herself, and them, total honesty and fidelity to their own opinions, unswayed by socially accepted views, and she demands respect for others, whatever their opinions. It is no accident that she so admires Jane Austen. I believe that, in her heart, she is a person of faith.

It is beyond my comprehension why she is tempted by Clive Bell's courting of her.

At six o'clock in the evening, when the sun was hiding behind the summits of the Galilee mountains, and the entire expanse was infused with a golden stillness, we arrived here, at Jilin, and after a tour of this wretched place, and a meal in the company of Mr. Farhi and Mr. Ginzburg, I went to the room I had been given.

(Lord of all Creation you know and see that throughout my entire stay in this country I looked upon the beauty of your handiwork and never ceased blessing You for having created it—please save me from my hatred, my desire for revenge and from the evil thoughts…. Let me take pleasure in the beauty of Your world without terror of the demon that is burrowing in my womb.)

The white lily!

At eleven o'clock in the morning, when we were in the field on the far side of the Zizon stream and I was collecting flowers whose names I did not know, Mr. Aaronsohn called my name from afar in a voice that heralded good news, and walked towards me, holding a large white flower on a long stem, its petals spread like a funnel—

"You were looking for this flower, were you not?" He handed it to me, "Here it is, the white lily, *lilium candidum*, and you should give thanks for this miracle. It is quite rare in this area! Indeed, in the entire country!" As I stood there, speechless, thrilled by the sight of the white flower, inhaling its intoxicating perfume, he placed it on the lapel of my vest. "A gift from the land of Horan!"

"You were looking for wild wheat—and found a white lily..." I mumbled.

"I was looking for the useful, and found the beautiful," he said, laughing. "Who can say which is more important?"

Tears of excitement and gratitude filled my eyes.

He once again said it was a miracle, since the Crusaders had torn the bulbs of that rare flower—considered by Christians to be the symbol of purity and innocence—from the soil of this country and taken it with them to the gardens of the European nobles and kings, to be reminded of the holy land from which they had been expelled; that is why so few of them are left in this soil.

"And now, because of you..."*

It rained in the morning, a fine drizzle, and we thought we

---

* As I have already indicated, the white lily is a consummate phallic symbol, which also holds the opposite of its erotic meaning. It is interesting that here it is given to B. by the agronomist, Aaronsohn, who represents a figure of paternal authority

would be forced to stay in Jilin the whole day, but after eight, the clouds dispersed, and the sky turned blue, no longer overcast except for some light cirrus clouds sailing by; we mounted our horses and set out. This time, Mr. Ginzburg joined us.

Many small streams flow in the channels that crisscross this plateau, and at ten o'clock, after we crossed the bridge over the El-Akhrir stream, we reached the town of Muzarib, whose streets bustled with animals and people—the peasants and Bedouins from the area who come to buy and sell. We did not linger there, but continued southwest, crossed the Hejaz railroad tracks that went all the way to Zemach, which is on the shore of the Kinneret, and went down to the Zizon stream. We tied up our horses and walked along the bank. Much water flows in the stream, leaping over the rocks in cascades, many of which are used to drive flour mills. A. examined the soil, collected limestone and flint stones, discussed colony matters with Mr. Ginzburg, and as we ascended from the stream bed, a panoramic view of green fields of grain and wildflowers spread out before us.

That is where Aaron found the white lily.

I put it in the cardboard flower press I carry in my rucksack.

At the foot of the hill along which the railroad tracks pass is the train station, a stone building surrounded by yards for holding merchandise. Freight cars stood on the tracks, and Arab workers were loading tree trunks, beams, sacks of grain and wheat, camel saddles, carrying them on their backs and running—as policemen urged them on, prodding them with their whips—along narrow planks from the lot to the freight car, from the freight car to the lot. We stood there watching them for a bit, and A. remarked that the cargo was being sent to Ajlun and Damascus, "and how primitive that loading system is. Slaves, as in the time of Pharaoh."

On our way back to Muzarib, we saw an amazing sight: hundreds of camels wandering across a grain field, grazing freely on the vegetation. In the distance, along the edges of the broad field, we

---

for her, and is perhaps a substitute for her biological father, from whom she was estranged, and her relationship to him is coloured by guilt and conflict regarding her relationship to her mother.—P.D.M.

could see some six or seven mounted horsemen who had swords in their belts, and wore brown *abayas*, kaffiyehs fluttering from their heads. Aaronsohn and Ginzburg were astonished too, and, astride their horses, watched this spectacle for a long while, rooted to the spot. When we turned to continue on our way, A. said: "Bedouins. Bandits. They invade the peasants' fields and destroy their crops. The government doesn't care, and the victims dare not drive them off."

From Muzarib, we returned to the place from which we had started out in the morning—Jilin. It was already four o'clock when we arrived there, and two or three hours still remained until nightfall. (Dear God make all the evil that has befallen me disappear as if it had never been like a nightmare that terrified my errant spirit.) Mr. Ginzburg, a fat man whose smooth face reflected kind-heartedness, invited us to his room, which was furnished with a sofa, armchairs, and carpets. He offered us tea and biscuits. His wife, he told us, refused to come to that remote place, and stayed in Safed. He also told us that at first, ten families had come from Romania, five from the United States, and two from Canada to settle there, and they had planted grapevines, almond trees, and olive trees, and built houses and stables. They had high hopes, until one day it became clear that one of Baron Rothschild's officials, who lived in Beirut, had registered the land in his own name, and a clause in the contract of sale prohibited foreigners from settling on it. The government in Damascus issued an eviction order, and most of the settlers were forced to leave. Now, he was seeking to have the injustice corrected.

When I later entered this gloomy room, where I spent the previous night, I thought how far I had come from the world in which I had spent the thirty-two years of my life. I had been pampered by the pleasures of our Jacobean estate, whose large rooms were appointed in velvet settees, and Louis xv silk armchairs; huge vases imported from India and China stood by its sideboards, and the length and height of its walls were hung with oil portraits of our ancestors; servants would tiptoe around, bowing before us, ready to respond to our every request, and I had governesses from the time I was a baby—

Silk, gauze. I recall the ball in the Savoy Vanessa seduced me into attending with her. I wore a gauze dress, which made me look even wider than I was. Vanessa, despite her beauty and strong character, and despite her privileged family, was embarrassed and lacked self-confidence in the elegant company of the nobility, and more than once told me that she "hates society matrons"—yet she nonetheless would go, nearly every week in fact, to salon parties and balls, perhaps to bolster her sense of femininity. She did, however, need some sort of "protection." So she would take one of her brothers—George, or Toby—to those balls. They both happened to be busy on that evening—meeting with the Cambridge "apostles" if I am not mistaken—so she turned to me, and I was happy to consent. She spent the entire evening dancing with Roger Fry, who by then was a well-known art critic, often present at the Bloomsbury Group meetings, and apparently in love with her. No one asked me dance that whole evening—perhaps because I looked too large and clumsy to glide lightly across the dance floor. I sat at a table at the far side of the hall, watching Vanessa circle like a butterfly in her partner's embrace, and I sipped from my champagne glass, which the waiter filled again and again. In the carriage on our way home, she placed her arm on my shoulder and whispered: "How I do hate all of this..." and before we parted, she kissed me: "Thank you, thank you, and forgive me for dragging you to that den of hypocrites."*

Could I ever have imagined, through all my years in England, that I would spend one night and then another in such a remote place, in such filthy digs, and that I would sleep on a straw mattress, with bugs crawling all round me? Could my parents have imagined it, my fellow art school students, my friends in Bloomsbury?

Yes, Florence Nightingale too spent many weeks in army camps on the Crimean Peninsula, sleeping in a tent, or on the ground, tending to the war injured twenty hours a day without rest—even though she was the pampered daughter of a well-to-do family, and Lord Hewton had asked for her hand—but she heard the voice of God calling her to serve the suffering and the afflicted, the wounded in body and soul, and I—

---

* "Den of hypocrites" is an apt expression, and it is sad that B. was drawn, against her will, into that society that brought upon her this mental calamity.—P.D.M.

Here, on the eastern side of the Jordan, in these wild expanses, where high weeds and low shrubs grow, where camels wander freely, I sometimes think I am in Africa. What is more, the residents of this village, Jilin, are terrifying, black Sudanese people. Only the sight of the Kinneret in the distance, and Aaronsohn's stories about the ancient Jewish colonies that flourished here in the mountains and in the valleys in the time of Jesus, remind me that this, too, is the Holy Land.

And perhaps I really shall follow in the footsteps of Laurence Oliphant, and build a house on the Carmel, where, like him, I shall live out my days...

Tiberias, 12th May, 1906

The Grossman Hotel. In the same room.

We rode for seven hours from Jilin, arriving at two o'clock in the afternoon.

At first, we rode along the railroad tracks, and then along the banks of the Yarmuk stream, filled with rapidly flowing water and crossed by many bridges. In several places, the river entered a deep, narrow ravine, twisting sharply and bursting forth amongst the rocks on the far side. Tamarisks, jujubes, and wild almond trees grew in its bed and along its banks.

We stopped only at the El-Hama hot springs. Their source lies in a valley encircled by high mountains, and they are surrounded by many ruins from the first centuries AD—ruins of a Roman amphitheatre and bathhouse, and a fourth-century synagogue on whose foundations a basilica was built in the sixth century. Mr. Aaronsohn explained that those springs and the bathhouse built on them in ancient times are mentioned frequently in the Talmud.

From there, we turned north towards Samach—Zemach in Hebrew—which, apart from a small train station and several grey clay houses, boasts very little—and we rode along the shore of the Kinneret. The water was as smooth as a mirror, and the strong light and rays of the sun were refracted on the surface of the water, flashing like bolts of lightning, blinding us. Reeds and grass grow on a narrow strip at the lake shore, and on the mountainside to our left, we could see white tombstones planted here and there amongst the thorns, on the graves of the Jewish sages and holy men, the grave of Maimonides amongst them.

When we arrived in Tiberias, Mr. Aaronsohn went straight away to a business lunch, leaving me at the hotel. I took the flowers

I had collected from my rucksack, and began to draw them. Many days have passed since I held a pencil or brush.

The flowers I drew looked like flames in the wind.

And the thought that at these very moments, a foetus might be growing in my womb tormented me constantly—a dagger piercing my heart.

Where could I turn? And when I return to London, will I go under cover of darkness, to one of those clandestine clinics in Harley Street, like a harlot from St. John's Wood, or a kept woman, to have the foetus removed from my womb with a forceps?

In my mind's eye, I saw a large pool of blood issuing from between my spread legs.

I mustered the courage to ask Aaronsohn if he were prepared to extend our trip one more day, if his schedule would permit it, because I wanted to see the place where Peter was born and from which Jesus set out to walk on the water. "I would be happy to do so!" he said, laughing, adding that since he had already returned our horses to Toufiq, who had surely taken them to the far side of the Kinneret, he would rent two other horses, here in the city.*

---

* There, in Tiberias, I located Mr. Turov, Aaronsohn's agent—a shrewd Jew, present wherever things are happening in the city amongst Jews and Arabs alike—and asked him if he recalled a young English woman tourist who had joined their trip east of the Sea of Galilee. He remembered her, and when I inquired whether he noticed something unusual in her behaviour, he replied that she had impressed him as a modest young woman, curious and eager to learn, but, for some reason, she was depressed and did not speak a great deal. Is there something unusual in that?—he laughed—after all, the English tend to speak very little…He was quite astonished when I told him that, for the last several weeks, she has been lodging in the village of Magdala. Was she perhaps carrying out an anthropological study there?—he inquired…—P.D.M.

Zichron Ya'acov, 17th May, 1906

Dear Vanessa,

You write, with your characteristic irony related to anything having to do with religion and faith, that my love for the Holy Land will turn me into a saint as well…

No, Vanessa, there is no danger of that. To become a saint, one needs more than to love, one needs to act. And I do nothing that might cause others happiness, or prevent their suffering, or please God.

And I am incapable, no matter how hard I try, of obeying one of the first Christian commandments—to forgive. To forgive those who have treated you badly. I am vindictive. Sometimes, during sleepless nights, I plot revenge. In my imagination—I kill. You are not familiar with this trait of mine. Nor was I myself aware of it. And here, of all places, in the Holy Land, I have discovered it in myself. Perhaps it is due to my proximity to Jews, whose God is "a jealous and vengeful God…"

But here, in this Jewish colony, I am surrounded by good people, whose influence upon me is only good.

Last weekend, I returned here from a five-day trip with the agronomist, Aaronsohn, my host and a most generous person, that took us to the eastern side of the Jordan and the shores of the Sea of Galilee. Every evening, I recorded the day's events in my diary, and when I return to London, I shall read you what I wrote.

Aaronsohn's noble aim on this trip was to find "ancestral," or wild wheat. This is a genus from the neolithic age, that is to say, from the eighth or ninth millennium BC, which was common in this part of the Near East, and A.'s aspiration—or so I understood from what he said—is to hybridise a cultivated species of wheat with this wild wheat, so as to improve it and make it more resistant to natural diseases. He believes that if he succeeds in doing so, it will be possible to grow wheat in arid areas throughout Asia and Africa and save millions of people from hunger.

He is much closer to "holiness" than I, as you can see...

He did not find "ancestral" wheat on this trip, but he did find—to my great happiness—a white lily.

This is the "rose of Sharon, a lily of the valleys" mentioned in the Song of Songs—a symbol of virginal purity.

Have you noticed that in Annunciation paintings, the angel telling Mary of her pregnancy carries a white lily in his right hand? As in Simone Martini's painting, for example.

And in the mosaic I saw several days ago in the courtyard of the Church of the Annunciation in Nazareth, Mary is portrayed sitting in a "locked garden" (which is also a symbol of virginity), and the angel hovering above her, who tells her of her pregnancy, is carrying a white lily.

When I return to London, I will give you the flower we found on the eastern side of the Jordan.

On the final day of our trip, we set out from the city of Tiberias, where we had spent the night, and rode north along the shore of the Kinneret, towards Capernaum. By doing so, A. was granting my request, with considerable generosity on his part.

It was a day filled completely with radiance—the radiance shining from the serene blue surface of the water, embraced by a series of sun-washed mountains, and radiance shining upon us from the cliffs of the Galilee mountains, and radiance pouring from above, from the infinite expanse of the heavens above us.

In the heat of early afternoon, we arrived at an oasis on the lakeshore, a grove of eucalyptus and palm trees surrounding a hot spring, called Ein a-Tabiha. This is where—I must tell you this, even though I know you have no patience for such things—as related in Mark, Chapter 6, the miracle of the loaves and the fish took place. A small colony of The German Catholic Society for Palestine is located here now, consisting of a number of God-fearing Germans who welcomed us cordially and gave us some of the delicious bread they bake.

Not too far north from there is Capernaum, called El-Khum in Arabic, which is the birthplace of Peter, John, and Andrew the fisherman. It is where Jesus walked on the water when he descended the mountain and saw that a great storm on the lake was threatening to drown them.

Today it is the site of a small Franciscan hospice for pilgrims, which has neither beds nor furniture. The large area in front of it, enclosed by a stone wall, contains many antiquities: the ruins of a synagogue from the time of Jesus—a mosaic floor, rows of column bases and tall columns with Corinthian capitals, and stone panels with Hebrew and Greek inscriptions; all these are scattered randomly on the rock-strewn land.

Do I believe in miracles? In man's ability to walk on the surface of the water?

As I stood on the edge of that blue lake, the gentle tongues of water rustling against the grains of sand and the pebbles strewn on the shore, undulating quietly in a monotonous rhythm, so that it seemed to have been that way from primordial times, and will continue to be that way to the end of days, I felt that it had not been many hundreds of years since the fishermen saw Jesus approaching them here, like "the vision of a ghost," but yesterday or the day before, and I felt that I might see it happen now, too. And I thought that through the power of faith, a person can accomplish things we call "supernatural." But do we know what the boundaries of "nature" are, and where the "supernatural" begins? The discoveries and inventions of science itself, which is ostensibly the opposite of belief in miracles, bring it beyond the province of "nature"! We "enlightened" people are used to thinking that only knowledge, education, and reason have the power to perform miracles; did not faith precede them? Do not the Indian fakirs—even in our time—walk barefoot on burning coals, just as Jesus walked on the surface of the water two thousand years ago?

On our way back to Tiberias, we once again passed the village of Magdala, which is the birthplace of Mary Magdalene, the "sinful" woman who became Jesus' faithful and devoted disciple, anointed His feet with oil and dried them with her long hair, and who witnessed His crucifixion and resurrection. I asked Mr. Aaronsohn if we could stay in the village for a while, which, though quite squalid, contains several stone shacks on an almost barren hill where low shrubs and two faded palm trees struggle to survive. I dismounted—he himself remained at the lake shore—and went up to the village to feel—you will say: How absurd! How naive!—what it is to be born and raised in such a place.

Grey dust, hot as ashes, covered the small square in the centre of the village, and even before I could turn this way or that to look down from the hill at the lake or at the mountains and valleys in the west, a group of bare-buttocked children gathered round me—they had undoubtedly never in their lives seen a woman like me, dressed as I was. Laughing boisterously, they extended their hands for alms. I had nothing to give them, for I had left my rucksack with A., and I gestured an apology, which did not silence them. A woman of indefinite age stepped from one of the shacks. A torn dress trailed down to her bare feet, her black hair hung in a braid as thick as a rope and rested on her flattened breast, wrinkles lined her face, and the corners of her eyes and mouth were smeared with kohl. She looked at me for a moment and immediately shooed the children away from me as if they were chickens. She then stood before me and asked something in Arabic, her tone hostile. When I spread my arms to indicate that I did not understand her language, she continued speaking, her voice growing increasingly louder and more irate. She gesticulated angrily, pointing once to the lake below and then to the mountains above it. Her voice became a shout, and my assumption that she was reviling me and demanding that I leave the place so frightened me that I rushed down the hill and returned to Mr. Aaronsohn, who was waiting for me on the shore.

I was quite agitated. A., seeing my pallor, asked if something had happened. I said, "A woman from the village cursed me."—"Cursed?" he said, looking up at the hill, "Mad, probably."—"Or a witch," I said. And I thought, she was right, that woman. I, my strange appearance, my elegant clothes—was there not something about my standing there, in the middle of that wretched village, which provoked its poverty-stricken residents? Perhaps I deserved to be stoned…

And now, as I write you about it, Vanessa, I am reminded of

Titian's painting that hangs in the National Gallery, *Noli me tangere* (which our pedantic teacher, Professor Tunick, believed was painted by Giorgione and only completed by Titian), in which Mary Magdalene is shown falling at Jesus' feet upon seeing Him after He had risen from His grave, extending her hand to touch His feet, and He, wrapped in His burial shrouds, says to her, "Do not touch me, for I have not yet ascended to my Father in heaven." The village shown in the painting, where this scene occurs, bears no resemblance at all to the village I had stupidly climbed up the hill to see. The village depicted by Titian is a group of low wooden houses with gabled roofs and arched doors, of the sort you see in an Italian or German village; and yet, the hill upon which it stands, the white path leading down from it, the hints of water in the distance…and there is such innocence, such sincerity and faith in Mary's face, her long hair cascading from her shoulders to the ground…

Whenever I recall this story from John, about Mary Magdalene coming in the early morning darkness to Jesus' tomb and weeping upon discovering that the stone had been moved and the crucified body was gone, I am choked with tears. This is one of the most moving stories in the New Testament, for its humanity arouses profound compassion for the heart-breaking grief of an innocent soul.

And I am reminded of another *Noli me tangere*, the one painted by Giotto, which I saw in the Scrovegni chapel in Padua, in which Mary Magdalene is wearing a royal purple robe, her head crowned with a halo, and she kneels before the Lord who has appeared to her, her arms extended towards Him, an expression of great longing on her face, as if her soul were reaching out to grasp Him—she is surrounded by several leafy plants, perhaps white lilies—and He, just resurrected, wordlessly expresses His wish, "Do not touch me."*

---

* B.'s identification with Mary Magdalene—which is what ultimately brought her to the village of Magdala—is reminiscent of many cases in which mystics, in ecstatic states, identified with New Testament figures. Theresa of Lisieux, for example, writes in her autobiography that one day she heard a voice from heaven—*Sanctus, sanctus, sanctus*—and then felt Jesus kissing her forehead, and so she identified with the Virgin Mary. This is the condition known as delusion infatuation, from which mentally healthy people do not suffer. Could it be that

And by the way, when I told Mr. Aaronsohn about these paintings as we rode back to Tiberias, he remarked that there was a species of acacia in Palestine known as "do-not-touch-me," because if you do, its leaves constrict and wither.

I decided to stay in Zichron Ya'acov another few days before leaving for Jerusalem, and when we returned to the colony from our prolonged trip, the Aaronsohns found me lodgings in the Graff family's hostel, not far from their house, on the same street. The room is small, comfortable, and best of all—its window offers a lovely view of green-covered mountains and valleys, pine tree branches graze the glass, and a bird lights upon the sill every morning, waiting for me to scatter some bread crumbs. For a small sum, I receive my meals at the hostel. I spread my paper on the table in my room, and draw. For several hours a day, I work beside Sarah, Aaronsohn's sister, in the garden and in the vineyard.

I lack sufficient words to enumerate the virtues of the Aaronsohns. They are a working family, warm and united, each one doing the work he has been assigned, like bees in a hive. And while they are farmers in every respect, dedicated to earning their bread from the plants and animals of their diversified farm, they are also educated and well read. The father—who is religious and prays every morning and evening, before going to work and after returning from it—spends the few hours of leisure time he has reading the Hebrew holy books in his library; the girls, Sarah and Rivkah, read the latest and best literary novels in Hebrew and French; and the boys delve into reference and scientific books taken from their brother Aaron's library. He himself is busy with his research, his experiments, and his trips throughout the country.

A friendship is forming between myself and Sarah, who is some fifteen years younger than I, though I sometimes think she is older than I in her knowledge of the earthly world in which we live.

in B.'s case, it alludes to latent schizophrenia? I must ask Mrs. Campbell-Bennett whether her daughter suffered from the mumps or typhus when she was a child, as these are diseases which might induce various psychoses in adult life.—P.D.M.

I never cease to be amazed by the rare blend of naive idealism and sober pragmatism she possesses. When we walk side by side amongst the rows of grapevines, pruning the dry twigs before the vintage, she talks to me about her desire to act "for the homeland"—to help her brother in his experiments, to teach new settlers about agriculture, perhaps to travel to Europe to influence Jews to come and live in Palestine; and in the evenings, I find her sitting at the desk, bent over a large accounting ledger, writing long columns of numbers, calculating the day's income and expenses, the wages of the Jewish and Arab workers, the amount of hay sold, and so on. Yesterday, she read me a letter she wrote in French to a debtor of theirs who lives in a colony called Hadera, something about 500 francs he was supposed to give her father for fodder he bought from him and was late in paying for, and she hoped she would not need to remind him again...And another letter, to someone from Haifa who had received 1200 francs from Odessa for them, as payment for a plot of land, and had not yet given them the money...And she is beautiful, Sarah, so beautiful, with her long hair, her large, deep grey eyes, like the colour of the sea on an autumn morning! Everyone who sees her falls in love with her!

She offered to teach me Hebrew...I said I would have to stay in Zichron Ya'acov several months to do that. "And why not?" she looked at me warmly, "We could put you up in our house when Aaron is away. Why, he has been invited to go to America next month..."

This afternoon, Vanessa, I tried to paint in watercolours, as I looked at the mountain rose so common here amongst the mastic shrubs. I painted a few strokes, and gave up. You might say I had no "inspiration." I recalled, with great emotion, your painting: a table, and on it, a sugar bowl, a small bottle of perfume, wrapped in a greenish mist. A small distance from them, in the foreground, is a short-stemmed red poppy that looks defeated, a casualty. Like a little girl who has been run over and is lying on the sidewalk, bleeding. I think my first sight of that painting—which moved me so greatly, for in it, I discovered how it is possible, with a few lines and a single splash of colour, to invoke religiosity from the recesses of the soul—led me to the decision to paint biblical flowers.

Yesterday, walking on the mountain and seeing those modest wild roses that hide their white innocence amongst the green bushes, I recalled the poem about wildflowers in the field, written by Emily Dickenson, the American poet we both recently discovered:

> *Alter! When the hills do—*
> *Falter! When the sun*
> *Question if His glory*
> *Be the perfect one—*
> *Surfeit! When the daffodil*
> *Doth of the dew—*
> *Even as herself, Sir*
> *I will of you.*

Yours,
Beatrice

Zichron Ya'acov, 22nd May, 1906

A mother's sensitive, long-rage antennae. This morning, I received a letter from my mother—which had apparently been delayed quite a few days in the Austrian post office in Jerusalem, even though I left them my new address before coming here—and an enclosed check for fifty guineas. The letter was written on the fourth of May, that is to say, the day of the same night that dreadful thing happened to me in Nablus. Towards the end of the letter—after two pages brimming with details about what was new at home and on the estate, the births in the stable, the hiring of a new stable boy to replace Tony Saunders; the marriage of our neighbour, Laura LaBonet, to Sean O'Toole, the deputy mayor of Norwich; the impressive church ceremony, and on and on (and not a single word about Father)—she expressed her concern about my health, cautioning me against those who "prey on women," natives for whom every white woman, especially if she is beautiful, is likely to be "quarry for licentious designs." Particularly, she stressed, since I wrote her that I was being escorted on all my trips by a young Arab dragoman, she cautioned me against entering "dark alleys and unlit rooms" in his company, and spending evenings alone with him. And, as is her wont, she concluded with a scriptural verse, this time from The Letter to the Hebrews: "Let marriage be held in honour amongst all, and let the marriage bed be undefiled, for God will judge the immoral and adulterous."

I put the letter down, engulfed once again in darkness. My anxiety grows greater as the date of my period approaches. Thoughts of how to extricate myself from these straits scurry about in my mind like mice in a trap. One minute I tell myself that if indeed—God help me!—I am pregnant, I will return to London straight away for an operation, and no one will be the wiser; the next minute—that I should be condemned to a tormented conscience for the rest of my life if I do that deed, which is like the murder of a human creature; and then I see myself finding sanctuary on some isolated farm in Kent, or Devon, or Scotland, where no one would know me, and where my belly would grow until some peasant midwife extracts the baby from my bleeding vagina…but even there I would be ostracized, a fornicator who has given birth to a bastard…and how can I raise a child that is the seed of a vile rapist? …. And what would I do with it…? Other times, as I lie awake in the early morning, my room in darkness, hearing from outside the first dawn chirps of a pair of sparrows that built their nest in the pine branches—I think: perhaps I will stay here, in this Jewish colony, and perhaps—because of young Sarah, who likes me as I do her, who understands me, to whom I can reveal my secret—the people here would not condemn me, neither during my pregnancy nor at the birth of the child, but would be compassionate, and would abide my presence amongst them…*

In the meanwhile, I attract their attention. People look at me when I walk in the street, and I catch the sound of their whispering. They are not used to a foreign woman staying alone here in a hostel for more than a day or two. Sarah laughingly told me that the boys who saw me riding a horse on the street call me "Lady Godiva." One of them knew the legend about the eleventh-century lady from Coventry, and told it to his friends. "Who is the Peeping-Tom here?" I asked, remembering that only a single one of the city's residents dared draw open the curtain and look through his window at the lady astride the horse, her naked body covered by her long hair. "The boys look at you…one of them will certainly ask for your hand if you stay here a few more days…"—"My hand?" I said, laughing and blushing, "I'm already past thirty, and, besides, I'm a Christian…"—"So you'll convert…and besides—you look younger than your age…"

Last night, she gave me my first Hebrew lesson. *Aleph, Beth.*

---

* This is a typical case of "hysterical pregnancy," similar to that of "Anna O." who felt labour pains and believed she had been impregnated by her doctor, Dr. Breuer. B.'s repressed libidinous desire has led to neurotic hallucinations and to the belief that she is indeed pregnant as a result of that imagined "rape," which did not even produce virginal blood; this is a pathological condition which, in many cases, also causes delayed or interrupted menstruation.—P.D.M.

From right to left. *A-ba, a-dam, a-hava*...But I was distracted. The suntanned arm touching my elbow made my body burn with the heat of the sun it had absorbed in the field during the day; and the fresh scent, cool and sharp, of the salvia that grows so abundantly in the woods surrounding the settlement, clung to her hair, which hid half her face, and it wafted over mine; and the spark of innocence emanating from her eyes—all this dizzied me somewhat and distracted me from the book lying in front of us. "Shall we learn a Hebrew song?" she asked, seeing my distraction. "I don't know how to sing," I said, laughing, feeling suddenly like a bashful child in her presence. But she continued encouraging me to sing with her, syllable by syllable, *"Im-ein-ani-li-mi-li..."* and we both laughed. Then she showed me a letter she had written when she was fourteen to "the man who had revived the Hebrew language," the linguist, Ben-Yehuda, in which she asked him to coin Hebrew names for plants, stones, and agricultural tasks, so she would not have to use the foreign terms.

Yesterday afternoon I went into her brother's "herbery" with her—it was as stifling as a hothouse—and we leafed together through the hundreds of samples of dried flowers, and all the fields and forests and groves and ravines and deserts of this land, their colours ranging from intense, joyful green to dry, desolate yellow—rose before our eyes.

But we did not find the mandrakes.

She turned the pages agitatedly, one after the other, mumbling ceaselessly to herself: "But they were here...I must find them...they cannot have disappeared...nobody could have taken them...."

As if she felt responsible for their absence, she promised me as we left: "I will make sure you get them."

Today, I painted all morning, until noon. With the help of the hostel owners, I improvised a makeshift easel, placed a large sketchpad on it, and painted in watercolours. I was in a kind of ecstatic state, imbued with the spirit of vigorous work, and painted twelve flowers, one after the other, on three pages. Four on a page. And I painted the flowers—I myself do not know why—crucified on poles. A white mustard flower on its stem, two shoots spreading from it like arms, nailed onto the horizontal shaft of the cross. And next to it, a yellow briar, the two elongated leaves growing from its stalk fastened to the second cross. And next to that, a thistle, its head like a green parasol, its two shoots extending to the edges of the horizontal shaft of the third cross. And I gave the pink flower of the wild-rose two long, thorny arms, which I fastened to the fourth cross. And so on.

Standing and looking at what I had painted, a great, twilight sadness engulfed me. I asked myself why I had crucified the flowers. How had they sinned that I punished them in that way...?

In the morning, I went down to the Aaronsohn's vineyard. From afar, I saw Sarah walking amongst the rows of grapevines; she was clad in short trousers, her head covered with a white kerchief, pruning shears in her hand. Leaning over a vine, lingering beside it, straightening up, continuing to walk the length of the cordon, bending over once again, as if examining the foliage...I entered the vineyard from the side closest to the grove. The sound of bees buzzing amongst the grapevines seemed to permeate the entire vineyard, and butterflies with yellow-spotted wings flew above me, crossed my path, landed fleetingly on the large, emarginated leaves, and took off again. The vineyard glowed in the sun; a latticework of light spread above it, and the green needles of the pine forest on the mountainside glittered like silver splinters.

The world was so beautiful, so bathed in sunlight, that I thought: This is where I belong. Here, in this ancient East, that illuminates all.

I surprised her. "Oh, it's you! How lovely that you've come!" After she inquired how I had passed the night, whether the mosquitoes had bitten me, whether the hostel-keepers were treating me well, she asked me to walk with her as she examined the grape clusters in preparation for the next vintage. As we walked, she occasionally bent down to the plants, and gave me a lesson in growing grapevines. She told me of the phylloxera blight that nearly destroyed the settlement's vineyards several years earlier, and of the American strain they had imported and grafted onto the stalks of the old grapevines, making them resistant to the disease, and of the improved strains of wine grapes her brother had brought from Turkey, and of the sulferization of the vines against moths and mildew...And she told me how much she loved working in the vineyard, adding that the grapevine symbolizes the Jewish people, which is why its image is imprinted on ancient coins, on the mosaic floors of synagogues, and on the capitals of columns…She said, too, that the grapevine is the symbol of female fertility as well, as written in the Psalms, "Thy wife shall be as a fruitful vine…"

When she straightened up, she smiled at me: "We Jewish women love having many children. 'They shall be like olive plants around your table'." Then after a moment: "I haven't forgotten the mandrakes. I looked for them again in the herbery, with no success. But have no fear—I will find them! And if I don't, then Aaron will when he returns from Jerusalem."

I was so grateful to her for thinking of me and my request, that I embraced her shoulders and kissed her on the mouth. Her eyes rolled back momentarily as if I had surprised and bewildered her, and then she bent down and began to fuss with the vine beside her.

I was alarmed at what I had done. Had I done something bad? Should I ask her forgiveness?

"Will we see each other this evening?" I asked.

She stood up, hesitated for a moment, and said, "This evening? My brother Alexander is coming back from Beirut this evening…. Perhaps tomorrow evening?"

On my way back to the hostel, a bitter childhood memory drifted into my mind. I was nine years old. A chubby child, with plump, rosy cheeks, nicknamed "Peach," often changed into "Bitch" by the other girls whenever we fought. On Good Friday, my classmates and I went to the village church for prayers. The minister stood on the pulpit beside the altar, its base lined with bouquets of carnations, gladioli, roses, lilies, and violets, and read from the biblical portion of that day. We girls responded in chorus and sang hymns to our Lord, and the mournful song about his crucifixion, and songs of that holy day, on which He and his apostles sat at the last supper. Then we read together, "Dear God, our Father, look kindly on your family. It was for this family of yours that your Son, our Lord Jesus, suffered and died at the hands of cruel men. May your Holy Spirit that filled Jesus, lead us to spend our lives as He did, in the loving service of others." In his sermon, the minister spoke of the obligation to help the poor and the suffering, as commanded by our Lord the Messiah, saying that children, too, can help people in distress. As an example, he spoke of a girl in our village who, upon seeing children in the street crowding around "Crazy Kathy"—taunting her, mocking her, pulling at her tattered dress—drove them off, thus saving her from humiliation.

The girls rose to leave, and I remained seated. After they had gone, I climbed onto the pulpit and went behind the screen, to see the minister. Norman Lewis was his name, a Welshman of fifty-five, a fat man, with a large head, florid cheeks, and watery blue eyes. "Yes, my dear, did you want something?" he said, placing his hand on my shoulder. "May I ask you something?"—"Certainly, certainly! That's what I am here for, to answer questions! Come with me, I want to remove this robe…" I went with him into the vestry, a small room where his vestments were hung on the walls and in a cupboard, and amongst them were sacramental objects—a silver goblet, a sceptre, a censer, and others. He removed his ornate robe, its edges embroidered in gold, a large purple cross embroidered on the back, and sat himself down in an armchair upholstered in a lily pattern, and said: "Now, tell me what is bothering you, my child." Standing opposite him, I said that the prayer we read that day says we must love our fellowman, and I, no matter how hard I try, find it difficult to obey this command. "So…it is difficult for you…" The minister looked affectionately at me, "Of course, it is not easy to love our fellowman…but what makes it so difficult for you? Think about the times you have difficulty doing so…" I said that when the girls tease me and call me derogatory names, I hate them, I want to hit them, and I find it hard to overcome my evil impulse. "What do they tease you about? Tell me." Stammering, I said I didn't know… "Of course you know! Tell me, don't be embarrassed, come on," he said, tapping his knees with both hands, "sit here and tell me." I was frightened. I had never sat on the lap of a strange man. But he encouraged me: "Don't be afraid. Whisper it as a secret in my ear," he said, taking my hand, pulling me to him and seating me on his lap. "Now, tell me, why do your girlfriends tease you, whisper it in my ear," he said, putting his hand on my neck and drawing my face close to his ear.

I was frightened. I stopped breathing. Hot fear filled my chest, my mouth. I began to speak, "They say I…" I wanted to say they didn't like me because I didn't associate with them, because they thought I was conceited, since my father was a well-to-do landlord, because I was prettier than they, even though I was fat…but the words stuck in my throat. "Yes, what do they say about you, those simpletons, tell me," he said, pressing my body against his. I suddenly burst into tears, pulled myself away from him and ran outside.

I have never told this to anyone all these years—how frightened I had been when I felt the growing hardness in his trousers pressing against my flesh!

The confusion I felt choking me all the way home!*—

Now, I stopped for a moment as I walked through the vineyard, hesitated, reconsidered—and went into the office. I bought a bottle of Carmel wine and carried it under my arm.

Few people were walking in the main street at that hour in the afternoon, and those who passed me greeted me with a smile. I couldn't make up my mind whether the smile was affectionate, or whether it concealed irony for some reason or other. As if the sight of me—wearing my white hat with its purple ribbon tied in a bow, and the long, loose dress embroidered in violet purchased in the Old City—aroused a mixture of wonderment and scorn. In a carriage harnessed to a white horse, sat an official of the settlement's holding company, the Palestinian Jewish Colonization Association—these men are recognizable by their elegant suits, their ties, their smug and authoritative expressions—the carriage stopped beside me, and the moustached, well-groomed man greeted me in French, "Bon-

---

* The trauma described here confirms the supposition I raised earlier regarding childhood trauma as the basis for B.'s anxiety, particularly her anxiety about the male sex organ.

How astonishing it is that a man like the Reverend Norman Lewis, whom I have known for many years as an honest fellow and true Christian, is capable of such an abomination. There is, however, nothing new in this… even with ministers who preach morality…

I must learn whether B. masturbated in childhood or adolescence.— P.D.M.

jour, mademoiselle!" Continuing in French, he inquired after my health, asked whether I was enjoying myself in this lovely colony, if he could assist me in anything…I dismissed him with vague replies, and continued on my way.

Reaching my room, I opened the bottle, poured myself a glass of wine and drank it, gulp after gulp.

It was hot in the room. The heat of the day had tired even the two sparrows on the branches of the pine tree. They leapt from branch to branch with a sort of ennui. They flew somewhere, and then flew back. I drank another half glass of the sweet wine, removed my shoes and lay down on the bed. The room spun about—the whitewashed walls, the square table and two wicker chairs, the pages painted with flowers hanging on crosses…until I fell into a deep sleep.

When I awoke, the room was already in twilight. I remembered my dream: a desolate expanse of sand, from which a red flower was sprouting, as if it were being born that very moment from the belly of the earth, a single flower in the wasteland, a poppy or a tulip. While I was still marvelling at how a flower had suddenly bloomed in the sand—it withered and drooped to the ground.

When I left my room, the hostel-keeper told me that she had knocked at my door to call me for lunch several hours earlier, but when she looked inside, she saw that I was sleeping and had not wished to wake me. Would I take my meal now? I said I wasn't hungry, and turned towards the centre of the colony.

I entered a small restaurant near the public gardens across from the synagogue, sat down at a corner table and ordered a cup of tea and a slice of cheesecake. A gaslight lit the street, and at that early evening hour, groups of young people were already wandering idly about. Some girls went into the still-open clothing shop whose window displayed dresses in the "Paris Fashion," and remained inside for quite a bit, inspecting various garments and apparently haggling over prices. Some high-spirited young men joined them as they emerged from the shop, and the sound of their laughter and vociferous conversation in French intruded into the restaurant from the street. A sense of alienation overtook me: what am I doing here, in this small Jewish settlement in the far reaches of the East? How did I happen to be here? Who do I have here? Why don't I pack up and go home?

But whom do I have in England, my homeland? My parents and the estate are far from my thoughts. I do not fit in with the Bloomsbury group. And Vanessa.... Vanessa will soon marry Clive Bell...

I ordered a glass of brandy.

I sipped it and looked out at the street.

A large man with a thick, yellow, handlebar moustache—a kind of Falstaff—entered the restaurant and looked around. Seeing me, he froze for a moment, and then came directly to my table, smiling. "May I sit with you?" he asked in English. I gestured for him to sit. He sat down across from me, placed his thick, hairy arms on the table, and, smiling broadly, said: "You, I believe, are the Aaronsohn's guest..." When I replied that I was, he extended his hand, a peasant's hand: "My name is Uriel. Rosenstein. A long-time resident of the settlement. And your name is Beatrice. Zvi, Aaron's brother, told me. Welcome to our colony."

And he launched straight into praising the English, whom he admires. They are the most enlightened nation in the world. They have brought progress to all their colonies. It is their sense of justice that guides them in everything they do...He had narrow, smiling eyes that were sunk in his cheeks, and a thick shock of hair that was either blonde or grey. He must have been fifty or fifty-five years old. I wondered why he had approached me. He talked ceaselessly. He asked where in England I was from, and when I replied, he said the knew the area well. Yes, he had been in Essex, in Colchester. There is a castle containing Roman ruins in that city. And he had been in Norwich—the city with the huge eleventh-century cathedral. He remembered quite distinctly a long, narrow street lined with houses all painted yellow, preserved from the Middle Ages, on Elm Hill, if he wasn't mistaken; and he had been in Bury St. Edmonds ...

"Did you really go to school there? Unbelievable!" Why, he had been there more than once, and he remembered the Norman tower—which had an arched gate the chariots used to pass through, replaced today by automobiles...When I asked what he had been doing in England, he said he had a wealthy uncle in Northampton, with whom he had stayed for six months several years ago, and he had toured the whole of eastern England with his uncle's two older sons, on horseback and by bicycle…

"Will you be staying with us for long time yet?" he inquired. I said: Another few days. "You must stay here at least another week or two," he said, to become acquainted not only with the colony itself, but with the entire area, the neighbouring colonies, the Carmel forest, Caesarea. He said I absolutely had to see Caesarea and its ancient port, strewn with so many Roman ruins. If I so desired, he was prepared to ride there with me, for he had seen how remarkably well I rode…. I asked what his occupation was, and he said he owned large plots of land below, in the plain, where he raised grain, hay and corn, but he could be available for several hours during the day, even for a full day, since he employed workers from the Arab village of Furidis, and he could depend on them to do their work properly even without supervision, for they had been working on his farm for many years. He had recently employed some Jewish workers too, from amongst the "Moscovites" who had arrived from Russia, and though he could not depend on them, for they were not trained for physical labour, it was a good deed to provide work for Jews who came to live in Palestine; a large group of them had come to the colony—he said—and they lived together in a shack on the hill behind the wine cellar; poor fellows, they lacked for food, and malaria was devouring them. For this, he blamed Baron Rothschild's functionaries, arrogant and lazy men, who strut about the town like lords, haughty, carrying whips, living like parasites off the labour of the farmers, mocking and bullying the Jewish workers…. Had I noticed the red tarbooshes they wear? Had I seen the red flag with the crescent hanging on the facade of their "palace," the Administrative House?—all to ingratiate themselves with the government officials, the Turks…. On Saturday afternoon, he had to go to the adjacent town of Shffeyah—a half-hour's walk—and if I had not yet visited there, he could escort me. He recommended it—a small but lovely colony. Moreover, I could meet a special person there, his friend…I said I would consider it. Would I permit him to knock at my door at the hostel on Saturday to ask my decision?—One may always ask, I said.

I rose and, even before I could open my purse, he hurried to the counter to pay for me. He then shook my hand and said how happy he was to have met a representative of the country he loved.

I am not familiar with the customs of this country, the nature of its people are terra incognita for me, and now, too, as I write these lines, I cannot decide whether it was openness and unaffectedness, which are perhaps typical of Jewish farmers in this colony, that brought him unhesitatingly and unceremoniously to my table and allowed him to speak so volubly; and whether it was out of generosity that he offered to be my guide on a tour of the area, or whether he has hidden motives? I am sure that if Vanessa were in my place, she would politely but firmly dismiss him from her presence. I, on the other hand, fear that I will offend him, which makes me uneasy…His broad, candid face, his smiling eyes, and his warm, fatherly voice project a kindness and sincerity that dispel suspicion, but only God can see into our hearts…

25th May, 1906

Almost midnight, and I have only just returned from the Aaronsohn
house. Aaron accompanied me to the door of the hostel.

This is the first time in my life that I dined in a Jewish home
on the Sabbath.

An air of sanctity prevailed. The table was laid out, and on it
were silver candlesticks, wine goblets, a bottle of wine, two braided
loaves of white bread, known as *challah*, covered with a white cloth,
and prayer books at every setting. Several moments after we entered,
the mother, Malka, lit the candles and said a blessing over them,
raising her hands as she did so, a kind of veil covering her head, her
face glowing with an aura of purity as the Sabbath drew near. After
a while, the father, Ephraim-Fishel, and his three sons came into the
house, from the synagogue, and all began to sing a hymn that began
with the words, *Shalom Aleichem*. Sarah, who took it upon herself
to explain to me all the details of the ceremony, whispered that the
song was about the angels that accompany a Jew from the minute
he leaves the synagogue until he reaches home, hovering above him
and sheltering him, as he welcomes the Sabbath. The father kissed
his wife, and began, in her honour, to sing the psalm, "Woman of
Valour" from the Book of Proverbs, and when it was translated for me,
I realised that I too knew the words, and all the family joined in the
song. We stood at our places around the table, and Ephraim-Fishel,
who was at the head, raised his wine glass, said the prayer blessing
the Sabbath, blessed the wine and took a sip, then removed the cloth
from the *challah*, blessed it, tore off a small piece and sprinkled it
with salt, tasted it, and passed small bits of it to each one of us for a
first taste, which is apparently a religious custom.

I was seated between Aaron and Sarah, and both took pains
to explain the customs to me. To make it easier for me, Aaron gave

me a prayer book with an English translation opposite every page of the Hebrew prayers and hymns.

It was a meal in the Jewish tradition: slightly sweetened stuffed fish, clear chicken broth, two kinds of roasted meat, steamed and cooked vegetables, and a compote of prunes, raisins, and apples.

Between courses and sips of the red wine, I, a Christian, and my Jewish hosts engaged in a kind of theological discourse. Ephraim-Fishel asked me—assisted by Sarah, who translated his words—why the Christians had changed their day of rest from Saturday to Sunday, for Jesus and his apostles were Jews, and as is well known, they too obeyed the commandments, as did the other Jews in that time. I replied that I was not knowledgeable in such matters, but as far as I knew, Sunday was the day Jesus rose from His tomb after the crucifixion, and that is why it became the holy day of the week, and it is even called "the Lord's day." Rivkah, Sarah's younger sister, asked: If Jesus was resurrected, then where is He? Does He walk amongst the living? I tried to explain, briefly, that according to Christian belief, Jesus ascended to heaven after He was resurrected and revealed to His disciples, to His mother, and to Mary Magdalene, and He would reappear in the era that would be a kind of "end of days," when he would redeem all of humanity. "Something like our Messiah," Sarah said. Aaron interrupted the conversation and demonstrated his knowledge of history: Sunday was established as the Christian day of rest only at the beginning of the fourth century in an edict issued by the Byzantine emperor, Constantine. He supposedly chose that day because before he converted to Christianity, when he was still a pagan, he worshipped the sun, and Sunday was literally "the day of the sun," which is its name in many languages today. Malka, who knew a bit of French, told me that amongst the Jews, the Sabbath is "a bride," and those who observe the Sabbath are considered her lovers…" "Not only her lovers," Sarah said, "but also her bridegrooms. In the hymns we sing to usher in the Sabbath, we say, 'Like a groom's rejoicing over his bride,' and 'Enter in peace, O crown of her husband.'" Aaron pointed out to me the English translation of these sentences, while Sarah's father corrected her error: the bridegroom is not flesh and blood, but God Himself, who is the bridegroom, the husband of the Sabbath, for an eternal bond has been forged between them. "If that's so," Rivkah asked, "why do the Hassids in Safed go out into the sunset on Friday evening to welcome the Sabbath, singing 'Come in, bride; come in bride,' as if *they* are the bridegrooms?'" Her question stirred a casuistry amongst the diners that I could not follow, despite Sarah's efforts to translate their words for me. But I thought the image of the Sabbath as a bride so beautiful—an image not only of pure festivity, but also modesty and intimacy between man and the sanctity of the day of rest—that their debate seemed utterly unimportant to me. "But how can the Christians believe that a man is God?" Rivkah disconcerted me with her question. But even before I had opened my mouth to answer her, Aaron rescued me from my embarrassment with an older brother's smile: "If God can be a bridegroom, as we have just heard, then a man can be..." His father, who did not like this remark, broke into song so as to cut off his son in mid-sentence, and they all joined him in one of the popular Sabbath hymns.

After we had said grace following the meal, and sang several other songs, Malka asked me what I thought of their colony and how I had spent the last several days since returning from my trip with Aaron. I said I had painted a bit, walked about a bit, had observed the activities of the residents a bit...and then I recalled last night's strange encounter in the restaurant, and told them jokingly about the man I did not know who approached my table and began speaking to me of England, where he had spent several months, and of the Baron's officers who conspired against the farmers, and when I offered a brief description of him, they all rejoiced: Ah! Uriel! Uriel Rosenstein! adding laughingly, "What a character!" They told me he was one of the first farmers in the colony, a hard worker who had done very well and increased his property. Since having been widowed five years earlier, he had become quite restless. He roamed the country, wandering from the Jewish colonies to Arab villages, making friends with the Druse who live in the Carmel, and finding other "characters" like himself amongst the workers who had come to Palestine from Russia—they were his fellow countrymen, for he too was from Russia—and spending his evenings with them singing, arguing about socialism, revolution... "He's half adventurer, half buffoon," said Alexander, and his brother, Zvi, asserted: "But he's a good man." This assertion brought a sneer to Alexander's face. "Really?" he whispered. I said he had suggested that I go with him to Shffeyah the next day, and asked their opinion. "Why not?" Zvi said, "He has friends there, and if you haven't yet visited that colony, it's an opportunity…" The others remained silent, or shook their heads, so I did not know what they thought.

I thanked my hosts, and Aaron, who volunteered to escort me to the hostel, brought me first to his house across the yard, took a small book from his library, and handed it to me: "Theodor Herzl's *The Jewish State*, in English. You don't have to return it. Take it with you to England." I promised I would read it while I was still in Palestine and tell him my opinion of it.

On our way to the hostel, he said: "Sarah told me you were looking for the mandrakes in the herbery and couldn't find them. I was surprised. We have only one example, for it is a rare plant, but it will be found. I shall find it." At the hostel door, he shook my hand warmly and said, "We shall meet again tomorrow, then. Come by when you return from Shffeyah."

I sat down on the bed, engulfed in sadness. I was overcome by longing, even while I was still here—longing for this colony, for the Aaronsohn home, for Aaron, for Sarah, for this land that I would soon have to leave. And Sarah's wise eyes gazed upon me, and I did not know how I could forget them.

Haifa, The German Colony, 27th May, 1906

Early this morning, I left the hostel with my suitcases, dragging them to the centre of the colony, defiled, violated, swallowing my tears, and stepped into a diligence going to Haifa. I told Mrs. Graff—who was quite surprised, even frightened, upon seeing me with my bags at six in the morning, asking to pay my bill—that I had received a telegram from my mother, and I was obliged to return urgently to England. "You're very pale," she said, looking at me, "You don't feel well?" Tears choked me. I could only shake my head, and bolt.

I slipped away from the colony like a thief. My eyes downcast, I was careful to avoid being seen by anyone who knew me. The street was bustling with people even at that early hour, but fortunately, they were Arab workers hurrying to work in the fields and vineyards, and the Arab women on their way to the farmers' yards.

But I was known to the Jewish residents. And the passengers in the diligence stared at me in astonishment. One of them even ventured to ask slyly, insolently, why none of the Aaronsohns—big, strong men—had helped me with my suitcases...I shrugged. I did not have the strength to utter a sound.

As the diligence descended the mountain to the plain, I did not look back, for the last time, to see the colony to which I had grown so attached.

An hour and a half later, we reached Haifa.

The carriage had travelled quite a distance along the seashore, and I occasionally gazed upon the sea—smooth and calm, only its rippling waves murmuring on the sand, the water azure close to the shore, deep blue further out, seagulls flying above it—thinking that the world could be pure too.

I found lodgings in the Krafft family's hotel in the German Colony. It was a clean, quiet house. As if I were the only guest.

I do not know what I shall do. Perhaps I shall stay here several days and then sail home.

Perhaps not.

It must be my fault. I attract adulterers and lechers. Apparently.

They smell my weakness.

My defect: the inability to discern evil.

I am the open door that beckons the thief.

They are drawn to me, not like bees to honey, but like mosquitoes to the swamp.

But how could I have foreseen it?

At five-thirty in the evening he knocked at my door and came in, carrying a long-stemmed purple orchid. Bowing, he gave it to me: "Allow me, a small gesture...I heard you were interested in flowers. This is from my garden." I was quite embarrassed. I thanked him and put the flower into a glass of water. "Well, what have you decided?" Will you be so kind as to accompany me on a short walk to Shffeyah?" The sight of him made me smile: he was wearing a short-sleeved white shirt and khaki shorts of the sort worn by English soldiers in our colonies. A fifty-year-old in shorts? I wondered. But I had been told that he was a "character—half adventurer, half buffoon...."

We went down to the vineyard, up the hill behind it, and then turned left to the trail that wound between the vineyards. To make the trip pleasant for me, he related anecdotes the whole way. He told me that one winter's day, several of the first settlers riding in a wagon from Haifa had been caught in a downpour, and when the wagon sank into the mud, they fled to an Arab village, which they could not leave for three days, until the torrential rain let up. "What happened?" I asked, when he smiled at me. "What happened is that one of the young men fell in love with an Arab girl," he said, laughing, "and has remained there to this very day..." He told me that eight years earlier, one of the Baron's officers had tried to do away with the women's gallery from their synagogue, where they sat separated from the men, as is the custom amongst orthodox Jews, all the residents objected, and mutiny broke out, threatening the well-being of the colony, until the Baron himself intervened and restored the previous arrangement in the synagogue…I asked what this custom of separating men and women in the synagogue meant, and he replied, smiling at me: "Since Jews have strong passions that must be restrained…" adding immediately: "Do you know why Shffeyah and Bat Shlomo are called "the daughters of Zichron Ya'acov?—because our men love girls…" I did not like these clumsy jokes, and I did not find them amusing. Observing my dissatisfaction, he pointed to the expanse of vineyards that surrounded us, and said: "You see—all of this was wilderness when we came here. Rocks and shrubs. And there, on the hill, was a single hovel we used for shelter. That was Zammarin. Do you know what 'Zammarin' means in Arabic?—pipers. And that's what the Arabs called this place, because there was nothing here but shepherds, playing their pipes."

He began to hum something in Arabic: "Zammarin, Zammarin…"

We climbed to the colony of Shffeyah, which was on the top of the hill. A single street of twenty or so small houses were surrounded by well-kept gardens, and a larger, two-storey house that was used as quarters for refugee children from Russia. Carobs, oaks, and pine trees grew between the houses and in the central square. As we walked around this small village, he pointed out various houses, saying that their owners were hard-working farmers who had succeeded in building prosperous farms, and said that the farmers of Shffeyah were cleverer and more educated than those of his own colony, for they lived from their own labour. We passed through a small, murmuring pine grove, the carpet of pine needles rustling under our steps, and he picked a pine cone from one of the trees and gave it to me as a gift. We then entered one of the yards, and he knocked on the door of a wooden shack. Receiving no answer, he called out: "Zeid! Alexander!" and then: "Hankin! It's me, Uriel!" Two or three moments later, the door opened, and a thin, but sturdy man of about twenty stood on the threshold, rubbing his eyes like someone who had just awakened. He was a handsome young man, likely to enchant women: a black, rectangular moustache adorned his face, a shock of black hair concealed his forehead, and he exuded the charm of bold youth. The two embraced, patted each other's backs, and exchanged some remarks in Russian so vociferous that it was hard to tell whether they were salutations or curses, and I realised that my escort was apologizing to his friend for waking him, and the latter responded with something that satisfied him. The farmer from Zichron introduced the young man, "Meet Alexander Zeid. A native of Siberia. He arrived in our country only two years ago, and he knows its roads better than those who arrived twenty years ago. He's been in the south, he's been in the north, he's learned to talk to the Arabs, and he is a watchman. A guard in the vineyards. A hero!"

He pounded him on the back. The young man smiled, invited me to sit on a crate, hurried to cover his bed—which had only a wrinkled sheet and a pillow on it—with a grey blanket, and my escort translated his Hebrew words for me, saying that he apologized for the mess and for his rumpled appearance, as he was wearing only trousers and an undershirt. He had been on guard duty that night, had gone to sleep in the morning, and in the afternoon, had been roused to identify some Arab caught trying to steal a sack of barley from one of the stables, and had gone back to bed at three…

"He's a hero!" Uriel repeated, "and he's a gentile!" he laughed, "His mother was a 'Sobotnik'—that is a Russian sect of Sabbath observers—and had converted to Judaism…. He's a Cossack! When he was a child in Siberia, he learned how to fight like the Cossacks! To shoot a rifle, to beat up others…" Uriel said that once, when Alexander was guarding a vineyard in Zichron Ya'acov—the only Jew amongst the vineyard watchmen, who were all Arabs—the Arabs tricked him. One of them was sent to steal fruit from the vineyards, and when he ran to apprehend the thief, the other ten of them fell upon him and snatched his rifle, leaving him with only a dagger. Though he did manage to overcome them all, he was wounded in the head…. And here the farmer from Zichron turned to the young man, who was sitting and listening to Uriel's English without understanding, and asked him in Russian to show the young woman proof of his wound. He approached me with obvious reluctance, kneeled beside me, and moving his head towards me, he parted his black hair and showed me the stitched scar. After that incident—Rosenstein continued his story—the farmers in Zichron fired him, and he moved to Shffeyah.

He and his friend, Hankin, were the only Jewish watchmen in the colony. The Zichron Ya'acov farmers—he said—employ only Arab guards, for they work quite cheaply, for fifty piasters a night, and apart from that, they don't trust Jewish watchmen…"

"Did I get it right?" he asked the young man, and translated into Hebrew what he had told me. The young man laughed, said something, and my escort translated: "One of our farmers told him that a Jew could not be a watchman, for he doesn't know how to steal…"—and all three of us laughed. "I myself," he said, "also employ an Arab watchman. Because except for these two, Zeid and Hankin, there are no Jewish boys in the area willing to be watchmen. Those who have been in the country for a short while don't know how to hold a rifle, and don't understand Arabic…" He once again spoke to Zeid, whose reply he then translated for me: "He says that soon, there will be many Jewish watchmen, because a group of several dozen young men who believe this to be their calling are already in training." He then added his own words: "He dreams of establishing a 'Jewish Legion' here that will conquer the country from the Turks. With your help, the English…am I right, Zeid?"—The latter smiled and shook his head.

It was already dark in the room. Zeid rose, went to the corner where two or three boxes containing food were piled one on top of the other. He removed a bottle and three glasses from one of them, placed them on the table, poured vodka into them, and handed one to me and one to my escort. He approached me, clinked his glass against mine and his friend's, and we all drank. They conversed together, a bit in Hebrew, a bit in Russian, Zeid poured again, emptied his glass in one gulp, as did his friend, and I drank about a quarter of my glass. My escort apologized for speaking in a language I did not understand, saying that the subject of their conversation was horses: Zeid had an excellent mare of the fine Arabian breed that he bought from a Bedouin sheik in the Galilee, and he himself wished to buy a similar mare from the same thoroughbred family. They were consulting, therefore, about when Zeid could be available to ride with him to the tent of that Bedouin tribe and act as a go-between with the sheik.

Zeid lit the kerosene lamp, but I said that I had to return to the colony, for I had promised Aaron Aaronsohn to come to his house in the early evening. "Already?" Rosenstein said resentfully, and hurriedly swallowed another glass of vodka, "We'll stay another little while! When will you have a second opportunity to be under the same roof with such a valiant man as Alexander Zeid?! There are no such fellows in England!"

I said to myself: I actually would be willing to stay a while longer with the fellow with the black shock of hair on his forehead and the black moustache, even if we do not have a common language. I liked his silence. There was a modesty about him that projected strength, a kind of inner determination. But I was beginning to find the Zichron Ya'acov farmer very tiresome.

At last he got up, asked his crony something about their friend Hankin, then we said good-bye and left.

The colony square was empty, and as we walked away from it, he put his arm around my waist and asked if I had enjoyed the visit. I said yes, and extricated myself from his arm. As we descended the hill, he continued to ask my impression of Zeid, and what I thought of his being a bum of sorts, a vagabond, wandering from place to place like a gypsy, and so on and so forth. He was a bit drunk, his face was flushed and his speech slurred.

As we reached the edge of the first vineyard, the moon rose in the east. A full moon, large and rose-coloured, it climbed between two mountain flanks painting the rows of vines a gunpowder, copper colour until the whole vineyard was a crimson carpet. "Moon, moon! Why do you blush so? From shame?" He extended his hand towards the moon and stopped on the path we were on between two vineyards. And suddenly, his voice rose in song, a sort of nostalgic song, in which the howl of a jackal could be heard, a song that echoed through space, and of all its Hebrew words, I could discern only "Canaan" and "Rachel." I stood at his side and marvelled—captivated too, by his voice—at how an elderly person such as himself could behave like a wild young man, and bay into the night. He stopped singing, held my shoulders with both his hands, and spoke into my face, alcohol breath emanating from his mouth: "That's a song you must learn!" and translated it: How beautiful are the nights in Canaan, how beautiful and clear...and Rachel, my Rachel...I laughed. The lyrics, like the melody, were lovely. They held something ancient, eastern, suffused with love and longing.

We moved forward a bit along the path, and then he again halted and pointed to a shed in the centre of the vineyard, to our right. "Hankin should be there now, Zeid's friend. It's his turn to guard tonight, that's what Alexander told me." He shouted towards the hut: "Hankin! Han-kin!" There was no response. "Let's go over there," he said, "he must have fallen asleep. We'll wake him."

I feared going with him into the vineyard, thick with shadows, but not wishing to appear cowardly, I followed him.

We entered the hut. No one was there. On the floor was a straw mattress, and on it, a rolled-up green blanket. Moonlight filtered into the hut between the braided eucalyptus branches.

He embraced me forcibly, kissed me and mumbled, "You're wonderful...you're so soft, so desirable...I've never met a woman like you..."

I pushed his face from mine, his mouth from mine, but as he continued to kiss and compliment me, he pulled up my dress, shoved his hand into my undergarments, and slid it down to my groin—

As I was trying to pull his hand up, to extricate myself from him, we fell onto the mattress. He lay upon me with the full weight of his heavy body, continued mumbling words of affection, and penetrated me, ignoring my pleas to stop, my whispered protestations, how dare he do such a thing to someone who trusted him...

For a long while after he had spent his seed in my womb, I could not move from where I lay. I turned my face aside and cried silently.

And after all he had done to me, he tried to comfort me! He again showered me with compliments, how "good" I was—as if I were a receptacle for the satisfaction of male lust—and asked forgiveness again and again, saying that he had been "swept away," that he could not control his passion when such a juicy, sweet, and tempting body was so near at hand...on such an enchanted, moonlit night...

When I rose (how amazing: this time, too, not a single drop

of blood!) to return to the colony, he would not desist, and when he tried to hold my hand, I recoiled from him in nausea and began to run along the path between the vineyards, leaving him behind. I ran as fast as my legs could carry me, all the way to the hostel.

I fell onto the bed, unable to forgive myself: why had I submitted to him? Why had I not fought him with all my strength? If I had struggled with him, I could have pushed him off me! If I had shouted, he would have become frightened and run off! If I had warned him that I would tell my hosts, that I would tell everyone in the colony…

Did the liquor I drank render me powerless?*

---

* The repetition of the "rape"—with such ostensibly accidental symmetry: once by an Arab, once by a Jew (only twenty days apart)—strengthens my opinion that Miss Campbell-Bennett is in urgent need of psychiatric treatment, and perhaps even hospitalisation. The entire matter of forced intercourse is utterly unthinkable; it is impossible that a man over fifty years of age, a "prominent" man, as Miss B. says, a propertied farmer known to all in the colony, would "rape" a young English woman who is the guest of the most distinguished citizen of that colony, a man whose fame has gone beyond its boundaries. If there was intercourse here—which itself is doubtful—it was consensual, and it appears that B. herself is aware of this, for she tries to blame her "submission" on her intoxication…. Does she require a Jewish "rapist" lest she suffer pangs of conscience for racism against the Arab people?

And the most striking evidence of the incredibility of the story: after this "rape" too of the virgin Beatrice—not a single drop of blood was shed!—P.D.M.

My period should begin tomorrow.

If I do not bleed menstrual blood tomorrow—I will not know whether the seed of the Arab or the seed of the Jew is growing in my womb.

Whichever it is, I shall not kill it.

I tossed and turned all night thinking about it, and that is my decision.

In the morning, I looked up at the Carmel, the green mountain on whose other side is the colony, the Aaronsohn family, Aaron, Sarah. And that scoundrel.

It is a lovely, clear morning. On one side, the turquoise sea spreads to the horizon, and far in the north, beyond the bay, emerging from within the fog like a fortress, is the grey block of the city of Acre. And behind—the mountain, rising erect, a kind of castle, or perhaps a church, on its peak. And between the mountain and the sea stretches the clean, ruler-straight street of this German Colony, of the Templars, its boulevard lined with palm trees spreading their fronds over its rustic, red-roofed houses.

I thought about what has happened to me in this country over the course of the past six weeks. Jerusalem, the Russian pilgrims kneeling and weeping at the rock of the crucifixion...the leper carrying his cross on the Via Dolorosa...the blazing heat pounding against my face...the rocks bleached by the sun...the road to Jericho and the mounds of salt...Bethlehem, Hebron...the arid expanses, and the camel caravans swaying slowly, as if dozing, in the desert...the white lily blooming miraculously in the fields of the Golan...the Holy Land, Holy Land ...

How Shechem, the son of Hamor, defiled Dinah, the daughter

of Jacob...that dark night in Shechem, the open wound screaming, with no one to hear...

The vineyards, and Sarah walking amongst the rows of vines, pruning the branches, her eyes shining with love and happiness...the vineyards, and the vines laden with juicy clusters of grapes, ready for vintage...and the full, rose-coloured moon rising in the east, pouring its blood-red light over the field of green foliage...the concubine in Gibeah...and the killing of innocence, and the killing of faith, and the killing of the soul...and the rage of the Prophets...and the defiled land...

And I will never be able to eat grapes again.

I climbed to the summit of the mountain at noon. A marble statue of Theresa of Avila stands in the church of the Carmelite monastery, Stella Maris. In one hand, she holds an open book, and the other is extended before her, as if seeking to keep away someone who is approaching her. Behind the altar is a painting of the Holy Family: the Father, the Mother, and the Child, who is four or five years old, standing between them. Beside the Father is a vertical staff, and the Mother is holding the Child's hand, and in the Child's other hand is a kind of green copper ball encircled with a gold hoop. The Child has curly hair and a mischievous gaze. I have seen hundreds of paintings of Jesus the Child—in most of them, He is a plump baby in the arms of His Mother, the graceful Madonna—but never, in any church, have I ever seen such a painting, in which He is an impish and clever child, one of the playful boys of the neighbourhood, and His parents, too, standing behind Him, are simple people, proud of their child. For a long while, I could not take my eyes from that adorable Child, who I thought was smiling at me.

Suddenly, an organ began playing a section from Bach's *Magnificat* and the empty church filled with the glorious sounds.

My heart nearly broke from the intensity of my emotion. I fell to my knees, and tears burst from my eyes. Here is my baptism in purity, I whispered to myself. With those sounds, I purified myself of all the contamination that clung to my flesh.

I recalled the verses of the Magnificat from the first chapter of Luke—the verses in which the Virgin Mary gives thanks after

Elizabeth, the mother of the future John the Baptist, tells her that she already feels the foetus moving in her womb—and I murmured them: "My soul magnifies the Lord, and my spirit rejoices in God my Saviour, for He has regarded the low estate of His handmaiden…for He is mighty…and holy is His name…"

I felt as if I were ascending, together with the divine music, above the earth, and hovering, hovering amongst the angels, and I felt I was no longer here, in this country, with its Muslims and Jews, with its ancient ruins and tombs of its holy men, with its blazing heat and its madness hiding under its stones, leaping out from amongst them like snakes and scorpions—

A mad country.

A male, violent country.

The god of the Muslims—a jealous male, a bloody sword in his hand.

The god of the Jews—a wrathful, vengeful male.

It was no wonder the Jews had driven off that gentle, delicate, frail son, His pale face suffused with mercy, the shadow of death like a cloud above it, His slender fingers whose touch healed the sick, His soft eyes that consoled the suffering, His lips that silently whispered love—for He has nothing of their violent masculinity. It is no wonder His disciples fled this harsh land and dispersed beyond its boundaries, to bring his message to the Corinthians, the Galatians, the Romans, and the Hebrews, who had left it.

I am no longer here.

But neither am I in England. Nor am I in the gloom and fog and soot that fill its air. Nor in those salons, with their stifling politeness and manners and fine words, their self-aggrandizing wit, and its restrained arrogance, hypocrisy, and pomposity—

I thank You, God, for giving me the strength to cut myself off from all of that, both here and there, so I can ascend and approach You, with love, only love, without complaint, bitterness, or vengeful thoughts, in my longing to be cleansed of all that.

"Jesus, our Lord, meet us as we make our way and yearn to reach the kingdom of heaven, so that we shall walk straight and never stray into the darkness of night that covers the universe. For You are the way, the truth and the light, and You will shine within us, for the sake of Your grace."

When the sound of the organ died, I remembered that in another couple of days, on the 31st of May, the Catholics celebrate the holiday of the Visitation, the day of the Magnificat—the day Mary visited the house of Elizabeth in Judea to tell of her pregnancy.

Haifa, 1ˢᵗ June, 1906

I ripped to pieces all the paintings of flowers I had done over the last few weeks and tossed them to the wind.

I painted all the flowers again. In red. Bleeding. The white lily bled too. A large sheet of paper—all of it a pool of blood.

And in any case, I hadn't found the mandrakes.

I went to the Lloyds' office in the old city, where the Austrian post office is located, and sent a telegram to my mother. I told her I was staying here, in this country, for another several weeks, and asked her to send me fifty guineas.

Then I wandered the streets idly. I went to the small port, which has only one pier, and where only a few ships were moored, and gazed at the sea. Far off, in the bay, a boat was anchored—Italian, from its flag—and its barge, packed with large boxes, had been separated from it and was being towed by the cable of a motorboat that churned the waves around it. I could sail away now, beyond this place, I thought. To Europe. I could go to the office of Messageri Maritime, which I had passed by earlier, and buy passage to Greece, Italy, or France. But I had no desire to do so. I am not from Europe. Nor from here.

The die has been cast, and I am alone, whatever happens.

I walked along narrow streets bustling with people—Arabs in kaffiyehs, Turks in uniform, clerks in red *tarbooshes*, customs agents and merchants coming out of the customs house, clerks from foreign agencies, Jews hurrying from one shop to another, and commercial establishments selling textiles, house wares, flour, and grain. I reached the colourful bazaar, whose crowded stands were laden with fruits and vegetables, copper objects, carpets and cheap clothing, the shouts of the peddlers hawking their wares filling the air. I walked as if in

189

a daze, seeing-but-not-seeing my surroundings, wondering if all this was happening in reality or in a dream—

I returned to the main street near the port and turned westwards, and on my way back to the German Colony, I passed a mosque, and the Convent of the Ladies of Nazareth, and the Latin cemetery, and the Greek Orthodox cemetery, and the blue of the calm sea, resting securely between the arms of the bay, always at my side—and I entered my room in the hotel—

And knelt beside my bed.

Our Father who art in heaven, hallowed be Thy name, Thy kingdom come, Thy will be done, on earth, as it is in heaven…

And lead me not into temptation, but save me from evil.*

---

* This is the last page of the two notebooks that make up Miss Campbell-Bennett's diary, which I was able to obtain from her through various contrivances. It may be that she has other pages I will see as therapy proceeds, if it does. We meet twice a week in the office of the Ein a-Tabiha church. Beatrice walks there from the village of Magdala, and I ride from Tiberias in a rented carriage.

In truth, however, I am sceptical about the benefit of this "talk" therapy: B. answers most of my questions with verses from Hail Mary, such as *Blessed are you amongst women, and blessed is the fruit of our womb!*; or from the Lord's Prayer, such as, *Forgive us our debts, as we also have forgiven our debtors*, and so on. She responds not at all to my mention of the name, Vanessa Stephen—as if she does not know her; as if everything she wrote in the diary has been erased from her memory. She frequently looks at me silently, her face suffused with a beatific smile.

I do not know how long I can survive here. The heat of these summer months is unbearable. The mosquitoes bite day and night. Tiberias is a filthy town that offers no diversion in the evening other than sitting on the wharf on the lake shore, sipping iced lemonade brought from the Arab restaurant, and observing the surface of the water, on which fishing boats sail. I greatly fear that the lethal malaria, now rampant amongst the residents here, will not fail to visit me as well.

Sometimes, like today, when the heat reaches 40 degrees in the shade and there is no air to breathe, I begin to fear that I too am losing my mind in this Holy Land.

Perhaps we will have no choice but to take B. to England forcibly and hospitalise her there.

Dr. P.D. Morrison, M.D.

Magdala, 28th August, 1906

My dear good, beautiful, Sarah.

I am here, in the village of Magdala near the Kinneret, the village of Mary Magdalene.

I feel quite good here. I am happy.

I am delighted to tell you that I am pregnant. In my fourth month already. I think I have twins in my womb. Like Rebecca.

I arrived here some twelve weeks ago. I travelled by diligence from Haifa to Tiberias for the price of fifty francs, which is not a great deal, and I spent my first night in the same hotel I stayed at with your brother, Aaron. How is he? Please remind him that he owes me mandrakes. He promised. I'm waiting.

I walked from Tiberias to Magdala. I found a room with the Jamil family for one majid a week. The room is small and dark, for it has only one window that faces west, and the lavatory is in the yard, but do not be concerned about me. The Jamil family, especially the mother, Halima, treat me well. They have three children: Mahmud, who is eight; Said, who is five; and Fatima, who is three. They walk past the door of my room quite often, peer inside and laugh. They are curious about me. They look at me and laugh, and I laugh with them. I have already learned to speak a few words of Arabic.

In another six months, I too will have children. Two. Halima says there will be only one, because my stomach is small. But I think she is wrong. I can already feel them. The way Elizabeth, John the Baptist's mother, felt her child moving within her when the Virgin Mary visited her before giving birth to Jesus. Or the way Rebecca felt Esau and Jacob stirring in her womb.

The first two weeks were a difficult for me. The young men in the village thought I was a prostitute, owing, perhaps, to my clothes, of the sort they were not used to seeing—my wide-brimmed hat and the muslin off-the-shoulder dress that I had brought from England—and perhaps because of my long hair, worn loose. They came to lie with me at night, and I could not refuse them, for they are good lads.

After two weeks, however, that stopped. Thanks to Father Thomas Oswald from Ein a-Tabiha, to whom I am grateful.

I go to Ein a-Tabiha and Capernaum every day. Three hours walking there, and three hours walking back. I immerse myself in the Kinneret and light candles before the altars of both churches. The miracle of the loaves of bread and the fish took place in Ein a-Tabiha. Peter, the apostle of Christ, was born in Capernaum, and it was from this shore that our Lord went down to the water and walked upon it to reach the fishing boat. All of this is recounted in the New Testament. I shall send you a copy of it. I have two.

When Father Thomas Oswald saw that my eyes were always red—from crying—he asked what was wrong. I told him that the young men come to lie with me at night, and I find it most unpleasant. I told him that I was apparently to blame, and asked him to exorcise the seventy demons from within me. He came to Magdala, spoke to the head of the village and with the village elders, and since then, the young men have stopped coming to me in the night.

So now I am serene and happy. Halima has found a bathing costume for me, albeit a bit small, and in the early evening, I swim in the Kinneret. The water cleanses me of all infection, both internal and external.

Yes, another unpleasant thing happened.

The last time I was here, with your brother, Aaron—

Give him my regards, and please remind him of his promise to me—

I had entered the village then to see the place where Mary Magdalene was born and lived. A woman stood before me and cursed me.

So when I came to the village this time, she recognized me, and every time she saw me on the street, she would cast an evil look upon me and spew at me all sorts of Arabic words, like the venom spewed by snakes.

But that too stopped, from the day Father Thomas Oswald came here.

So now, as I have told you, I am quite happy here. I eat little, but the food I do eat is healthy. Pita bread, goats' cheese, olives, vegetables such as lettuce, cucumbers and peppers, and fruit, which I dearly love, such as figs and dates. It is quite sufficient for me. And I wash my own clothes and bedding on the shore of the Kinneret. If my mother could only see that—she would not believe her eyes. She did not understand why I do not come home, but when I wrote her that I want to live near the place where Jesus walked on the water, she understood, and sent me money.

In the evening, when I return from Ein a-Tabiha and Capernaum, and after my swim, I read the Old and New Testaments by candlelight, drawing courage from that holy book.

Please tell your brother Aaron that I have read *The Jewish State*, the book he gave me as a gift, and in my opinion, Dr. Theodor Herzl was a prophet.

My mother thinks that when you have a state, and the prophesies of the Jewish Prophets are realised, you will believe in Jesus, who is a scion of the royal house of David son of Jesse, as written in Isaiah.

I sometimes spend hours gazing at the Kinneret. On nights when the moon is full. Gazing thus upon it, I am infused with divine peace. The blue of the lake spreads within me, within my soul, like waves spreading along the sand, absorbed into it. Sometimes I think I myself am blue.

I had a friend in England, Virginia, who was blue also.

Now, at the end of August, it is frightfully hot here. I perspire terribly. There is no air in my stifling room. At night, I take my bed out to the backyard and sleep there. Father Oswald has given me a mosquito net, and I spread it over the bed like a tent. He has also given me quinine, against malaria. Whenever I am bitten, I say to myself: Job suffered more than you, he sat in the ashes and scraped himself with a potsherd.

I will tell you something funny about my landlady, Halima.

When I told her I was pregnant, she asked who the father was. I pointed upward and said, "Our Father in heaven knows."—"Then perhaps you are pregnant by the Holy Spirit, as the Christians believe the mother of Jesus was," she said, laughing. And I laughed with her.

Several nights ago, I had a truly prophetic dream. A tall acacia tree stood in the desert of the Dead Sea, and I heard a voice coming from its foliage: "Behold, you shall bear two sons. You shall call the first one Immanuel, and the second, you shall call Azriel." When I woke up, I remembered that it is written in Isaiah, "Behold, the young woman shall conceive and bear a son, and shall call his name Immanuel," and in Hosea, it is written that his wife of harlotry would conceive and bear a boy child whose name would be called Jezreel. And it is well known that the names Isaiah, Hosea and Jesus are from the same root. So I asked myself why my second son should be called Azriel, not Jezreel. But I did not know the answer.

The very next day, several Jews arrived to buy the village land so that they could establish a Jewish colony here. I asked one of them what Azriel meant in Hebrew, and when he told me that it meant "God shall help," I was very happy.

And that night, I dreamed that my son, Azriel, was planting mandrakes, and they grew from the earth and blossomed before my eyes. The fields filled with mandrakes. The whole country was covered with the blue love-flowers.

Bless me, dear Sarah. My heart is full with love for you. And I bless you too, that you will be "fruitful as the vine," as you once told me. I hope you will bear healthy boys and girls and be happy.

And come to visit my two boys when they are born. I shall be waiting for you.

I embrace and kiss you.

With love,

Beatrice

About the Author

Aharon Megged

Aharon Megged was born in Poland and came to Palestine at the age of six. He was a member of Kibbutz Sdot Yam between 1938–1950, and later, a literary editor and journalist. He has been a pivotal figure in Israeli letters since the 1950s. His many novels, short stories and plays reflect the complexities of Israeli society over the past fifty years.

Megged's work has been translated into several languages, including English. The president of the Israel PEN CENTER (1980–'87), and the cultural attaché at the Israel Embassy in London (1968–'71), Aharon Megged is a member of the Hebrew Academy. He has won many literary awards, amongst them the Bialik Award, the Brenner Award, the Agnon Award, and the much-coveted Israel Prize for Literature, 2003.

Foiglman, published by *The* Toby Press in 2003, was awarded the Koret Literary Prize, 2004, in its English translation (by Marganit Weinberger-Rotman).

Aharon Megged is married to the writer Eda Zoritte and they have two sons, Eyal, who is also a writer, and Amos, a lecturer in history at the University of Haifa.

The fonts used in this book are from the Garamond family

Other works by Aharon Megged
published by *The* Toby Press

Foiglman

The Living and the Dead

The Toby Press publishes fine writing,
available at leading bookstores everywhere. For more
information, please visit www.tobypress.com